Like the
Red Panda

Like the
Red Panda

ANDREA SEIGEL

A HARVEST ORIGINAL • HARCOURT, INC.

ORLANDO AUSTIN NEW YORK SAN DIEGO TORONTO LONDON

www.HarcourtBooks.com

This is a work of fiction. Although some actual places and
organizations are named, any resemblance to actual persons,
living or dead, events, or behaviors is entirely coincidental.

Library of Congress Cataloging-in-Publication Data
Seigel, Andrea.
Like the red panda/Andrea Seigel.—1st ed.
p.   cm.
ISBN 0-15-603024-1
1. High school students—Fiction. 2. Orange County (Calif.)—Fiction.
3. Grandparent and child—Fiction. 4. Foster parents—Fiction.
5. Teenage girls—Fiction. 6. Orphans—Fiction.   I. Title.
PS3619.E424L55   2004   2003017164

Text set in Garamond MT
Designed by Cathy Riggs

Printed in the United States of America

First edition
K J I H G F E D C B

For Brian, Eileen, and Larry

Like the
Red Panda

One

FRIDAY, JUNE 13

This afternoon in drama (I'm taking it because Mrs. Amis said I needed to show interest in the arts on my transcript, and I can't draw) I was supposed to be throwing a fake beach ball up and down, but I just couldn't do it anymore. Last semester I was ready to drop out the day Mr. Nichols made us have fake arguments with our scene partners and Danielle Reinhardt theater-slapped me for "stealing her boyfriend" when everybody knows she's a lesbian. I was there onstage, realizing the complete pointlessness of debating about things that don't exist as she slammed me across the side of my face and forgot to cup her hand the right way. My eye was throbbing so I turned to Mr. Nichols midscene and said, "Can I please go to the nurse?" because I honestly thought I might have a broken blood vessel. But he just said,

"Tell it to Danielle! Tell her how you feel!" I wanted to give him the evil eye, but couldn't, and thought to myself, "Tomorrow I'm getting a drop slip."

But then Mrs. Amis, my counselor, said that Princeton probably wouldn't look favorably upon my dropping a class three months into the semester, especially since I had written my personal statement about "my love of performance" (the topic being in no way my idea, sorry). So I went back to drama the next day and played fake tennis and did depressing monologues about the circus and generally dealt with it. But then today, when Mr. Nichols told me that my beach ball wasn't going high enough (and considering that it's invisible, how did he know?), I knew I was done. That's it. There comes a point when you're just too exhausted to pretend to have fun at a beach that doesn't exist.

So, essentially, I let the ball drop. Ha. Ha. Ha. And when I did, the smell of the room hit me. That smell that seems to come straight from the hard orange carpet that they like to put in all the classrooms. It's the smell of countless sweaty high school bodies and the nervous energy that emanates from their armpits whenever they're put on the spot. And I looked over at John Steiner's acne, which is the kind that's so deep under the skin that you want to rush the kid to the emergency room before his face dies. His forehead and nose were so shiny under those hot lights and he was smiling up at his fake ball, beaming, and I just couldn't take his naive optimism. John looked like he was having the most fantastic, perfect, idyllic fake day at the beach I ever saw. I don't want to be too mean, and I hope he never reads this, but the guy exhausted me.

So as Mr. Nichols stood next to John asking what color

his ball was, I started to back toward the corner where the piano sits. Somewhere in my mind I heard John happily yelling, "It's rainbow colored!" but mostly the blood was rushing to my brain as the extreme stress of being somewhat bad hit me. I ducked down behind the piano, my heart beating ridiculously fast. I've never even gotten a U (unsatisfactory) in P.E. and I never talk when a teacher is talking. Not because I think it's wrong, but just because I know I shouldn't. So sitting behind that piano was huge for me. Huge. I can't even say exactly why I did it, except for the smell and John's acne, and maybe also because of the lights. Just imagine thirty people throwing their arms up and down like they're crazy, and every time they do this warm air hits you in the cheek. It's awful. I told myself to breathe out and I tipped my head back against the wall. I opened my eyes and saw Mr. Nichols was standing over me.

"Did your ball roll over into the marshlands?"

"What?" I asked.

"I'm wondering why you're ducking behind this sand dune."

If Mr. Nichols had gotten me on any other second besides this one, then I would have said, "I lost control of my ball in these high winds. They're blowing mighty fierce today." But like I said before, I was just exhausted and wanting to put my index fingers on my nostrils and close them off forever. So I just said, "I don't know what you're talking about."

He kind of laughed a little. You don't expect these kinds of things from the students who've done everything you've asked for nine and a half months straight.

"Stella, just pick up your ball and get it going again." His mustache twitched.

The twitch made me nauseous, and all I could think to say was, "No."

"What?"

"No. I'm sorry. No." I got light-headed. Mr. Nichols looked so disappointed I almost couldn't take it. I was almost about to do what he wanted, but his disappointment wasn't strong enough to change how tired I felt.

"Stella, you won't throw the ball?" He asked this like he was hopeful, like I still had time left to save everything. But I was surprised to find out that for the first time at school, I didn't care about fixing things, so I told him, "No. I'm sorry. I'm done."

Mr. Nichols had no choice but to make an example out of me. Because by then everyone had stopped playing on the "shore" and they were all watching us. He told me to go to the principal and he trilled the *l* at the end. His face turned red and then white.

The only other time I've been in the principal's office was when I went to pick up my Warrior award sophomore year. You get a Warrior award if a teacher nominates you for being exceptional, and there's this whole awards ceremony, but I couldn't go that particular year because of the flu. Anyway, you have to pick up your certificate from the principal because he shakes your hand and tells you how proud he is. The real irony is that the students that get the Warrior awards are the ones who are completely anonymous to the principal because he only sees the bad kids on a regular basis. So really, the kids he's got a deep relationship with are the ones who steal keys from teachers' desks and throw freshmen against walls. Normally I don't cause problems, so I don't think he knew my name before today, but maybe he knew my face.

When I walked across campus to go see Mr. Frankel, I tried not to look at the kids in the quad who never seem to go to class at all. I know one of them, Larome Nolans, has at least one period of ceramics because I've seen him carrying around ugly vases and what I think are ashtrays, but every time I go past the lunch tables, he's there sitting on top of one of them. Last year he was suspended for offering to sell a gun to an undercover policeman, but I guess he was just loosely offering and didn't have an actual gun to hand over. He spent some time in juvy and then came back. I'm a little bit fascinated with him partly because he laughs all the time and partly because he's one of maybe twenty black kids that go to my school.

When you think of the bad kids, you think they're the ones who are bitter and hating school. But today I realized that they're actually happy. The narcs come by and threaten yellow slips and detention, but then the narcs just end up laughing with the kids and making up inside jokes. And then, like I said before, the principal watches out for them, and the teachers want to make a difference in their lives, so the bad kids are probably the most beloved people in the entire school. If Princeton stopped caring about grades and extra-curricular activities and started admitting some of these people from the quad, it just might end up with a more likable student body.

As I was passing the cafeteria, Larome (in the middle of laughing) yelled out, "You've been a good girl, girl?"

I knew what he was talking about because I have this habit of dressing like a Catholic schoolgirl. Over the years I've built up this collection of pleated skirts until they're pretty much all I have in my closet. I must like them. I mean, that's what you've got to figure when you end up with thirty of them. Today I was wearing a yellow-and-black plaid skirt and even a tie, so I knew what he was talking about. Still, I said, "What?"

That made him laugh, obviously. Then he stopped long enough to say, "Yeah, yeah, you're good. I can tell. That skirt's pretty damn short though, girl."

In that moment I wished I could find everything as funny as he did. He must see things on some kind of higher plane, where the essence of everything ridiculous comes to him in these sharp, pleasurable spasms. I think that today I ended up on the plane where I see the same essence, except it makes me sick to my stomach.

I only had a half hour until school let out and everything Larome was doing made my head hurt. The sun was shining from under his chin, bringing every single hair out of his face. I could see hundreds of them. His hairs were so obvious that they made him look fake, but then when I changed my focus to his actual head, it was so sharply defined that everything in back of him started to look fake. That right there shows just how useless perspective is, since it can always change.

I said, "Yeah, I'm good, I guess." I gave him a weak smile because I didn't want him to think I was an uptight white girl, and then I walked quickly to the office because I couldn't wait to get out of there.

Mrs. Green, the secretary, had me sit on the hard blue

couch outside of Mr. Frankel's office, and it was right under the air-conditioning vent. I was wearing one of my thin bras and when I looked down, my nipples were poking out of my shirt. I crossed my arms and thought about how Mr. Frankel would probably read my body language as a sign of difficulty. I started to make up scenarios in my head where I would be so difficult that he'd end up calling me a bitch and I'd kick over his desk. He came out of his office five minutes later, but I chickened out and uncrossed my arms.

He raised his eyebrows and asked, "Stella?" And I wanted to say, "I've shaken your hand so many times. You've handed me so many awards. Yes, my name is Stella." I almost did because the exhaustion had crept into my mind and was just about at my bottom lip.

But instead I said, "Yeah. Hi." We went into his office and both sat down. Mr. Frankel always has bags under his eyes, but today he looked like he was going to put a gun to his head at three. I sympathized. I really did. He was wearing one of those polo shirts with the pony on them, and I imagined it running off his shirt, up his nose, and into some major artery in his brain. (Brains have arteries, yeah?) It would neigh and start digging its hooves in until Mr. Frankel had become completely and peacefully catatonic.

He smiled and sighed simultaneously while picking up the papers Mrs. Green had laid out for him.

"It's Friday the thirteenth."

I nodded. "Yeah."

"Not only is it Friday the thirteenth, but you're also graduating in two weeks. Right?" He talked slow.

"Right."

"I'm getting the feeling here that this ball throwing incident is nothing more than a typical case of senioritis."

I stopped him right there and said, "I don't want to be argumentative, but there was no ball to throw."

He squinted. "In Mr. Nichols's mind there was." And what can you say to that but, "Hmm?" He took a look at my transcript.

"You're a smart girl. You're probably a little impatient with your classes, and you're all set to go to..." His eyes got wide. "Oh, Princeton. Very good. You must be very excited."

But, exactly then, hearing that I must be very excited, I was instantly hit by how unexcited I actually was. It's just like when you lie in bed at night thinking about a word and you say it over and over again out loud until it makes no sense anymore and you're not even sure if you have the right word for the idea? Or, and here's a drama class example to warm Mr. Nichols's heart, it's like the time when I was Lizzie Borden in this class play called *Blood Relations* and all my movements were completely choreographed, but then I got up there and wasn't even sure which way I should face. You'd think that, logically, I could figure out that the audience was one way and the scenery was another, but I looked around and there were people in the wings and people on the stage with me and people in the pit. And they all looked exactly the same. I was standing reciting someone else's words and decisions that had been preset before I even got to sixth period, and suddenly the room was a globe and there wasn't any particular direction that seemed to stand out. So it's like I've heard Princeton, Princeton, Princeton since my big envelope came in the mail, and maybe four months ago when I heard the name I thought about the gargoyles in the brochure. There was something to picture then. Princeton was an actual concept because it was the end of a very rational equation, as far as good grades plus drama class plus glowing teacher recommendations equals going there. But then I'm thinking that my brain kept repeating the idea over and over again, even when I wasn't associating that idea with the word, and the two got worn out when I wasn't even paying attention.

You need to be happy to be sad, yeah?

Anyway, now I know what it's like to surprise yourself with apathy in the afternoon when you woke up in the morning believing you cared.

I looked down at my watch and it said 2:41 and I memorized the number by thinking two times the two dots in the colon is four, times the one to the right is still four. I still had to give an answer to Mr. Frankel, so for lack of any desire to communicate, I told him, "Yeah, I'm real excited."

He blinked four times and I only know this because I was watching his eyelashes. Like repeated words stuck on his lids, the hairs also stopped making sense the longer I studied them. I wondered, Hey, why not pubic hairs stuck onto the top of his eyes instead? Curly lashes. Just another option. Four times, not five times, and definitely not three. He had lashes to keep out the dust and the dirt, but we (and by we, I mean all us human beings) could also throw in bugs and countless other dangers until so many were listed that we couldn't consider ourselves having ever made a list. If I listed everything in the world, then that would just be everything in the world, and not any sort of organized statement.

"You don't say that like you're very excited," he said.

I apologized.

He asked, "Are you having problems with your boyfriend?"

I told him I didn't have one.

He breathed. His skin even breathed. I swear I felt bad for just wanting to get away from him. I think he knew it, too, and he said, "I think this is probably an isolated incident. I don't think we need to call your parents."

I corrected him. Guardians.

"We don't have to bother them then."

He stood up, tipped his head toward the window like some sad plant, and instructed me to "have a relaxing weekend."

I walk home because I don't have my own car and I don't have a friend that I can carpool with. I wouldn't say I'm unpopular because if you asked other kids about me, they would say, "She's so smart" first and "She dresses like a Catholic schoolgirl" second. They'd know who I am. And even though I don't really have any friends as far as having someone to hang out with on the weekend, everybody at my school would tell you I have lots of friends because I have so many acquaintances. The thing with acquaintances is that one acquaintance probably assumes that the other acquaintances are your best friends, and then the latter group assumes that the original acquaintance is your soul mate, and that's how everybody stays at arm's length.

I live in a village of what is technically a city (I guess) called Irvine. Sometime around the sixties the Irvine family must have been taking their horses out for a spin, and one of them thought aloud, "A lot of people have cities named after them, but how many people have cities that turned out exactly how they imagined?" So I'm assuming they pulled out a piece of graph paper back at the ranch and drew up a dream plan, and they got really excited by the idea of seeing the future and the part they'd play in making it true. The Irvines plotted years ahead so that even Southern Irvine, the later part of the city to be developed, was already a gleam in North Irvine's eye by the time the original houses were built there.

Being older, Deerfield (the extreme back end of the North Irvine) is quieter than its newer counterpart and earthier, too. I mean, as earthy as a place can get where the homes will still run you a half million. This part is where families try to resist divorce because they've been in their houses since the dawn of planning, and I think subconsciously they figure, "The city was started here and we remember when it was all orange groves, so what the hell. Let's stick it out." The houses feel safe like purified log cabins and the trees loom taller and grow bushier and Deerfield even has a 7-Eleven, which the South wouldn't be caught dead with. The existence of a 7-Eleven says that someone somewhere got lazy.

And that's the thing about Woodbridge, the village where I live now. When I hear people talk about upper-middle-class America, they rattle on about the mediocrity of the homes and the scenery and the lives contained within them. But Woodbridge was created with what I can only identify as intense passion. The Irvine family took stock of Deerfield's flaws and then they gazed forward, knowing their next baby would be better-looking and smarter, too.

The man-made North and South Lakes went up, marking

the top and bottom of the lasso known as the Yale Loop. This is the continuous circle of a street with amazingly wide lanes and grassy dividers and airy trees placed at equal intervals (they stay deliberately green in the winter and sprout purple blossoms in the spring and summer). Everyone always says that nature has an incredible sense of balance, but they need to come take a look around here. One white gazebo at the South Lake? One white gazebo at the North Lake. One faux-rickety wood bridge (hence, the name) at the South Lake? "Aw shit, I got that, too," laughs the North. A "lagoon" with concrete rock slides and imported sand? Both ends of Woodbridge raise their hands and then fight over which one has less duck crap in it.

And so it goes. Absolutely nothing has been left to chance. I think Irvine even let Costa Mesa and Santa Ana pop up next to it on purpose, so it would have somewhere to put its maids and gardeners.

But you can't call it a mediocre or deadened place. You just can't. There's incredible focus in the streetlamps that light up the night like the whole city's an accident on the freeway. There are lush parks and sparkling pools to be shared between every hundred homeowners, even though tons of them already have parks or pools in their backyards. The grocery stores are bright and elegant, with marbleized floors and women that get dressed up to buy Lysol.

See, everybody is involved in keeping the game going. Even the bronzed John Wayne (at the airport named after him) looks fantastic and clean despite having worked so hard in so many Westerns to protect his various towns.

There's definitely passion in the air, and while it seems to scoot everyone else along, allowing them to move on to the more complicated tasks of making money and planning Saturday-night dinner parties, sometimes it just makes me dizzy. Like I'm inside a honeycomb watching everybody scurry to preserve their efforts when nobody's even coming to take it away. But the people around here don't believe that what they're actually doing is taking up energy. It's natural— natural balance.

Today I see their movements and decisions like my eyes can take thermal photographs.

On my way home I walk past the South Lake, where citizens can rent small boats and drift around if they feel like it (don't worry, the North Lake has got all this, too). Today there wasn't a single boat out. In this town, if you build it, they won't come. Ha. Or actually, I think it's just that the people here recognize the lake for what it really is, which is a sculpture of a lake instead of an actual living body of water. Maybe it soothes them to drive down Alton (the street bordering the lake) and feel the sun bouncing off the water and streaming into the car through the passenger window. They don't even have to turn their heads because they see the reflected light out of the corner of their eye and they feel the warmth and they can just sense there's a lake.

Anyway, while I was looking at the sun on the water, I heard a honk and then a girl call, "Stella!" I turned to see who it was, but my eyes were shot with the sun and iridescent orange hexagons were everywhere, even on the driver's head.

Like an idiot I said, "Who's there?" My voice reminded

me of those trembling girls who call out to really dark basements in the movies. It was daylight and I was on a main street, so I must have sounded so lost.

It was Ashley Wakefield calling out, "It's Ashley Wakefield!" I kind of blindly stumbled toward the sound of all the cars whipping along and started to wonder what it feels like to get hit by a truck. By the time I was within two feet of her black Rabbit I could make out Ashley's face. She's amazing looking and that's one of those facts that everyone has to accept unconditionally.

I leaned over, put my elbows on the lowered window, and said, "Hey, sorry. I had the sun in my eyes."

She took off her sunglasses. "Oh god, I didn't even realize it was a sunny day out. That's how good these things are." I firmly believe that Ashley has a perfect life because she knows how to do all things. She knows how to grow straight, fine hair and she knows how to protect her eyes from harmful UV rays. She reminds me of Nancy Drew. I used to read all those books when I was little, and Nancy was strawberry blond, too, and similarly possessed the uncanny ability to lead a productive, charming life. Somehow over the years Ashley and I have come to a mutual understanding that we are equally intelligent and kind of on the same page (and in the same classes), but we also silently acknowledge that she is more attractive and well rounded.

I asked, "So where are you going?" Then I rolled my eyes and finished off with, "Boating?"

Ashley smiled with only one side of her face and examined the split ends she doesn't have. That's her signature move. "Yeah, maybe I'll take out a canoe later, after I finish studying for the English final. Are you making flashcards or what?"

Again, I was struck with the strong sensation of surprising myself when I discovered that no, as of this moment I was no longer making flashcards. At 3:01 P.M. I would have believed that there were flashcards that were going to be made, but now it was 3:02 P.M. and not only was I no longer looking forward to college, but I was no longer intending to pass my English final, either.

I said, "I'm not sure yet" because I didn't want to explain to Ashley how different things were looking this afternoon and how a small idea was already forming in the back of my head. At that point I'd say the idea was still somewhat tiny, but it was definitely holding my interest in a way that I had never exactly experienced before. The best way I can describe it is when you have a massive headache and you roll around in bed at night until finally you figure out that if you stand on your head and squeeze your thumb or whatever, the pain goes away completely. I'm not saying that I've been going through my days with some kind of constant pain because I haven't. In fact, I've been completely fine. But like I said, you don't know anything until you know what it isn't.

One of my elementary school teachers had paper doll cutouts on her wall and a strip of paper underneath that said, "In order to discover who you are, first learn who everybody else is—and you're what's left." So this idea that started in drama class (and I wouldn't even say it was a full idea then) was so striking in its newness that it made all my old ideas seem like crap.

I was thinking about all this when Ashley's voice drifted

back in and she was saying, "So—what?—you think you're too good for flashcards now?" She was pretty much kidding, but I'm sure she was also trying to figure out what percentage I had going into the final.

Right then, I got sick of her, too, and especially her long fingers. She was stretching them out on the steering wheel, flexing them backward, and the tiniest cracking sounds were coming from her knuckles. When she did that, all I could think about was what she was made up of. If you start thinking about people in terms of their bones, then the whole mystery of something like beauty gets tossed out the window. Or actually, I don't know if that's true for the rest of the world since everybody at school is so continually entranced by her.

Suddenly I heard her say, "Why are you staring at me like that?" so I said, "Sorry, I'm just entranced by you." She looked hurt and told me, "Don't make fun of me. I can't help the way I look." And I just raised my eyebrows and informed her that sorry, but you don't have the right to feel insulted for being amazingly popular and beautiful.

"I get the feeling that you don't respect me sometimes," she said.

I told her, "No, that's not it at all."

"Sometimes I think you think you're smarter than I am."

"I don't know where you're getting that from. How could I think that when we have the exact same GPA?"

She checked her split ends one more time thoughtfully and then asked, "Where do you live? Do you want a ride home?"

I pointed over my shoulder and said, "I just live on the other side of the lake. I can walk."

"I live over there, too. I'm just picking up Ainsley at the bank first. Get in."

"I feel like walking," I said.

One time I studied in the library with her and Ainsley Cleveland, and being with the two of them was torture. They're the kind of girls that everyone makes Siamese twin jokes about (except Ainsley's the obviously uglier head). As long as I've known Ashley, Ainsley has been with her ninety-nine percent of the time. She's quiet and kind of invisible, but always there. Ashley talks and wins the class election for liaison to the athletic department and, really, I have no idea if Ainsley does anything at all except be Ashley's best friend. When I was a freshman I just figured that Ainsley must be really engaging behind closed doors because why else would Ashley choose her as her only confidant? But after four years I haven't seen any evidence of a spectacular personality lurking behind Ainsley's emotionless face. But, anyway, that one time I agreed to study with Ashley, Ainsley sat right next to her and kept talking in such a low voice that I couldn't understand a thing.

"You really don't want a ride? You want to walk?"

I said, "Yes."

She put her sunglasses back on. "Okay. Whatever. See you Monday."

I watched her pull away toward a tunnel of purple-blossomed trees ahead, and then I walked back toward the water. I began to think that maybe I should have gone with Ashley. Maybe we would end up talking for hours, going and getting frozen yogurt, and marveling at all the things we had in common. Maybe she would create (for me) a newly strong faith in the objective greatness of people. Then, by extension, I would see the natural goodness in certain government systems and ways of leading one's life. But deep down I knew that couldn't happen, so I bit my cheek and kept moving.

The rest of my usual path takes me around the back of the lakefront houses, where French doors open out from glass living-room walls. This is why the chandeliers and the couches tend to be pretty swanky. All the retiree dog walkers and corporate Rollerbladers go by and look in, and they wonder where the homeowners got their stuff.

Next I go through the middle of Springbrook Elementary where the tetherball chains clink and echo, even when there's no wind, and then I make a right. Go down the street, and I'm home. I live in a tract in the shape of a tadpole or a sperm where my house is part of the head. A curving line of homes extends from the main part and ends at Woodflower pool, which in turn connects to the lawn of Springbrook Elementary. Like I said, everything here comes full circle. Passion in planning.

The tract consists of about five different wood-slatted models with subtle variations. The high peaks above the rooms above the three-car garages fall in the middle, the left, or the right. The driveways alternate between concrete, brick, and stone. The two-story houses are pale blue at their most exotic, and a soft tan at their least. But all the houses have long walkways up to their doors because you're supposed to stop and admire the snapdragons and the ferns in ceramic Grecian urns on your way to the doorbell.

My parents are dead, so when I step through the front door I never want. Never mind. I don't feel like explaining that right now. I'd just rather discuss how today I had some sort of abstract revelation that showed me how arbitrary the world is, and as soon as I realized that, what was I supposed to do? Pretend it wasn't arbitrary? It's like I have X-ray goggles on that show me that Princeton is just a Kmart with a nice facade on it and John Steiner is just a skeleton with some skin (and acne, sorry) slapped on top of it. All these pieces of the puzzle are clicking together in my head. They were all floating around in my brain before, but I could never make sense of them. Every time I felt these hints of discontent I would just study a little more or do some extra credit or apply to another Ivy League college. But today, the beach ball—it's so clear how we make everything up.

I remember the first day of drama class when Mr. Nichols had us go around the room and say our name and our favorite animal. The last smart thing he said was, "Choose your animals carefully because that's how your classmates will remember you." What he was really saying was that we should probably lie to each other. When you think of the animals an average high schooler comes into contact with on a regular basis, you're in dog, cat, fish, and hamster territory. If we didn't have to work so hard to impress each other, I bet everyone would just admit that, god, our real favorites are our old, lame household pets. Those are the animals closest to our hearts. Those are the animals we love, yeah? When we have to tell anything defining about ourselves to someone else, though, we begin to lie and build these exotic layers. We don't want to be bogged down in the smelliness of doggy chow and pee on the carpet.

When everybody made their introductions in drama, I

found out there were a whole bunch of peacocks, elephants, lions, and flying squirrels in the room. That was John Steiner—not just a squirrel, but a flying squirrel. And I'm not above it at all. I said, "My name is Stella and my favorite animal is a porcupine." The last time I saw a porcupine was when I was something like six. But I thought that animal would impress the others in a punk sort of way, especially Nick Dalton, who's kind of sexy in an all-American kind of way.

I'm exhausted. I'm going to stop trying to explain things. I think I'm just nervous that when people find out what I've done they're going to think I did it for the wrong reasons. So I'm trying to write this thing and explain, but I'm not even getting close.

The other week in coordinated science, Ms. Stocks was teaching us about stars and how some are considered young when they die, even though they've been up in the sky for hundreds of thousands of years. Some burn out at two hundred thousand, and some hold out until they're a million. Some are dead long before we ever even realize it because of the time it takes for light to travel.

I hope that makes things clearer. Put a fork in me, because I'm done.

Two

The last birthday party I had was in sixth grade, and I haven't thought about having one since. At around five-thirty on a Saturday night I had eleven acquaintances and maybe one friend over to my house for a pizza dinner and a Miami-themed scavenger hunt. I was into pink flamingos, palm trees, and neon during that time of my life.

Before everyone arrived, I was up in my bathroom curling my hair, and my mom came and sat on the hamper lightly so she wouldn't make the wicker crack. There was still enough light from the window over the shower, so I didn't have the ones in the ceiling on.

"Aren't you so excited?" she asked. "It feels like a party night." I looked at her in the mirror and she was grinning at me with shiny eyes. You'd be amazed if you could have seen how much my mom's eyes could glint, even in a semidark room. I'm not naive enough to say she was beautiful, not even in the way that all girls say their mom is a beautiful woman when she's really kind of haggard. But my mom did have some form of rare charm that gave the impression you had just seen someone beautiful as soon as she left the room.

I said, "Yeah, I'm pretty excited." That made her jump up and come over and shake me. I could feel my brain rattling against the sides of my skull and was almost about to tell her to shake me a little softer if she was going to do it at all.

"You have to be more excited than that," she said.

She was still rocking me back and forth from behind while looking at me in the mirror. I remember getting kind of dizzy. I told her, "Mom, you're going to make me burn my head if you keep doing that."

So she took the curling iron out of my hands and started to do my hair very quickly and haphazardly. Like she would take unequal sections of hair and wrap them around the curling iron backward, so that the curl was bent out of shape. She told me, "There you go. Now you're free to be excited."

I swear a bolt of something just started right then in my stomach and rushed up to my head. She told it to be there, and there it was. For a second my shoulders twitched and I jumped up halfway onto the balls of my feet. In the mirror I kind of looked like I had just had an incomplete seizure.

My mom asked, "What the hell was that?" but she didn't say "hell" in a confused or angry way. The word *hell* was the part of the question that let me know she thought I was funny and that she knew what it was anyway.

I told her that I didn't know. She kissed the top of my

head and put the curling iron down on the counter, but she put it too close to the edge of the sink. It fell in and first made a clanging sound against the porcelain, and then a sizzling sound once it landed under the heavy faucet drip my parents never had time to fix. She started to reach in to get the curling iron, but I put my hand on her wrist and said, "I don't think you're supposed to pick it up when it's been in water."

She ran her hand down my curls. "Right. Of course. Well, I guess you can't finish curling your hair, so you should just put it into a ponytail." Really quickly she opened my bathroom drawer and got one of my rubber bands out and started pulling my hair together like she was in a huge rush. While she wrapped the band around my hair she was holding on to the ponytail so tight that my head started to tip backward. When she was done, there were bumps everywhere, but she patted my head like I was ready to go. She kissed the top of my head again and told me happy birthday. Then she walked out of the room.

I took my hair down and went to see if my mom had bobby pins, but the door to her bedroom was shut. I contemplated knocking, but there was something about the pure silence behind it that made me decide to go downstairs instead. In the living room I found my dad kneeling next to the wine rack and examining two bottles at the same time. He was holding one in each hand and kind of turning his head back and forth quickly between them like he was comparing labels without bothering to read any of the ingredients.

I went over to him and laid myself across his back like a blanket and put my arms around his neck. He hadn't shaved for a few days at least, so I remember his hairs scratching my wrists.

"Are those for my party?" I asked. With my parents, you kind of never knew. I'd been allowed to drink champagne on Christmas after I turned ten.

He pretended to hide the bottles under his shirt and said, "You weren't supposed to see these."

"Why not?"

"Because this is what we got you for your birthday. Your mom's giving you the pinot and I'm giving you the cabernet."

I asked, "Are you kidding?" With my parents, I might've really been getting wine.

"Why, would you rather I got you some tequila? I thought you were classier than that, Stella." He laughed and got up from the floor with me still hanging off him, except he couldn't keep his balance so he started to bend backward. It's a good thing I let go before he fell down. When he hit the ground the bottles left his hands, and one jumped across the carpet and the other rolled over to the two tiled stairs leading down into the room.

"When did you get so heavy?" he asked.

I said I didn't know. I was the right weight for my height. I've always been a little bit on the skinny side, too. He didn't respond or get up, so I asked, "Are you okay, Dad?"

"I'm fine. I'm fine. It just feels good to lay here."

He patted the ground next to him. "Come here. You try it, too."

I lay down on the carpet and he looked at me.

"Are you wearing makeup?"

"Yes," I said.

"Why? Are there boys coming to this party?"

"No. I'm wearing it because I'm eleven now."

That made him purse his lips together like he was thinking about something incredibly difficult. He looked like he was working out the final glitches in his cure for cancer.

Finally he shut his eyes and said, "I can't look at you right now. You're growing up more and more by the second."

I poked him in the ribs. "Dad,...Dad," I said.

He kind of murmured, "What." Like he was very tired.

Right then the doorbell rang. I rolled onto my stomach and saw that there was a dark and gigantic stain spreading underneath one of the wine bottles. We had white carpet. I jumped up, ran over to the bottle, and picked it up (the cork was loose). I yelled, "Dad! We made a huge mess!" He sat up and said, "Oh shit! We have to clean that up!" He took off his shirt and started pressing it down into the spot on the carpet. My mom came down the stairs and asked, "Who was at the door? I heard a bell, right?" I told her, "I'll go see, but me and Dad spilled on the carpet! You should get some cleaner!" She yelled, "Spilled what? What did you spill, Lance?" (That was my dad's name.) I went toward the door and my mom came running to the living room, still saying, "What did you spill? You weren't doing anything down here, were you? You didn't spill something in front of her?"

When I opened the door, a balloon guy was there with a whole bunch of helium flamingos and palm trees for the house. The man told me how much we owed him, and I turned to ask my mom for a check, but she was jogging on the soaked carpet trying to sponge up the wine with her socks. She told him to just bill us. He said he needed cash or a check. My dad looked up from the ground and it was like he only just realized the man was standing there.

My dad asked him, "How much do we owe you?"

The balloon guy said, "Two hundred."

After standing up, my dad took his wallet out of his pocket and gave the balloon guy the money.

When you're younger, you're selfish, and you're able to believe fully that the world revolves around you. When your parents act like they're doing coke, you just assume that they're all jazzed about your turning another year older.

At five past five-thirty Katrina Percy knocked on my door (she was my only friend). I opened it and her mom, Dawn, was standing behind her holding my present, which was big and wrapped elaborately like a professional at Nordstrom had done it. My mom ran up and hugged Dawn tightly and said something into her ear while Katrina and I just sort of nervously stared at each other. Even though we were friends, we weren't friends that touched. We didn't ever link our arms together like the other girls at school, and we didn't hold hands when we were scared or shy. Instead, we spent long hours seriously discussing what we should put in the time capsule we were going to bury behind a restaurant called Marco Polo once we got out of sixth grade.

Since Dawn had gotten a divorce she'd been spending a lot of time at my house. She'd show up at ten at night with Katrina, and while our parents went upstairs, we'd sit in the family room and watch hour-long dramas until we passed out around twelve. The other kids at school used to come up with elaborate stories about what their parents did after they put them to bed. Most were convinced their parents threw parties as soon as they were asleep. I guess mine really did.

Soon everybody else arrived (I won't bother going through the guest list, and I'm not even sure I could if I wanted to). My mom had spent an entire afternoon putting together a scavenger hunt list consisting of things like a palm frond, a bikini bottom, a pinch of soft sand, a cocktail umbrella. After me and my guests were split up into two teams, she told us we were only allowed to collect one item from each household. She even drew a line next to each item so the provider could verify that the exchange had taken place honestly.

I remember reggae playing from the surround-sound speakers in the house. I remember looking back at my mom and dad. The sun was casting a pink color on the wall behind them. Some of the other parents had been invited over for a barbecue, and they were all holding wineglasses between their second and third fingers and sloshing them around in the air.

My mom asked, "Is everyone ready?" She held her watch close to her face and stared at it intensely.

Evie Barrows tugged excitedly on my arm, but only because I was the one with the birthday.

"Yeah, we're ready," I said. Without looking up, my mom yelled, "You have ninety minutes. Go!" and then we were all running down my hallway and out through the garage. Even the parents were running behind us and waving from the bottom of the driveway.

This was when I lived in Newport Beach, when the houses in my neighborhood were sleek. Like blocks of ice and snow gracefully arranged to make houses. The air smelled like the ocean, obviously, and even from the outside you could tell that all the ceilings were high and concave.

Anyway, on the corner of Windover my team huddled together and everyone was fighting over which way we should go and which things we should get if a household was able to offer more than one item. Lesley Nussbaum, one of my neighborhood acquaintances, tried to take charge by saying, "We could go to my house and get the bikini bottom," but I knew that she just wanted everyone to see how great her bedroom was. It had art deco furniture and was done in pink and black.

I was having none of it, so I put my hand in the air and said, "The Wongs have a parrot. You can hear it squawking when you walk past their front window, so that's where we'll get our tropical feather. My mom says Mr. Landshim is an alcoholic, so he's bound to have one of those paper umbrellas in the house. The Trolleys have a shell wind chime hanging off the lantern by their door. Seriously, they have to have a palm plant in the backyard. I've seen the sailboat in the third-car garage of the Newstats, so maybe there's sand in the bottom of it or at least in the bottom of their beach shoes. Mandy Tilmon is a total Newport Beach slut who wouldn't be caught dead in the same bathing suit two years in a row. She'll give us some bottoms. And then we'll have forty percent of the list done."

We ripped through that whole list in seventy minutes and the only reason it took that long was because we got held up at Mr. Howarth's house. When I asked him if he had a coconut, he just stared at me for what seemed like forever. Then he smiled and stared at the rest of my team. His eyes went up and down our bodies and I wanted to scream out, "Jesus Christ! We're eleven!" but he said that he thought he could help us. He asked, "Do you want to come in and sit on the couch while I go look?"

"Sorry," I said, "but we're in a huge rush."

He gave me the most lecherous gaze and said, "It'll go faster if you girls come inside and help me look."

I glared at him. "It's my birthday." He gave me one final look, but then seemed to accept that answer. After we got the coconut we began to sprint back to my street, and I remember feeling warm with the thrill of having completed the hunt thoroughly. The sun was on its way down. I saw a flare in the corner of my eye and looked up toward the bedroom window of Grey, a neighborhood teenager with arsonist tendencies. He was at his desk, burning something in a vase, and the light in between his hands seemed like it was jumping outside and into the sky.

Katrina kind of galloped next to me, and she was shouting that we should save a piece of my birthday cake in Tupperware for our time capsule. She thought the people of 2047 would want to know what sheet deserts from Vons tasted like way back when. My team ran passionately down the middle of the asphalt as it curved down toward my street, punching our arms back and forth. We just knew we were coming in first and taking home the prize (which I already knew was notepads shaped like oranges that also smelled like oranges). The way I remember it now, the last thought that went through my mind as I rounded the corner and the streetlamps went on was that I hoped the other team wouldn't accuse me of cheating.

When I saw the police cars and ambulance parked on the gravel part of my driveway which wasn't meant to be parked on, I stepped up my pace and ran so fast that my knees became unsteady. I felt my cheeks beating next to my jaw. My skin felt so loose. Like if I ran harder it could fly off. Every time my feet hit the pavement, the impact ran up my back and banged against my skull.

I tore through our two front doors that were both wide open, and as I entered the house I heard the voices of what seemed like two stories of men. Men echoing from across the stair banister onto the tiles downstairs, men booming from beeping walkie-talkies, and men's heavy feet on the ceiling above me. But then behind that wall of sound I heard Dawn Percy's frail and incomplete instructions, like "press" and "heart" and "splash some water" and "they'll wake up."

I screeched, "Mom!" so loud that my temples screamed back.

I screeched, "Dad! Please!"

I screeched, "Mom!"

I screeched, "Please!"

One of my team members, Rebecca Shafer, asked, "Stella?" She stepped in front of me and tried to look into my eyes, like a kid wanting answers. I pushed her, and she hit the wall (which I didn't intend). But I didn't stop. I ran past her and took the stairs three at a time.

There were two policemen at the top and when they saw me, their arms went instinctively out to their sides and their brows furrowed, making them look angry. I tried again.

I wailed, "Mom! Dad!"

The policemen said something. I threw myself on the

ground and aimed for the gap between them, in between their calves. I tried making the space bigger with my arms, pushing outward with everything I had left. They both bent over and I felt two arms pulling on one of mine, and two arms pulling on the other. They were trying to pull me up, like you see parents doing to their kids in a shopping-mall parking structure after they've counted to three. All I know is they were hurting me.

I screamed, "You're going to pull my arms out of their sockets!" My eyes welled up with tears as soon as I said it. I threw all the weight of my head, neck, and stomach toward the ground, trying to become so heavy that they'd be forced to drop me. But then I felt an arm across my breasts, and the shock of being touched there was what made me realize that the policemen had changed their tactic. Now they were cradling me across my chest, almost swinging me back and forth as they attempted to balance me in the middle of them. The blood rushed to my head and I tossed my head backward, the very same move I do at the end of an exhausting day, and finally their bodies weren't blocking my view of my parents' bedroom. I only saw my mom's head. The rest of her body was out of my line of sight. She was already on a stretcher, and her head would jump a little every couple of seconds as something mysterious was done to the rest of her.

I said to them, "Oh god, it's my mom!" A paramedic opened one of the double doors to my parents' room a little farther and I saw my dad on the ground. His eyes were open and he was blue. In the background, some of my acquaintances' parents stood with their fingernails blocking their mouths. Dawn sat on the edge of my mom and dad's bed, already cried out, and the Fields paced back and forth while grasping on to each other. They were both shaking. They were both wiping their noses.

For the past six years I've thought it incredibly romantic that my parents died within seconds of each other, their usual coke having been cut with heroin. It was like their bodies possessed the exact same thresholds and weaknesses. Their hearts snapped in tandem.

I remember them being very much in love with each other, and even when I looked back and realized that they were probably always very high together, I still used to comfort myself with the idea that they died together. I wondered who my mom would have been if she had survived and had to bury my dad, and then I decided she would have killed herself anyway. I specifically know that she found the song "Don't Fear the Reaper" really passionate. The singer is practically begging his girlfriend to die with him, and the way he sings it, anybody would have to admit that by the end of the first verse his argument starts to sound reasonable.

It's good they died on the same day, but I don't think I find it as romantic as I did before. Today I had the idea that romance is just something people decide on so they can make their intentions understood. There's nothing essentially romantic about things like roses or jewelry. Romance starts as some blank concept, and then you just fill it in with objects so you can have something to point to when you want to make it real.

Anyway, as for me, my parents' death was something that I just accepted. I spent about five minutes waiting for them to come back to me as ghosts or whatever, but then I had to roll my eyes at how far up in the sky I had let my head drift. My parents didn't believe in God, and they raised me not to, either. So then, who did I think was going to send them back to tell me how much they wanted to be with me, and how did I think they were going to appear.

I went to stay temporarily with the Percys and for a while I wouldn't talk to Dawn. I'm not sure why, and I know it's considered really rude to ignore the person who's volunteered to be your interim caretaker, but...I guess the silence had something to do with the fact that Dawn had been doing drugs with my parents for months, and a part of me wished that she had been the one we all cremated. Soon after I moved in, Katrina entered an early rebellious stage, so not only was she smoking cigarettes at twelve, but she wasn't talking to her mom, either.

There were times late at night when I couldn't sleep and I'd hear Dawn get on the phone. Then I'd hear the garage go up and her car pull out. One night I heard the phone ring at three, so I left my sleeping bag and went out into the garage in the dark. I stood there barefoot until Dawn came through the back door. Her keys jingled. I could make out her outline since my eyes had adjusted to the dark, but she had no idea I was there. Her slippers shuffled along the concrete, and I could even hear her breathe because I was exhaling and inhaling as slowly as possible through my nose. She came closer and closer, making the hairs stand up on the back of my neck.

Finally she bumped into me and as soon as her arm touched my shoulder, she jumped back against the car and made a thud against the driver's side door. She screamed like she was under attack by a murderer. She started pleading with me, not really knowing it was me, promising that she had drugs upstairs and would give me some if I'd just let her live. All I said was, "Dawn," but she must not have recognized my voice because she dropped to the ground and passed out.

Dawn told Social Services that she didn't feel comfortable around me any longer and that they needed to hurry up and find me a real guardian. My parents were both only children, so I didn't have any aunts and uncles or close cousins. My mom's dad was the only one still living, and he was already in a home. I mean he was in a convalescent one. My mom hadn't been on very good terms with him anyway.

Eventually it was decided that I would be placed in foster care, since no one would want to adopt me at my age. Also, since I wasn't that close to any of my acquaintances, it wasn't like I had some best friend begging her mom to make me her sister.

I ended up with the Roths when I was eleven and a half. God knows what made them volunteer to be foster parents, and I've never asked.

Three

The first time I met my foster parents, Simon and Shana, I thought the Social Services lady had brought me to the wrong house because they seemed so surprised to see me. Shana opened the door and looked at me with wide eyes like I was a parking ticket. Simon came up behind her and tentatively put his hand on her shoulder, like he was saying, "Don't worry, sweetie. It's only thirty dollars and we'll pay it." I stood still on the welcome mat, waiting in the shade of the spruce breezeway.

After a few seconds, Shana said, "Yes?"

And I said, "Yes" back, but without the question mark. I really thought she was asking something along the lines of, "This is our new child, yes?" So that's why I was confirming things for her. I just assumed she was happy or in shock and not able to get out a complete sentence. On the drive to the house I had imagined the Roths as people who had been dying to have children for years. Maybe they had gone through a couple of miscarriages.

But Shana didn't say anything back or throw her arms open for me. Instead, her cheek began to twitch right under her eye. The skin hopped like there was a miniature Mexican jumping bean under the muscle. And she stayed silent. That's when I realized she had been saying yes like my mom used to say yes when a telemarketer asked if she was indeed Amelia Parrish and if she was in charge of making changes to our long-distance service. I kept waiting for the Social Services woman to step in and announce me, or at least turn me back around and take me to a more excited family, but instead she put pressure on my neck and kind of nudged my head forward. I guess she was trying to hint that I should enter the house.

I couldn't take the awkwardness anymore. "Hi," I said, "I'm Stella."

Simon, a very gangly man, leaned over a little and said quietly, "Not anymore. We'll be renaming you."

Panicked, I looked to my agent to tell them that she didn't think that renaming was a good idea because I wasn't a puppy, and I wasn't one of those kids taken out of Russia who arrives with a name that has no vowels in it. I was positive I would be reassigned and thought, "Oh well. The next family will be better." But the Social Services lady was smiling slyly at Simon in the way that adults smile at one another when a little kid gets upset over something stupid. I've seen the same smile given to the parents of children who are bawling over some guy in a Mickey costume at Disneyland. Then I knew that she had actually picked up on some imperceptible sign that Simon had made a joke.

But, just in case I didn't, Simon said (without cracking any sort of smile or without changing the expression on his face), "I made a joke."

And I just said, "Oh."

The agent's pressure on my neck was getting ridiculous. I gave in and kind of stumbled into the house. Shana took a step back as I tripped over the doorstep on the way in. There was a brief look of alarm on her face. I mean, I think she would have produced the same expression had I had been running with scissors and come "thisclose" to stabbing her. Anyway, I didn't end up falling down, so after I steadied myself I gave Shana eyes as if to say, "I'm sorry." I'm sorry for startling you—I guess that was what the sorry was for. She looked like she needed it.

Simon thanked the Social Services woman for bringing me while Shana tucked her hair behind her ear so softly that the hair fell back out of place within seconds. When the woman wished us all luck, Shana reached out and patted me on the shoulder so lightly that I wondered if I had hallucinated the patting in the first place. Then the door shut and we were all alone together.

Without any signal to each other, Shana and Simon headed toward the stairs and I still stood by the brass coatrack, not sure if I was invited, too.

I asked, "Should I bring my bags?"

Shana's head whipped around like she suspected a rapist was following her in the dark.

"Oh! Hi."

I didn't get it. But I said, "Hello" with my *o* drawn out to demonstrate that I was confused and completely unsure about why she was greeting me now.

In her dazed, eternally startled way, she said, "There's a bedroom for you upstairs. Your own bedroom."

"Great," I said.

Simon did a sideways shuffle toward me and then bent down to lift up my suitcase and two bags. At first he pretended that my stuff was really, really heavy and that he couldn't lift it. Again, he didn't make any of the appropriate comical facial gestures to go with this "joke," so he looked like a guy having real difficulty. Except I knew he wasn't. The bag he was trying to lift had underwear, socks, and a Costco-sized box of tampons in it (which isn't heavy).

He asked in a thin, reedy voice, "What do you have in here? A dead body?" At the time, I thought, "Didn't they give these people any background about what's happened to me? Shouldn't they maybe be avoiding the topic of death?"

But I was eleven and a half, and I badly wanted them to like me, so I tried continuing the joke and said, "No, I have solid gold in there."

Shana cut in, as much as someone whose voice is barely perceptible can cut in, and said, "Have you ever seen the show?" She finally sounded vaguely excited.

"*Solid Gold*?"

"Mmm-hmm."

I told her, "I think so, when I was little."

All of a sudden Shana began to kind of twist her body and do some sort of low-kick combination. The two steps didn't particularly flow together, and she looked extremely self-conscious.

"That used to be our favorite show. We still have all the episodes on tape in the family room."

Simon added, "We used to love to dance. Loved to cut the rug."

And then he bent down and began pantomiming actually cutting the rug, using his second and third fingers as fake scissors. That's the moment when I knew what deep crap I was in.

Over the years, nothing's really changed. In the mornings we kind of eat breakfast together, which means that I push cereal down in the bowl with the spoon until it's soaked with milk and it looks like I ate something, and Simon and Shana chew on theirs dry. They ask me about things like movies that I've told them I've seen, and I make up a scene to talk about. They barely go to the movies anyway, just dinners and coffee afterward. They don't know that I'm probably describing a movie that's better coming out of my mouth than it actually is on the screen. I had a version of *Lost Highway* that was a hysterical road comedy about a husband and wife who couldn't read maps.

Shana is almost always home at three o'clock, watching old tapes or sometimes just sitting there at the kitchen table, staring at the oven. In the beginning, when I was younger, I'd stay in the family room for a while and she'd give me apple juice, and I'd drink it out of a straw because the straw kept me busy. I'd look down at it, or I'd bend it into shapes, whatever. And then, when I got into high school, I realized I could just go upstairs and start working on my homework, even if I didn't have that much left. Only once, out of the blue, Shana asked as I left the room, "Would you say school is the most important thing to you?" and I asked, "In terms of what?" and she asked back, "Huh?" She stared at me with dead eyes. So I started to explain, "Well, it's important in a lot of ways," and she told me, "I don't remember doing much homework when I was a girl."

I used to think all you needed was time and then you could love anybody. At one time I had myself convinced that eventually Simon's sense of humor would become comfortable, like the way my dad's sweat didn't bother me when he used to come home from playing tennis. He'd be dripping and his shirt would smell like dead animals had thrown up on it, but I'd hug him anyway. And, okay, admittedly, I don't know exactly what qualities Shana had that I expected to turn into something positive, but I thought at least she'd have some more tricks up her sleeve besides a mild obsession with *Solid Gold.* To this day, when I come downstairs in the morning and say hi to her, she whips around like I'm a poltergeist and I've just sent a pot flying across the room. It's hard for me to believe that she continually forgets I live in the house, but I can't really come up with a better explanation.

Also, the house never changed. When I got there, the couch was a blue floral, the wallpaper was a blue floral, and there was a lot of that blue glass (you know the kind) on the shelves and tables. The funny thing is, I never found out if it's Shana that likes blue or Simon. But it's all still the same color, and I don't think anything's been added or taken away.

My old house used to be pretty minimal. I liked the sound my mom's favorite leather chair made when I jumped onto it from the counter in the kitchen. And the counters were all marble, even in the bathroom, and they always made everything feel clean and simple. There's too much wood at the Roths. I feel like wood sucks things in, even if that's irrational. When you look at all the curvy lines in it, you feel like they're made up of trapped smells and old air. What sucks is my current bedroom has tons of wood cabinets along the top rim of the room because the Roths used it as an office before I moved in.

A few months into our arrangement, Shana was sleep-walking one night and came into my room and tried to fax something through my headboard. I guess that's where she used to keep the table with the scanner and the fax machine. She started to dial out on my forehead and that woke me up, so I grabbed her arm and shook it to wake her. I didn't shake very hard, but she gasped, made a little squeal, and walked backward out of the room. Every once in a while Simon comes in to get some white paper out of the drawers by the window, but besides that I hardly ever see him upstairs.

The Roths are Jews and the only times they seem to realize they're raising me is on occasional Sunday mornings and Friday nights, when they seem to want me to go to temple with them. Their temple is so reformed that everyone believes God doesn't care what day of the week you choose to worship on, as long as you make the effort. Simon told me that ten years ago the congregation held a vote and unanimously decided to move Saturday services to Sunday, mostly so everyone could be on the same worship schedule as their Christian friends. This benefited cross-religion plan-making on the weekends.

On the first Friday I spent at the house, the intercom buzzed in my room and then I heard Shana going, "Hello? Hello?"

I got up from my bed and pressed the speak button. "Hi."

Shana said, "Hello?"

I pressed the button again, and shouted, "Hi, Shana!"

Shana said, "Hello? Stella?"

I told her, "Yes, it's me."

"Oh!" It was like I had rung the intercom from outside of the house, and she was only just discovering who had come to visit.

Anyway, since the sun was going down, I asked her, "Should I come down for dinner?"

There was silence. I pressed the speak button. "Hello?" Shana didn't answer. I tried a few more times, but then figuring it was easier to go and talk to her in the kitchen, I opened my bedroom door and headed toward the stairs. Shana had the same idea because when I got to the top of the stairs, she was at the bottom. However, the second-story landing creaked under my weight when Shana was halfway up the first step, and as soon as she heard the sound she immediately retreated back down. This was even before she looked up at the top of the stairs to see why the floor was creaking.

I watched her trying to decide whether she should restep or not, and she seemed smaller than ever, the kind of woman who should live in a condominium and not a house. I said, "I'm sorry. Did I scare you?"

Shana stayed put. "Of course not, honey." That was the warmest thing she had said to me since we met, so I was sort of touched.

"Well, did you need help setting the table or something?"

"Oh, no. No. We're going to temple."

In retrospect this seems pretty stupid, but I asked, "Is that your favorite restaurant?" Because I really thought that since we had made it through our first week, Simon and Shana were going to take me out to eat and maybe we'd go see a romantic comedy afterward.

Shana was visibly confused. "The temple. It's just a temple. But there are cookies after the service."

I asked, "You mean like a Jewish temple?"

"That's right."

I leaned against the railing to try to look casual. I didn't want to alarm her, as I told her that, "My family wasn't exactly Jewish."

"Hmm," Shana said.

"Oh." I think there's no possible way to come up with a suave retort to that kind of setup.

Maybe she was feeling more in her sphere of comfort because Shana began to climb the stairs and make her way toward me. Her feet didn't make any noise. The entire time it took her to climb was this gigantic pregnant pause, but pregnant with awkwardness and not meaning. I remember having trouble grasping her as a tangible human being since she was such a wisp of a woman. The best example I can think of is when you feel a hair lift from the back of your head and it makes you think there has to be a breeze outside, but there's no tangible proof of a real wind anywhere. The leaves on the trees stay still and the water on the lake is completely flat, but you're still pretty sure you felt a hint of something blowing around and making your scalp tingle.

We went in my room and things were still so quiet between us that I imagined hearing the sun going down even farther. It was a shock when Simon poked his head in a few seconds later and said, "Picking out a dress?"

I said, "I guess?" because up until then, I seriously had no idea what Shana and I were supposed to be doing.

He nodded and continued, "Nothing too short." I didn't know if he was kidding. I didn't know what to do, and I was especially tired of feeling this way every time he said anything, anything at all. But after we looked in my closet I found out he actually wasn't kidding, so I ended up going in one of Shana's floral dresses. It buttoned all the way up to the neck, had no shape, and made me feel like a Mormon.

That first time at temple was so boring that I spent the entire time trying to figure out how I could get out of it in the future. The thing was, I wanted to bail on the temple sessions without making the Roths hate me. Initially I came up with the idea that maybe I could just fail to get in the car next week and they wouldn't even notice I wasn't with them. I wanted to test their perceptive abilities, so I waited until the rabbi finished his silent prayer and then I started (softly, but noticeably) thumping the prayer book against the rim of my chair. I did this for at least thirty seconds as the woman on the other side of me went from making small eyebrow raises to glaring shamelessly. I watched Shana's profile during this entire time, and not only didn't she look at me, but she also didn't blink. I'm not kidding — this was the first time I noticed that Shana can go ten minutes straight without blinking, and her eyes don't even tear up.

Sixty seconds in, the situation was getting ridiculous and another guy started singing a song in what I have to assume was Hebrew. I didn't want to be entirely disrespectful, so I began to tap the book to the beat of the song. I had almost banged out the entire song when suddenly Simon reached across Shana's knee. He started tapping my knee to the same beat while maintaining very intense eye contact with me. I don't know if his intention was an eye for an eye or if he was just trying to bond, but he noticed me nonetheless. I thought, "Simon, you sly fox. You just might figure out if I'm not here one day."

After that I ran through some obvious options, like regularly pulling an "I have too much homework" or an "I don't feel good," but all those excuses seemed to have limited potential. I shut my eyes to think.

Soon the woman next to me elbowed me and said, "Open your eyes." I did. Still, even though I had done what she asked, she hissed at me, "Rude!"

I hissed back at her, "You're not my mother." She rolled her eyes and it made me feel terrible, but I still was glad for what I said. I hated the woman's perfume. Or maybe I just hated the thick body odor seeping through her perfume because I definitely remember that being an issue.

Anyway, I kept my eyes open, but I concentrated on the ark on the stage. It was at least twenty feet tall, but what really got me was the bush on fire on the doors. The flames were made out of some kind of metallic fabric so that they actually seemed to twinkle and leap. I stared at the flames so long that it was like I was really staring at a candle. You know how it is when your eyes start to see inside the flame, and the rest of the world drops off. I stared until I almost got to the point of imagining that I could see the threads that made up the pieces of fabric. When I finally looked away, there were spots everywhere, like I had just looked into the sun. While I was blinking and trying to get them out, the rabbi's voice drifted back in.

He was quoting a passage about "thy brother" and how if thy brother is so poor that he has to sell all his things, then his friends and family should step in and pick up the slack. Then he went into a lecture about how we should extend this notion to an immaterial level, so that when our common man is at a loss and needs anything at all, he has a figurative family that's always willing to step in and help. If he needs love, then he should have love. Love or twenty dollars. They should both be given equally freely.

In the middle of all of this, I realized the one thing the Roths couldn't hold over me was family. Because I still had a little bit of family left. My mom's dad is my last real living relative, except I didn't see him much during my childhood because my mom was pissed at him for cheating on my grandma over and over again until finally she died. Not that she died from the heartbreak exactly, but the guy just wasn't faithful to her, not even in the end.

After my parents died, the people at Social Services went looking for relatives, but I could have told them that was a futile search. My maternal grandpa, Donald (who I just call Donald), was already too old and living in a home, so he obviously wasn't deemed fit. I know I have cousins a million times removed somewhere in Florida, but who knows if they were ever tracked down or what they said about the idea of meeting me.

Prior to moving in with the Roths, the last time I saw Donald was at my tenth Christmas when we had him over to the house and he came without a single present. I was very quiet around him because I didn't understand what kind of person he really was. If, back then, you had asked me to describe three additional personality traits of his besides being an asshole, I swear I couldn't do it.

Anyway, it wasn't like Donald was bouncing me up and down on his knee. At one point during Christmas dinner my parents went upstairs and shut their bedroom door, and I was left alone with him. We were in the dining room sitting at the table, and how hard is it for an old man to think of questions to ask a young girl? Donald could have asked me what my favorite school subject was or if I knew how to roller-skate. The things you can ask little kids are endless, and that's why you never remember having awkward moments before the age of ten. You always have something stupid to talk about. Have you ever heard little girls having a debate in a public place? They literally sound insane. Even I used to be able to join in on conversations with complete strangers before fifth grade, and I've never been the poster child for social well-being.

But Donald had nothing to say to me. He just raised one lazy eyebrow and stared at me like he had something on his mind but no desire to express it. I didn't want to seem rude and stare back, so I practiced folding my napkin into a bra like Jane Stenson had taught me at school. Donald watched.

I finished with the bra and I felt a little proud about that, so I decided to try smiling at him. When I did, he put both of his hands under his chin and rested on them while thumbing the skin on the side of his neck. I did the same — not as any way of connecting with him, but because I got curious about what the skin on my neck felt like.

That made him ask, "Are you making fun of me?"

"No," I said, and immediately put my hands back down at my sides.

I was getting braver by the second, so I asked him what was under the Band-Aids on his arm. He had four in a vertical row and you just couldn't look away because of the way the skin puckered around them. The skin was already loose from age, and then the way that elastic tugged on it — it was just all too much, especially with all the sunspots.

Donald asked, 'You really want to see?"

I either nodded or said yes. Who knows now. He pulled back the first Band-Aid and I saw a lot of red skin with something purple and slightly wet in the middle.

"What's that?"

"Maybe you have to see another one to figure it out," he said.

I shrugged. I was a kid. Donald pulled off another Band-Aid and held out the arm, presumably so I could see the wound better. The skin around the second one was bubbled a little.

Donald told me, "You're looking at cancer."

Before that day I had heard about cancer, but really had no idea what it was. Sort of like how I saw a story about the AIDS crisis on the cover of *Newsweek* when I was younger and because a woman was on the cover, I thought the crisis was about teachers' aides in the public school system. I seriously wondered, What could the aides possibly be doing that was so bad? The word *cancer* pulled me into the same vague territory, where I recognized that it was a crisis of some sort, but didn't know if the crisis was the wound itself, the area around the wound, or a greater physical clue that I was overlooking. (The sunspots?) I thought cancer had to present itself as one tangible thing, and not just an overall condition.

So I asked, "Are you talking about the blisters, the scab, or the wetness on the purple part?"

Donald replied, "I'm talking about me," and that really threw me at the time. There was now the possibility of cancer being an adjective, as in "I am smart/I am cancer/I am confused." I also thought about it being a person, as in "I am grandpa/I am cancer/I am Stella."

Donald took off the third Band-Aid and asked, "Do you think these are disgusting?"

I looked carefully at his skin and said, "Yes."

He said, "Females think everything is disgusting."

I was stumped, so I just took another piece of chicken from the serving tray by my plate and ate without stopping until my parents came back down with red eyes and stuffy noses.

In temple, it occurred to me that I could start visiting Donald. Specifically, I could visit him on Fridays and Sundays. If the Roths started eyeing me suspiciously, I could say, "I need to feel connected to (maybe a tear?) my family," and even though that might be a little insulting or hurtful to them, they couldn't argue with that universal fact. Also, I did kind of think it might be nice to go and see him. My parents were gone, my house was gone, and my acquaintances were gone, so I thought to myself, "Yeah, I probably should see him." The whole idea clicked for me, and I got the same flash of content that I get nowadays when I figure out a thesis sentence for an English essay. The feeling of something making sense is a powerful and definite one, like a loose arm being popped back into its socket. This is exactly what I was trying to explain on Friday.

So the next Thursday I came home from my new school, which was Lakeside Middle School, and I found Shana in the kitchen paying bills. When I walked into the room, she did a troubled double take. She must have recognized me on the second look because then she asked, "Oh, how was your day, Stella?"

I had butterflies in my stomach because I'm really not very much of a confrontational personality, and it's not in my nature to make waves. That I was doing this at all should tell you just how boring practicing Judaism is when you're not actually Jewish.

I said, "My day was okay. I did well on my math, science, and social studies quizzes." I'm remembering this conversation exactly as it was since it caused me so much anxiety at the time. It's slammed somewhere in my brain.

Shana was punching numbers into a calculator and said, "Shoot," like she had pressed the subtraction button instead of the addition one.

"What's wrong?"

"The balance is coming up short."

I said, "I'm kind of good with math. Maybe I could check your numbers for you?"

Shana chewed on the clicker of her pen for a while, and then she said, "Oh, I forgot to add the money we're getting for you!"

"So now your checkbook will balance?" I asked.

"Yes. Perfectly now."

I thought that catching her when her checkbook was balanced was a perfect time to bring up the anti-temple issue. I got onto one of the padded blue floral chairs at the table.

"Can I talk to you about something?"

She started biting on her pinky nail. "Well, sure. Yes. Sure."

So then I just went into it. "The thing is, and I don't want you to feel bad about this, but lately I've been feeling like I should have more of a relationship with my grandpa. He's family. And please don't feel bad when I say that (because I understand that we're all trying to form a new family here), and I don't want to hurt your feelings. And I'm definitely not trying to fight against that family in any way because I think it's a good idea and I'm all for it. So please don't be hurt by anything I'm saying. But, you know, my grandpa Donald is blood, and I don't think I've been valuing blood as much as I should and maybe now's the time for me to start doing that. I called him and asked if he thought we should start seeing each other and he said, 'Why don't you come and eat breakfast with me on Sunday mornings? That's the big visitor breakfast.' They have a whole continental spread with muffins, fruit, orange juice, and all that stuff. He said there's some song singing, too. It sounded really important to him, so I said yes, even though I know that's one of our temple days. And then, before I knew it, I had also agreed to come and see him whenever he got lonely, because he said he gets lonely a lot. He is my mom's dad, after all, and I think that if she knew how lonely he was, she'd want me to do something about it." My stomach actually started hurting then because I was full of so much crap.

Shana had been listening with nervous eyes throughout the entire speech, and when I finally paused she said, "That's fine."

"It is?" I had so much more I could say on blood.

"Sure," she said. "It sounds delicious."

"The visits with my grandpa?"

"The continental breakfast."

I said, "Oh. Right."

Thankful for permission, I reached out to pat Shana's wrist, but as soon as our skin touched I shocked her. I mean, literally—I gave her some kind of electric shock. After the zapping sound, she pulled her arm back toward her chest like a dog with a thorn in her paw.

I told her, "Sorry" and went upstairs to get on the phone with Donald. I felt enormously guilty for telling my first lie in ages, but comforted myself with the thought that sometimes a lie is just a statement that hasn't become the truth yet. Really, it's just a matter of time in certain cases.

Today being Sunday, I walked to the bus stop and took the 8:07 bus to the coast, which I've been doing for almost six years now. Donald has a room in an assisted living home called the Horizon Villa, but the building is more like a weird preschool than a villa in the traditional sense. The first time he gave me the name I was expecting white stucco and bougainvilleas climbing the walls. I imagined Donald whiling away his days in a center courtyard with a running fountain (bearing a stone lion's head), thoroughly washed patio chairs, and frosted glass tables. After seeing the actual brown building, I thought to myself, "Do they deliberately try to make dying people depressed or what?"

Whenever I enter the Villa, I take a deep breath in preparation for the smell that hits as soon as I get into the front hallway. I don't need to explain that smell, since everybody in the world knows what old people and their places smell like. I sign in with Lupe at the window on the right, and she always tells me how great I am for visiting Donald. I guess I visit him more than a lot of other people visit their relatives, so she's under the impression we have a really fantastic relationship. Also, she keeps a daily list of the things that happen to him because she thinks I want to know all of it. So every Sunday she produces a paper with items like "ate his entire dessert" and "tried three jumping jacks" on it. I realize how much effort goes into documenting Donald's small achievements, so I always read the list in front of her and smile while I'm reading it. If Lupe's ever in a bad mood (which sometimes happens when someone dies or the ones living there just get to be too much to take), I take the pen from the sign-in clipboard and make her a list of all the nice things she's done for me. I mean, the things that I write that are "nice" are actually things I could definitely do without, like the calls every time Donald sees the doctor, but whatever.

This morning she gave me a list that included Donald's

sound nap and a Xerox of a macaroni art project he did yesterday.

In her Spanish accent she said, "This must make you very proud, Stella."

"Donald definitely did a good job with the macaroni," I said.

While shooing me with her hand and smiling, she told me, "Then go see him and tell him that."

I made a right past the sign-in window and walked down the hall while listening to the sounds of coughs, dishes clanking, and an old record playing in someone's room. There are shaky drawings all over the wall and I think it's pretty cruel to display them. They remind me of that old riddle about the animal that starts on four legs, then two, then three. You know the one — baby, man, old man. I see that third leg (the cane) as some kind of step back toward childhood, where man starts to hunch over again until he's forced to take back one of the legs he gave up before. It's all pretty depressing to me.

I went past the kitchen where the Mexican dishwashers were working and wondered how they deal with taking care of old people that aren't even theirs. It must suck to not only have to take care of someone else's grandparents, but also to take care of grandparents who probably have some kind of bias against you and who think you aren't understanding half of what they say. Two of the guys in the kitchen looked at me when I passed and said something to each other. Then they laughed. At least I can admit that I have no idea what they were talking about. But anyway, I can guess. I take French at school, but I know what those guys were poking each other in the ribs about. I had one of my short plaid skirts on with kneesocks.

At the end of that hall I made a right, and then went over to the second door on the left. Donald lives in room 103. He leaves the door unlocked for me, and I just go in because I come at the same time every Sunday. That way he knows to have his pants on by 8:25. Today I went right in like usual and I didn't see him immediately in the living room/bedroom, but there was a light coming from under the bathroom door.

I called, "Donald! I'm here!" so he wouldn't be alarmed when he came back out. But he didn't say anything back. His hearing is fine.

I called, "Donald!" again, and there still wasn't an answer so I went toward the bathroom and opened the door a little.

At first I thought he wasn't in there because I was just looking through a small crack, but when I pushed the door open farther I saw Donald bent over and floating in his shower. The best way I can describe it is he looked like one of those clowns in a county fair dunk tank. He has a glass rectangle shower with a plastic seat in it, and usually he sits while his helper, Gumer, turns the shower on and looks away. Anyway, what Donald had done was stop up the drain at the bottom of the shower, and then he had shut the door and let the water keep coming until it was high enough for him to duck under. It was probably up to four and a half feet by the time I got there. He was kind of crouched down, with his head bowed, gripping onto the bar inside of the shower door so tight that his knuckles looked like they were going to bust out of their skin. Unbelievably, he was dressed in his best and only suit. I saw he had tried to tie his tie by himself because the knot was all wrong.

I screamed, "Oh my god! What are you doing?"

He heard me through the water and looked forward while shaking his head like, No, no, don't do that.

I said, "Don't tell me no!" and I went to open the shower door, but I was a little slower to do it than I probably should have been. I wasn't sure if it was a good idea to release all those gallons of water in the middle of Donald's rented room, and I wondered if the water would run into the main hallway and ruin the carpet and maybe even somehow give one of the occupants pneumonia. I don't know. But just when my hand was on the shower door handle, Donald came up gasping for air, and I took a step back.

I jumped up and down with clenched fists and kicked the plastic hamper. Then I walked up to the shower and pressed my face against the glass and yelled, "Donald, you're fucking crazy!"

He breathed heavily, his eyes just about to bulge out of his head. The wiry, gray strands of hair on the side of his head were stuck to his temples and cheeks.

He said, "I"—*breath*—"was supposed"—*breath*—"to have this finished by the time"—*breath*—"you got here. I didn't forget"—*breath*—"you were coming."

I took a step back. "Well, aren't you wonderful."

"I can't"—*breath*—"do anything right anymore"—*breath*. "I bet"—*breath*—"I could have done it right"—*breath*—"if they let me keep my med—"*breath* "ication in my room."

Donald has been taking some arthritis pills and some other general prescriptions for the pains that come with old age, but he's not really "sick." Remember the cancer story? He never really had cancer. I found out later from my mom that he had some extra knobs of skin that had been burned off for reasons that were ninety percent aesthetic. He's basically in assisted care because his body is winding down and he can't do things like fix himself lunch anymore. It looks like he's going to be a guy who dies from natural causes in his sleep, and I know that sounds fairly stupid in light of today's incident, but I don't think he could kill himself if he tried.

Donald was still gasping, but still talking. "They cut our food for"—*breath*—"us, so we never touch"—*breath*—"a knife. I don't"—*breath*—"even think I could tie my sheet"—*breath*—"right. I don't know how to"—*breath*—"do it. My hands shake. I don't think"—*breath*—"I could keep my arms above"—*breath*—"my head for that"—*breath*—"long. The ceiling is made out of"—*breath*—"paper so that everything"—*breath*—"falls down. Oh"—*breath*—"Jesus..." He started to sob, which made the water slosh against the shower door. Some water went in his mouth and he started to choke and hyperventilate.

"Would you please just shut up and try to breathe!" I screamed.

As he paused to catch his breath, his eyes grew narrower and a more familiar expression returned to his face. His mouth shut and his lips tightened and the entire effect reminded me of this picture of a Roman coin I saw in history once, the kind with the eyes missing and the incredibly straight noses. Rationally I know that the Romans were supposedly really fun and adventurous (you have to be if you're using mice bodies as bowls and their heads as lids). But when

I look at any artistic representation of the Roman people, I just think, "There's a bunch that had no sense of humor about themselves."

I think that's the most important quality that anybody could ever possess, and my mom and dad both had it. They were really great at laughing at themselves. At their wedding my mom tripped on her way down the stone aisle (it was an outdoor wedding), and she skinned her elbow so bad that blood actually started to run down her arm. And she laughed then. My dad laughed, too. He took off his tie and wrapped it around her arm to keep the pressure off the wound. I guess my dad's mom wanted to stop the wedding right there. You know, take her inside and get cleaned up and then restart the ceremony when the bleeding stopped. But my parents thought the whole thing was very funny.

My dad was so giddy that he took his finger and wiped some of my mom's blood on it and then wiped it in two lines under each cheek. Next he swooped her off her feet and carried her to the altar while yelling, "My woman fall! I carry!" My mom said that made her laugh so hard that when he tried to put her back down in front of the priest, she was too dizzy to stand up straight. All the pictures in the wedding album show the blood on my dad's cheeks because my mom didn't believe in faking pictures before the ceremony.

Anyway, Donald was gearing up for his indifference again. I could see it coming. He inhaled deeply while staring at me, and then finally said, "I don't need you shrieking."

"I wasn't shrieking," I said. "I was just emphatically telling you to catch your breath. You could barely get out your sentences."

Donald peered at me, his eyes getting smaller by the second. "You just can't hear yourself. It's so rooted in your nature that shrieking probably sounds pleasant in your own head."

"I never shriek."

"You just did. All women do. Have you ever heard a man shriek?"

I looked him up and down and said, "I don't know. I've seen a man cry like an old baby though."

"You're crying."

I felt my cheeks and they were wet. I said, "I'm crying about something else."

He splashed some water over the top of the shower, but not at all playfully. Then he asked, "Have I ruined your visit today?"

"That's it," I told him. "I'm calling for help." I went over to the toilet and pulled the long white cord behind it. Donald's supposed to pull it if he ever falls, has a heart attack, catches on fire, or can't get off the toilet. It rings a bell in the main office.

Donald took a mouthful of water and spit it at the shower door. He said, "You want to know how I stopped up the drain? I've been stealing plastic place mats, and garbage bags, and a whole lot of glue. They count the scissors after arts and crafts, but they don't count the glue. I stayed up very late last night, pushing all of it down into the drain. I used my cane to push it down as far as I could. My arms shook, but I kept pushing it all in. And then I poured the glue onto the whole lot of it and then I lay down on the floor…"

I walked back to the shower and stared him dead in the eye and said, "I don't care."

"But you do. You shrieked."

I wondered if I did care about him dying. I realized I had been expecting it for years.

"I was surprised and kind of annoyed. Not caring." Right then the door flew open and Lupe, Gumer, and a couple of the guys from the kitchen came running into the room. From the front door Lupe was already calling, "Mr. Moonan! We're coming!"

"We're in here, Lupe!" I called.

When everybody saw Donald in the shower, they just about died themselves.

Lupe's eyes immediately started to tear up and her hand went over her mouth, but Gumer went over to the shower and pointed her finger so sharply at Donald that she looked like she was going to poke his eye out through the glass. With her long red nail she tapped on the glass so hard that the door shook (picture a hummingbird drilling into a tree—her tapping was seriously that hard and that manic), and I totally thought her acrylic tip would break off. At the same time she was shrieking so loud that I raised my eyebrows at Donald to say, "If you were wondering what real shrieking sounds like, here you go."

"Donald! Oh my god! Oh my god! They don't pay me enough for this crap! What, were you trying to take a swim, Donald?! Were you taking a swim? I can't let you out of my sight for five minutes! You're like a little child! And now what are we going to do? How the hell are we supposed to get all this water out of here? I should leave you there! I should leave you there until you're all shriveled! Oh wait! You *are* already shriveled!"

She was still going when I decided to walk into the bedroom/living room because the bathroom was getting too crowded. I sat down on Donald's old chair that's covered with beige velvet that's been worn down so far that it's not even fuzzy anymore.

I looked around at his room and decided it's better than mine. He has a nice big window, no wooden cabinets, and I like the way the sun comes in through the gauzy-type curtains. The wallpaper has floating peach and blue feathers on it and the paintings of the ocean (the Hamptons kind, not the Miami Beach kind) have matching peach frames. I guess the home puts the same wallpaper and paintings in all the rooms to brighten things up for the tenants who don't have the energy to do it themselves. But anyway, the decor reminds me of the kind you might find in a Marriot, and when I used to go on family vacations I always loved staying there. When you wake up in a hotel you always have a clean feeling. It's not just knowing that the sheets were washed yesterday. It's also more of a mental thing, where you know that any mess you make will be gone by tomorrow.

Speaking of messes, Gumer was yelling at one of the guys to go get "the pump from the storage closet! The one for the toilet!" Lupe added, "And get all the buckets we have here!"

Donald mumbled something about mothers. I couldn't hear.

I got up from the chair and poked my head into the bathroom. Gumer was showing Lupe how they were going to get the water out of the shower. She looked like she was milking an invisible cow. Lupe was wondering if they should call the owner.

I backed out of the room and then turned around and walked out the door. I went home, promising myself that when I go I'm going to do it correctly. Seeing Donald like that, it was just an eye-opener. I brainstormed some methods on a sheet of paper, and then I went on the Internet and did some research. I found out that I should be displaying certain telltale behaviors, like giving away my most treasured belongings, doing poorly in school, and telling people that the world would be better off without me. So I resolved to do all that, and then I spent the rest of the day doing homework and finishing my paper on *Huck Finn*.

Four

The crows were eating at the roof before my alarm went off. They started around 6:30 and were so amazingly loud that I couldn't even incorporate their pecking into my dream. It was about Donald and for some reason he appeared as a golden retriever, but when I looked at the dog I knew right away that Donald was inside him.

In the dream I was petting Donald like crazy while he gave this long monologue about the way weeds smell in the summer. He was saying things like, "When I was little, I always thought it was the caterpillars that made that smell. One time I put a little runt on my finger and actually sniffed him."

And believe it or not, in the dream this was all incredibly fascinating to me. I wanted to hear Donald wax poetic about the smell of weeds forever, so I kept on petting him. But after a while Donald (as a dog) threw up all over my lap. I didn't really mind because he vomited fragrant shampoo, but then the incessant tapping of the crows broke through my sleep and I woke up anyway.

I lay in bed for a half an hour listening to the birds and the sounds of the freeway. It's miles from the house and hidden by walls and trees, but Irvine's so flat that the sound washes over the walls and the trees and through the screen on my window.

I felt like something was wrong, like something was bad. I know that the obvious answer is Donald, but I couldn't figure exactly what it was about yesterday's visit that was stressing me out. I knew that I couldn't be mad at him for bailing out on me because I'm planning on bailing out on him. Then I thought that maybe I was having a selfish reaction because he had almost taken some of my thunder. Lastly I considered that I had always expected that someone would be around to say something personal about me, anything personal, and I didn't expect that statement to come from Shana or Simon. I reminded myself that I'm leaving this account, but then I worried that no one would bother to read it.

At 7:45, right when I was about to go out the door, Gumer called to tell me Donald had been checked into Hoag Hospital because they were scared he was going to do something crazy again. While I was talking to her, Shana was in the kitchen glued to the TV (one of her *Solid Gold* tapes was playing) and Simon was eating Golden Grahams. So happy together, him and his bowl.

After I hung up, Shana asked, "Was that a friend of yours?" The ringing of the phone in the morning had already freaked her out. You should see her with the doorbell around Girl Scout cookie time.

"Yeah," I said. "She was calling to ask if I wanted to walk to school together."

Shana's cheek twitched and she blinked rapidly. "Is she coming to the house first?"

I blinked back and said, "No, I'm meeting her on the corner and kind of have to leave right this second because she's nervous about getting to school on time."

"What's her name, Stella?"

"Celeste." Yeah.

Simon looked up from his toast, put his finger in the air, and said, "Wait, wait, Stella. Before you rush out, I've got something for you." He opened up this polyester bag he takes to work every day and pulled out a box of crackers. He works at Nabisco in product development.

"For me?" I asked.

Simon said, "No, they're for our other foster daughter. The one we're importing from the Philippines."

I'm serious, you can't tell with this guy, so I asked, "Are you really taking in another kid?"

Simon took a bite of toast and just chuckled like a zombie.

"Oh," I said, "I get it. Well, bye." I put the box of crackers under my arm and went out the front door.

I ditched the box in the trash by the South Lake (sorry, I'm not a huge cracker fan) and was smiled at, as usual, by the old Asian guy who exercises by the water. He makes these really slow and deliberate movements, except when I pass, he always winks and smiles. Which I find really weird. I think he should be in some sphere of ultimate concentration where he doesn't even know I exist.

His eyes are always shut as he does his exercises, but at the exact second I pass he snaps them open and makes direct eye contact with me. When he first started doing it I got kind of excited because I thought we shared some mystical connection. But at the beginning of this month I stopped and sat in the gazebo and watched as the man opened his eyes and smiled at the next five kids that passed. I couldn't see his left eye from where I was sitting, but I'm sure he winked.

If you spend enough time studying supposed mysteries, you find out pretty quick that they're not so mysterious at all. I'm guessing that the guy knows someone's coming because the kid's body blocks the sun from his face or he has good ears and hears shoes shuffling. Even when your eyes are shut, you just know it when the room gets dark.

So today I didn't smile back at him, and all I felt was a small wave of sad acknowledgment. I thought that, yeah, I was right about the complete chaos behind the way we all structure our lives. I really should have noticed all this before, but now it's glaring and obvious and headache-inducing.

Today in my mind I can actually see the way that every day is a chain of rules made up of completely random opposites, and there are even arbitrary ways of breaking those opposites down. I mean it's like this picture is floating around in my head (or a better way to describe it might be a chart) and the sheer number of branches on the chart is horrible. I can do this or this or this or this or this or this or this. And I know that a lot of people choose to see all those choices as proof of the great variety of life's paths, but what's pretty obvious to me is that when there are so many paths, they all become weak and shaky. Which one stands out among the others? Last week I was supposed to smile at the man because it's polite to smile, and today I choose to be impolite. I don't think I'm any different for the decision. I don't think there's any gratification in the choice. But what there is finally is some kind of satisfaction that comes with knowing that ending life is the last rung on the chart, and it's one that doesn't branch off in a thousand directions. And I don't have to pretend that it will, and honestly, that makes me a little calmer.

So the only one who might believe I *really* made a choice today is the exercising man, if he's that type of person. If he is, then maybe he'll spend hours wondering why today was the day I frowned at him, and maybe he'll waste time making up a deep meaning behind it all. And if I'm not giving him enough credit, then maybe he shut his eyes after I left and then rolled them inside his lids. Maybe he thought, "If she doesn't want to play along, then screw her."

Just like I said before. You don't ever know how happy you are until you remember how sad you once were and vice versa. Nothing is anything until I decide to hold nothing next to something, and declare that I see a difference.

It's like this time I gave my dad a nice razor for Father's Day and he immediately went upstairs and shaved with it. Then he ran back downstairs and into the living room shouting about how much smoother his skin was now. And he ran his right hand through his hair (it was black, but looked blue outside) while sucking in his cheeks and made me look at him close up until finally I was agreeing that he looked just like a cologne model.

My dad wanted me to see a change, and I wanted to see one, too. That doesn't make the change real or even important.

A switch has been flipped in my head. Like an actual switch. It's like putting on sunglasses, but internally. Look at me, trying to explain again. I still have that leftover need to be understood, even though it's stupid and I know it's stupid, but how true it is that old habits die hard.

Oh, and speaking of old habits dying incredibly hard, today I got to fifth-period English and saw on the board we were having a pop quiz. I put my bag down and Ashley Wakefield (who sits next to me) was pulling her hair back into a ponytail with her hands and sighing beautifully. I know it sounds dumb to admire a person for the way they breathe out, but Ashley does it with such pizzazz.

She moaned, "Is this really necessary?"

I slid into my desk chair and said, "In his head, yeah." I nodded in the direction of Mr. Muthler. He's the twelfth-grade AP English teacher and is known for being one of the hardest teachers, but not hard in an inspiring way. Mr. Muthler just gives tests on ridiculous things that no one remembers from the book. Like he'd seriously ask the name of Holden Caulfield's mailman if he could. On our winter final exam there were questions about the types of flowers in characters' front yards and whether or not they brushed their hair or teeth first before they went to bed. I'm not kidding.

So basically what he's taught me is to always have a pen while I'm reading. I go through and circle every name, date, and place I see, and then I underline the details that seem to pop out. Mr. Muthler went to Stanford, so it's not like he's in total confusion about the larger themes of the books. But for some reason he chooses to focus on the completely dispensable parts of the stories, and it really pisses everyone off.

The bell hadn't rung yet and Mr. Muthler was behind the pull-down projection screen at the front of the room. He hides behind it so no one can see the questions and cheat, but the screen bangs against his elbow and makes his writing shaky. And then, also, his questions end up sloping on an extreme diagonal since he can't tell if he's writing in a straight line when his face is that close to the chalkboard.

Today Matt Taketano must have been feeling especially invincible because he took a pencil and chucked it at Mr. Muthler's ass (the projection screen doesn't cover it). A lot of the smarter guys in the class are always kind of hostile toward Mr. Muthler, but never really in an outright way. In the past they've done stuff like jam the air-conditioner control with gum, and once they even drew a picture of him with a pencil up his ass, but they've never attempted to actually make the pencil meet the ass. But then Matt did this, and Mr. Muthler even felt it.

He ducked out from under the screen and just stared at us. The strange thing about him is that he has to be at least forty, but he only looks nineteen. It's not just that he hasn't exited his awkward stage. I think it's also that he wears untucked white short-sleeve shirts and the whole look reminds me of what (I imagine) boys look like at a seventh-grade dance.

Finally Mr. Muthler said, "Grow up." But he didn't say it in a very convincing way. As soon as he began to look like he was about to give up and run out of the room, he went back under the screen.

Matt smirked to his friends, who are these immensely boring white and Asian kids. Then he opened up his mouth really wide and let out a gigantic belch.

I thought, "What demon has leaped into this kid?"

Mr. Muthler's knees locked up, and from behind the screen he yelled (except it was muffled), "This quiz just became ten percent of your grade! Ten percent! That means if you don't have an A now and you don't get an A on this, you'll never have an A!" That really got everyone really worked up. All the kids started murmuring rude things to Matt, but it wasn't until Ashley shot him a dirty look that he looked like he was really sorry.

Ashley said to herself, "Oh, fuck me." And believe me, it was so soft, but every guy in the class looked over.

"You can't say things like that," I said.

She cocked her head at me and asked, "Why not? Have I offended you or something?"

I said, "Never mind." I find it really hard to believe that she doesn't know what's going on. The guys in our AP class are the ones that comfort themselves with the idea that Harvard actually makes a person attractive. They're the ones who say things like, "When I'm a world-famous economist, all the chicks are going to be begging for my jock." I don't think they necessarily believe this, but it comforts them anyway.

To them, someone like Ashley is beyond human because she's just as smart (if not smarter than them), and yet still sexually appealing ten years before they've set the sexual appeal deadline for themselves. It's like she's just so far ahead of schedule that they can't figure out how she can exist without imploding. The guys in our English class get hushed when she gives an opinion, but I just know they go home and make up amazingly complicated fantasies that involve leather binds and brainwashing.

Now the regular guys, and by regular I mean not especially attractive and headed to the lower-tier UCs or any of the Cal States, just try to make Ashley laugh and get as physically close as possible. It's not hard—the girl loves knock-knock and racist jokes.

Then there's the guys who are good-looking and have amazing social skills and it doesn't really matter if they're even going to college because they inspire confidence no matter what. Ashley has dated (I'm guessing) at least seventy-five percent of these guys at some point during her public school career (elementary included). All her ex-boyfriends are now her incredibly loyal friends who run to beat up the kids from the "bad" school on the other side of the creek when they call out lewd things. The "bad" school is where you go when you can't make it in regular high school, so inexplicably you get sent to S.E.L.F. (I'm not kidding, that's really the acronym) where the day ends at 1 P.M. I don't really understand the early leave since it seems to only give those kids more time to smoke and stare at us. I was thinking that maybe the school starts from a defeatist mentality, like "Well, we know they're going to ditch if we try to keep them here a whole day, so we'll just shoot for a few hours." I can imagine the teachers getting on their knees and begging the students to please, please hang in there until noon.

So when Mr. Muthler finished with his questions, he snapped the screen and it violently rolled itself back up. He said, "You have thirty minutes."

The first question was, "In *A Portrait of the Artist as a Young Man,* Stephen mentions a certain song playing as he's about to take the stage for his school play. Name that song." Mr. Muthler starts with the easiest ones. I knew the answer was "The Lily of Killarney" because I could mentally picture the way the words looked on the page, and I was almost about to write the answer down. I'm a sucker for tests. There's something rewarding about filling in a correct answer. I'm serious—when I left the SATs I felt like I could do anything in the world.

Then I remembered that I was supposed to be showing a difference in attitude and performance. You know how there's always the good neighbor on the street who commits a horrible crime, and all the other neighbors give local news interviews saying, "We never suspected she could do something like this"? I figure that the good people puzzle over this mystery for a few days at most and then just shrug. But imagine if those neighbors were all implicated in some way because the bad neighbor had sent each of them a small sign of what was to come. Then the matter would become personal. I think it's true that people only care about something when it becomes an inseparable part of their own lives.

So, basically, I didn't answer any of the pop quiz questions today. Instead I wrote Mr. Muthler a brief meditation on the way his classroom smells. Maybe later he'll look at it like the greatest puzzle he's ever seen. I think his first response will be to go through the essay and look for anything concrete. He'll end up circling everything. Maybe he'll count the number of times the letters of his name appear. It could be that he's felt detached from the books we've read because they don't speak to him. But (and I don't want to sound conceited) isn't it possible that maybe a statement from me to him will? Ha. Maybe.

While waiting for everyone else to finish the quiz, I studied Mr. Muthler's corporate motivation posters. His walls are covered with the ones that have images of idyllic landscapes and slogans like "Integrity," "Perseverance," "Dedication," etc., over them. It's like he didn't realize you're allowed to order posters from someplace other than the Office Depot catalog.

The room was completely silent except for the whir of the air conditioner and the scribbling of pencils. The thing about AP students is that they care about everything school related, no matter how small. If you assign an AP student to cut a lawn and tell him it'll affect a half a percent of his grade, your lawn will be incredible. I promise. I watched Ashley while she took her quiz and her forehead was about four inches away from the paper. She was on the last question, which requested a short essay that "listed at least twenty things Quentin did (in chronological order) during his chapter in the *Sound and the Fury.*" Ashley was on number eleven when I saw the classroom door moving out of the corner of my eye.

I looked up and there he was. He only had the door cracked open a little, but when you spot so much as your ex-boyfriend's nose hairs you know who it is instantly. Especially since he was the only boyfriend I ever had, and one of the few people I've been able to look at close up.

He (his name's Daniel Lorry) was trying to get someone's attention in the rear left-hand side of the room by saying "hey" very softly. But Mr. Muthler has incredible hearing (Is there a hearing equivalent for having eyes like a hawk? Ears like a dog?), and he jumped up from his desk and sprinted over to the door before Daniel even knew what was happening. When Daniel saw Mr. Muthler about to reach him, he shifted his eyes, and they met mine for just a second. I could tell he wasn't expecting to see me from the way his face lifted just a little. I think if he had had more time, he might have ended up smiling at me. But Mr. Muthler blocked my view of him and nearly started convulsing, saying, "I'm trying to give a quiz! What the hell is wrong with you? You can't just come in here!"

Daniel gets in trouble a lot, so he's actually really good at feigning innocence. He didn't move from the door, but opened it a little farther and said, "Listen, I'm sorry, but I had to give Jeff an urgent message." He was talking about Jeff Mahoney, one of the rare AP kids who smokes tons of weed but still always does well.

Jeff was sitting up straight in his chair and craning his neck to try to receive the message. Daniel was trying to tell him something with his eyes and eyebrows, but Mr. Muthler put his hand in front of Daniel's face and shouted, "That's it! What's your name!"

Daniel said calmly, "Golden Star in five minutes." That's what sent Mr. Muthler over the edge. He grabbed out for Daniel wildly like his first intention was to slap him, but Daniel backed away going, "Man, I'm leaving." Mr. Muthler lunged and grabbed again, and this time he got ahold of one of the sleeves of Daniel's shirt, but Daniel twisted his body and got free.

In a second he disappeared from the doorway and then Mr. Muthler was gone, too. We all sat shocked and silent for another second, and then we got up and ran out the door after them. In the hallway Mr. Muthler had Daniel slammed up against the lockers and he was kind of shaking him, but not hard enough to do any real damage. Daniel was yelling for Mr. Muthler to get his hands off him, but Mr. Muthler had his shirt crunched up in his fingers like he was never letting go.

Suddenly Mr. Muthler became aware we were all standing there and turned to look at us. While pushing against Daniel even harder, he pointed at me and said, "Stella. Take everyone inside. You're the teacher until I come back." When Daniel heard my name he looked earnestly at me and I felt pretty dumb. Like I was somehow betraying him by being singled out by Mr. Muthler. I felt even worse when Daniel dropped his eyes because he either seemed pissed, disappointed, or embarrassed, and I didn't want him to be any of those.

"What are you going to do?" I asked, and everybody in the class stared at me. They looked vaguely hopeful. Like they believed I was about to do something amazing and inspirational. I guess that comes from always answering questions right in class. When it comes to other issues, people just assume you know the answers to those, too.

Mr. Muthler gave me wide eyes, begging. "I'm taking him to the principal."

I bit my bottom lip so as not to seem like I was trying to show him up. I said, "Sorry, but that guy doesn't go to our school."

Jeff Mahoney snapped out of his permanent fog long enough to say, "Yeah, he doesn't."

I swear tears welled up in Mr. Muthler's eyes, but I can't be one hundred percent sure because he took off the other way down the hallway, dragging Daniel with him. Everybody in the class looked at me.

Tanya Morehead (and believe me, she gets massive hell for that one) asked, "Do we have to stay, Stella?"

I shrugged and said, "I can't make you do anything you don't want to do."

Matt Taketano, suddenly worried about getting detention or whatever, wanted to know if that meant I was going to be making a list of people who ditched or not.

I thought about it for a second. I knew I should say yes and go back in there and lead everybody in a review for the final, but I had to remind myself that it was time to stop caring about all that. So I told them, "No, you guys are free to go."

Darren Pinsky tried to high-five me, but I didn't hold my hand up because I find that whole mutual slapping thing lame. I just took his hand and put it back down at his side. "Yeah, you're welcome."

He looked a little astonished and said, "Stella, you're a character."

Everyone had gone back into the room by this time to pick up their stuff and now they were running back out, happy as can be, and some of the Persian crew (that's Reza, Amir, and Ali) were even punching lockers on their way down the hall.

Anyway, I asked Darren, "What do you mean?"

Then he looked shy, like he had said something he didn't mean to, and tried to casually toss off, "I don't know why I said that. I don't really know you."

"Well, we've had classes together for four years," I told him, even though I knew that meant nothing. I wanted to make him feel better.

He agreed, "Yeah, that's true." And then he gestured toward the classroom and said, "I'm going to go get my stuff. Do you think I should just leave my quiz on Mr. Muthler's desk?"

"Yeah."

"Okay. See you tomorrow."

Darren went back in. I didn't. I had my house keys in my right pocket and five dollars in my left, and didn't need my books since I wasn't planning on doing homework.

I went walking toward the social studies building, thinking about Daniel. He's another story for another day, but he was definitely on my mind. He had made my heart hurt for a few minutes back there.

When I passed the art building, I heard music coming out of the open windows and the song was "Box of Rain," which was one of the songs my mom used to love. She made a mix tape where the whole A side was just that one song. She told me that she knew ahead of time that she would want to hear it again and again, but wouldn't have the patience for rewinding. She told me, "I hate hippies. But damn, I love this song."

So I went into the art building, which is essentially a two-story room. The door was already propped open with a pot painted by someone tragically untalented, and no one even looked up at me when I entered. It's not that all the kids were busy drawing and painting, but they were busy talking, scratching stuff into the desks with X-Acto knives, and generally hanging out.

Ainsley Cleveland was one of the few kids who actually looked like she was attempting art. I saw her sitting over by the window (by herself) and she kept dipping her pen into a small jar of ink by her arm. I felt like I was having one of those dreams where I walk into a room and no one can see me. I just float by them and watch what all the people are doing and usually wake up feeling kind of crappy.

The art teacher, Ms. Silver, was over in the front left corner of the room with her back to the class, working on her own painting. Everyone says that she only took the job teaching so she could get supplies for free. I've heard she doesn't care if you're painting your crack as long as you don't bother her and have something to show for a grade at the end of the semester.

It felt pretty good to be in there and not have to worry about anyone realizing I wasn't supposed to be. There was an empty stool next to Ainsley, so I just went and sat on it. She looked up for a second to see who was blocking her light and there was the smallest flash of recognition on her face, but not any sign she cared it was me.

I said, "Hi."

Ainsley kept drawing this very intricate seal, but murmured, "Hey" anyway. She has this incredibly husky voice that I think guys would find really sexy if she had a different face. It's not that she's overwhelmingly ugly, but she's got one of those faces that might find its way in ten years. Maybe someday someone will tap her freckles and tug on her thin hair and say, "What, you? I don't believe you! You're lying about being a teen wallflower!" I can see how her face might need to be viewed from a different perspective. One day she might be called a natural beauty—it's just that her particular look isn't one that my high school is currently endorsing.

Today Ainsley had a long-sleeved thermal on. It's June. I don't know what her deal is.

For about five minutes I just sat there staring out the window and watching Larome Nolans at the candy machine, trying to get a self-made ceramic pick to stay in his hair. The kid with him was dying laughing.

But still, I could kind of see Ainsley out of the corner of my eye. I saw her arm move and thought she was gesturing to me or waving to someone outside, but she was just scratching an itch on her face. On the underside of her arm she had black ink all over her sleeve (she's right-handed) and I glanced at her paper and saw that a lot of her seal's spots were smeared together.

I don't know why I did this because I never, ever just touch people. I don't even put my hand on their backs when I apologize for accidentally bumping them on the street. But I reached over and tugged on Ainsley's sleeve (also touching her wrist underneath) and said, "You're getting your arm all dirty."

She looked at me and I let go. Then she said (not angrily or anything), "I know. It happens every day."

"Oh. Maybe you should draw on an angle. You're ruining your seal, too."

Ainsley took her thumb and dragged it through the seal's black nose, which was still a little wet. She made a streak across the page. "It was already ruined."

I can't help having order in my blood, so I was pretty shocked that she didn't think anything of making a mess of her drawing. I'll never understand why people ruin things deliberately. Maybe this sounds stupid, but she could have turned it in as her final project and probably have gotten an A for effort. Oh god, I've really got to stop thinking like that.

Anyway, I told her, "Well I thought it was really good. I can't draw, so I think people who can draw should take care of their stuff."

"I traced it. I was just coloring it in. I can do the same thing again tomorrow." She flipped the piece of paper and drew what I guess was supposed to be her version of a seal. It had a circle for the head, an oval for the body, and sloppy stick fins. "See, I can't draw."

"It's not that bad," I said. Right then the bell rang for sixth period, but I definitely wasn't in the mood to go to drama. I saw Ainsley wasn't packing up or anything.

I asked, "What do you have now?"

"More art."

"You have two periods in a row?"

She said, "Yes," and then got up and went to the clippings drawer to look for something else to "draw." I thought, "How about that. Two periods of art." I told you, I've never really been a drawer, but that sounded incredible to me. I felt great in that room. So I got a piece of paper from the rack in the back of the room and a pencil from a coffee can on the table. Ainsley came back with a photocopy of a fish and asked, "You aren't in this class, are you?"

I said, "Well, no."

"Then what are you doing here?"

I put my hand on the paper and started to trace around my fingers and told her, "Drawing, I guess."

Ainsley actually gave me a polite grin, but didn't say anything else to me for the rest of the time. I have to say, I don't know what it was, but I could kind of see why Ashley likes being her friend. There's something about Ainsley that makes you want to try a little.

Five

Today I drummed up all my courage and went to find Larome Nolans while everybody else was in the pep rally because last night, while lying in bed, I came up with the idea of asking for his help. I realized that I hadn't even thought through how I was going to go and was especially struck by the notion that just as people don't live in a vacuum, they don't die in one either. The thing is, I'm not the last person in the world (and I'm not saying I thought I was either). There will be someone around to find me and there will be bad *Irvine World News* reporters there to get the details for the newspaper. The last image I leave is what people will interpret as being the last thing I said about myself. I mean, it might be this stuff (this writing), but it occurred to me if everybody says actions speak louder than words, that might be how they really feel. Feeling something is true is not the same as it actually being true, but still, I think feelings go a lot farther than tangible proof does.

They'll remember the last way they saw me. And those people that didn't see me will want to know what I looked like from the people who did. And maybe stressing out over my last outfit and position seems kind of petty, but I just can't help but think that the way I ultimately look will affect everything that went before. If I look like I'm sleeping peacefully, they'll think I was an angel. If I'm crumpled up awkwardly, I'm worried they'll talk about how depressing I was. I mean, yes, I see all the effort that's going into making this an event. And I know that effort is exactly what proves it's all pointless. (Hey, I should make a bumper sticker of that and slam it up on the back of whoever's walking in front of me, so I can admire it. Since I don't have a car. Or a bike.)

But I guess a piece of a leftover fantasy is still stuck somewhere deep in my heart. It's just that once you know it's a fantasy, the whole dream doesn't work in the same way.

See. All night long stuff like this goes through my head nonstop and when I try to shut my eyes and make my mind blank it doesn't work. So then I imagine myself doing things like scanning items in a grocery store because I have to actively concentrate on the scanning. I imagine the customer and then think of all the things that that type of person would buy.

Anyway, today we had a pep rally and you have to stay on campus during it, but you're not actually required to attend. Really, the school can't force spirit upon its students. We don't even have to participate in the Pledge of Allegiance anymore if we don't feel comfortable doing it. So at around ten the band came marching through the school while playing the tomahawk song (we're the Warriors), and everybody filed out of class whooping and hollering. Personally, throngs of people freak me out and it's even worse when they're all following a red-and-gold marching band like they're in some freaky credit card commercial. Paulo Franchetti tripped and fell in front of me, and everyone around him clapped. I wondered if people at the turn of the century used to clap, too, because it seems like that routine never gets old for anybody.

The crowd headed for the gym on the other side of the school, but I hung back at the candy machines. I decided to get some peanut M&M's so I wouldn't look so intense when I was talking to Larome. I figured out that I could hold the bag in my right hand and pick the M&M's up with my left, and believe it or not, that whole plan relaxed me immensely.

The drums and the kids got farther and farther away until everything was eerily quiet, and that's when I started walking toward the quad. I rounded the corner by the library and, sure enough, there was Larome and three of his friends sitting on a lunch table. I put a lot of effort into not looking directly at them. Rubbing my eye like I had allergies, I casually went over to a nearby table and sat down. I brought a Xeroxed test review from second-period coordinated science and pretend-concentrated on the questions while I tapped a pencil lightly against the table.

Larome was loudly cracking up while telling a story about some girl, a knife, and a crazy bitch, and I thought, "Perfect." He would say a couple of words, break into a laugh, and then the rest of the sentence would disappear into mumbles and happy, exhausted *ahhhhhhhhs*. One of his friends was laughing so hard that he fell on the ground.

I thought it wouldn't be too big of a deal to look over in his direction since it's a pretty normal human reaction to want to find out what's funny. So I sighed, just to be safe, and raised my head and started intensely watching everything he did. I stared at him like I had a staring problem. I made myself not look away when his eyes crossed mine, and that was kind of tough because it's pretty embarrassing to just watch someone. After about two minutes of me staring at Larome he finally started staring back at me like I was a field rabbit hanging out on his lawn. Like he was curious, but not worried about my presence at all. Then he jerked his chin at me in the way that guys do before they're about to fight. The thing is, his eyes were still smiling. That blew me away.

All mothers think that their kids are a bundle of joy, but Jesus Christ, I'm not kidding, his mom really gave birth to one. Actually, maybe he's not a joy to her because he's got to be flunking every one of his classes and he split Andrew Kennigan's lip open the other day, but he sure amuses himself.

Larome did this exaggerated tiptoe toward me and raised his eyebrows. "You trying to do your homework or something? Do you think I'm being too loud?"

I said, "No," but in as friendly a way as possible. In my opinion, I used a tone that invited conversation. But I guess that one word was a good enough answer for him because he turned back around to his friends. I thought he would at least make a comment about the skirt that I was wearing. I got it two weeks ago from a Catholic school uniform supplier near Donald's home and it's pretty damn plaid and short. Anyway,

I just had to pick myself up by my bootstraps and remind myself that I didn't have time to be shy anymore.

So I said, "Wait!"

Larome looked at me over his shoulder. "Me, wait?"

"Yeah, I want to talk to you," I said.

He laughed. I told you, this kid just laughs and laughs and laughs. Two days ago I actually tried to mimic him in the mirror except when I tried to make myself laugh I looked halfway retarded doing it.

I just wanted to get that grin off of his face for two seconds and get him to talk to me. So I got up from the table and put my hand around his wrist. I was conscious of how hot his skin was and how sweaty my hand was getting.

Larome looked back at his friends and said, "Would you take a fucking look at this?" in the same way he'd ask about a cat dancing in booties or something.

"Can we please talk?" I asked, and then I dropped his wrist kind of rough for dramatic effect.

His friends had come up to get a close look at me and one of them, this white wigger guy (I forget his name, but I've been behind him in the lunch line before), asked me if I was pregnant and if Larome was the daddy. He put his hand on my stomach and instantly I felt my new touching people thing doesn't go both ways, because I've only just adjusted to dishing it out and I'm not even about to start being okay with getting it back.

I really surprised myself by taking ahold of the kid's hand and sort of bending back his fingers. I did it just hard enough until he felt it. As soon as the pain hit, he ripped back his hand and shook his fingers out, saying, "What the hell?"

"Please don't touch me," I said. And then to Larome, "Come on. I need to talk to you."

Larome chuckled and put his hand on my back, in between my shoulder blades, and gave a little push and told me, "All right. You've got me interested. Let's do it." He laughed especially heartily after that, too, so I have to assume that was some kind of sex reference. His friends were making groaning sounds and stuff behind us, and he kept looking back at them every five seconds. I'm guessing he was probably winking.

We walked toward the front of the school where the parking lot is, and I started to say, "Sorry, I don't really know how to broach this subject," but as soon as we hit the curb, suddenly there was one of the narcs speeding across the asphalt. I don't know his name because I don't get in trouble, but he's this big Samoan guy who rides around in a little white buggy thing. He always steers with one hand while leaning back, and I've noticed his legs are always spread really far apart. I mean, you can see his knees coming out the sides of the cart if you're looking at it head on.

The narc yelled, "Larome!" at the top of his lungs. He was still about two hundred feet away.

Larome put up his hands and started walking backward. "Not going off campus! Chill the fuck out!" I felt so dumb standing there, like I didn't have a place in all this. Should I yell to the narc, too, that I wasn't going anywhere, or did he just not care?

Larome tugged on the sleeve of my shirt and said, "Come on. I don't feel like talking to him. Annoying motherfucker."

I said, "Fine. Let's go in the library," and I walked over to the front entrance and he followed me. Inside the library was so still and quiet and shady in a good way. TV shows always show kids studying and hanging out in the library, but at my school no one sets foot in there. Our teachers drag us in at the beginning of the year and they do a unit on how to research things, but that's about it.

Mrs. Balsam (she's the librarian) is always at the desk doing god knows what, but I think she took the job because she likes the solitude. When we walked in today she didn't even ask us if we needed help or anything. She was reading something behind the check-out desk, but when we got close to her she quickly put it in the drawer and then she gave us (what I thought) was a kind of guilty and halfhearted smile. I like to wonder what kind of stuff she keeps in that drawer, but I'd never actually want to find out because I'm sure it's all boring and disappointing.

The library's walls are covered with anti-smoking posters (we have the lady with the hole in her neck, among others) and bad student artwork. What bothers me most about the artwork is the way it's framed in construction paper, which is such an ugly and cheap way to display something. Those construction paper frames just seem to say that all those paintings and drawings are ending up in the trash, no matter what. At the end of the year, when all the artwork comes down, it must have staples and holes in it and, really, who wants it then? In fact, I don't know why the school bothers putting the stuff up at all because no one takes the time to look at it and no one cares that anyone ever tried to make anything.

Anyway, I went to the bookshelves in the back left-hand corner where there aren't even windows, and Larome kind of sauntered behind me whispering, "Girl! What's all this drama about? Do I even know you?"

I stopped near the big atlases and said, "No."

Larome looked around at the towers of books and gave a short, bewildered laugh. "What, are you here to tell me someone's out to get my ass?"

"No. I just have a question."

"A question? Well, what is it? Go. Go." He was starting to look sort of nervous. Fidgeting with his pants a lot and sticking his hands in and out of the pockets.

I slid down against the bookcase behind me and squatted. I stared blindly at one of the titles ahead of me. "Listen, I'm not here to insult you, so if you leave here feeling that way, I'm sorry. And I'm not asking you this based on your race, but instead on somewhat solid verbal evidence that yeah, I know could possibly be rumor, but…"

Larome interrupted. "Look, I don't follow you. I just don't follow you."

I got up and said, "I'm not asking you this favor because you're black."

And then I don't even think I had time to blink before his face was coming toward mine and his hands were on my shoulders. Suddenly he was starting to kiss me and maybe I kissed him back for a second before I realized that I had no idea why I was making out with a complete stranger in the library. But when I did, I took a step back and put my hands against the books because he had upset my center of balance by holding me a certain way.

"Why'd you do that!" I asked. My whole face was tingling from having touched another person's. I felt totally strange.

He said, "Well, you're the one who started it all by asking that shit. You know. I'm just helping you out." He was giving me a sideways smile, but the slant it was at didn't look normal for him and I could tell he was feeling suddenly shy and insecure.

"But I didn't ask you anything yet."

"You've had that whole white girl and a black guy fantasy spinning around in the back of your head. Now you're graduating and leaving this place and won't have to worry..."

"Hold up a second," I said. "I didn't pull you aside to make out. Wait, did you think we were going to have sex back here or something?"

"I see. That was just too real for you. Too fucking real. Now you're gonna back down and play dumb."

I panicked that he was a sentence away from hating me and thinking I was this evil, manipulative Caucasian so I blurted out, "I pulled you aside because I wanted to know if you could get me a gun."

"Huh?"

"Sorry," I apologized. "Sorry about the mix-up."

He threw his hands up and whisper-exclaimed, "What!"

"Listen, I think you tried to sell a gun to a cop before. At least that's what I heard, and again, I'm really sorry for all the confusion, but that was my original question."

Larome bent over and twisted his neck so he was looking in my eyes from underneath. He said, "Who are you?"

I said, "Stella Parrish. Is that what you mean?"

He laughed. Back to the laughing. "You're a narc. I knew it! Every time I saw you around I thought, 'There's something off about that girl.' "

I told him, "No. No. You're completely wrong."

Larome looked happy again in a slightly pissed-off way. He was grinning from ear to ear. "Yeah, narc. I see you now."

I told him again, "You're wrong. I'm just a student."

Then I heard the band again as they came toward the far end of the library. They got louder at what seemed like a really quick pace, like they were all running to get back to class.

Larome was already backing away from me and shaking his head in a way that said he saw through me. He only said, "Elaborate. Elaborate, elaborate plan." And then he gave one-hundredth of a laugh. As soon as he got past the second row of bookshelves, he was out of my line of sight.

I leaned against the books and sighed. I felt like that had taken a lot of effort, and maybe too much. I was tired and I was nauseous again and smelling the tight carpet. Whenever the world reveals the way it works, it's like my nostrils open up and make me smell everything more deeply. It's kind of like the opposite of stopping to smell the roses. I'm trying to keep going because if I keep moving fast enough, I think I appreciate life more. It's when I take a pause and look around that I see the details I wish I hadn't.

I just realized, right now, that it shouldn't be taking this much effort. Forget the gun. I keep getting sucked back into playing along and I should really stop it.

Okay, there's my resolution for today. Forget the gun and the staging. Larome was completely right—I am elaborate, and it's not attractive.

After the band noises came the sounds of all the kids going to fourth period. Nothing makes you feel more detached than the sounds of groups of people going by. What I mean is that sort of thing always gives me the impression I'm on the outside of some giant universal conversation.

While I was waiting for all of the kids to pass, I left the stacks and went to one of the tables to look out the window. The library has those darkened kind that you can see out of, but can't really see into unless you cup your hands around your eyes while you look in the glass. No one was doing anything especially exciting (Ronnie Barlow, a kid I had P.E. with freshman year, was picking his nose with his sunglasses to impress some girl), so I spent some time reading the messages scratched into the table. There was a "David was here," which I thought was pretty clichéd, and there were a few so-and-so loves so-and-so, but always in bubbly girl writing. There was a poem that made me pause for thought: "I banged her all morning, I banged her all night, I banged her until she stopped being tight." I wasn't one hundred percent sure what the author was trying to get across as far as sadness at the sudden lack of tightness, or glee at ruining her for other guys? Then I decided that anyone who felt like scratching that into a table probably wasn't an enormously sad person, so I went with the latter.

I looked back out the window and saw that there were only a few stragglers, so I decided that it was okay to go back to class. I was getting up when someone said, "Stella" from behind me. I turned around and there was Mr. Muthler. He was holding one of the big blue books of quotations that kids have to look at while in the library, but teachers can check out. He put it down on the desk.

"Oh," I said. "Hey, Mr. Muthler."

He said, "I left you in charge yesterday because I trusted you."

My heart was already sinking. I know I shouldn't, but I always feel really terrible when people are disappointed in me. I don't know if this was just me imagining things, but I thought he was looking at me like I was the moral equivalent of a Charles Manson.

He went on, "So tell me, Stella," (he said my name so coldly) "is this about something I've done to the class? Is this retaliation for an unfair grading practice...or the paper I assigned last weekend?"

God, I felt so bad for him. It was like I was dumping him and about to give the "It's not you, it's me" speech, except I was doing it on behalf of the entire class. And really, for some of the kids, it kind of is him.

"It's not personal," I said. "It's just, you know, the end of the year."

Mr. Muthler put two fingers to his lips like he was smoking an invisible cigarette and thought deeply for about four seconds. That's actually an incredibly long time for a teacher to be standing there, not saying anything to you. Finally he inhaled deeply and said, "Of course it's personal."

The way I felt about him right then was the way I felt when I saw Mrs. Rayshell, my third-grade teacher, in the supermarket when I was eight. My mom and I were rounding the corner in the frozen foods and there she was, wearing a terry-cloth beach dress that cinched around her breasts. It wasn't an especially lewd outfit, but as she stood and talked with my mom I couldn't keep my eyes away from her chest because it was just so amazingly brown. I realized that I had never seen her chest before, or at least not in light that glaring. Her skin looked dangerously papery. Like her breasts might split it apart if they weren't kept close enough together.

I heard my mom ask, "Did you just get that tan at the beach?"

Mrs. Rayshell said, "I did. I go every weekend." She brushed off her shoulder like she was clearing off dead skin to let her tan shine even brighter. Then, out of nowhere, she said in this kind of desperate voice, "I go alone."

My mom said, "It's more peaceful that way, right?"

"Right," Mrs. Rayshell said without believing it. I finally noticed she had a basket and not a shopping cart. It had random things in it, like barrettes, a *People* magazine, and a plastic curly straw. The combination of them made me dizzy for a second, even though what they said to me was entirely abstract. But the general feeling was that of looking into her life and finding it vulnerable to my own judgment. I mean, third graders aren't supposed to see their teachers' lives closer and closer until they're aware that those teachers possibly have no friends and nothing better to do on Saturday afternoons than buy completely unneeded stuff at the grocery store.

And then when my mom tried to bow out of the conversation by saying, "Well, we'll let you get on with your weekend," she accidentally interrupted Mrs. Rayshell at the head of a new sentence. It was very apparent that Mrs. Rayshell had been about to start a fresh thread of conversation, but she didn't have anybody willing to stick around to help her carry it through. Her face kind of fell. I hadn't really said anything, but I felt like I had made her feel worse about herself.

I was struck with a mental picture of her going home and standing topless in front of the bathroom sink mirror, checking for any peeling skin on her tan, crinkly breasts. I had the same feeling standing in front of Mr. Muthler today—everything except the part about the breasts, obviously.

I didn't try to assure him it wasn't personal again. I thought that would sound fake. So I just said, "It was a lapse in judgment on my part. I'm really sorry."

Mr. Muthler said, "What's done is done." He sighed. "I have your backpack locked up in my room. You can get it during fifth period."

"Thanks," I said. He tucked the book of quotations under his right arm and started to leave.

While he was walking away, I called out, "Mr. Muthler?" and he turned around and said, "Yes?"

"What happened to Daniel yesterday?"

"Who's Daniel?" His voice was cold, and I realized that he had probably been expecting another apology.

I told him, "That guy you took to the office."

Mr. Muthler said, "Never mind that. Just be in class today." I wanted to explain to him that I wasn't just being a nosy girl, but he was already back on his way out the door.

I was already going to be late to fourth-period precalculus, so I decided to not go altogether. I didn't want to do something halfway, even though I know that's one of those qualities I need to chuck out the window. So I went to the back wall of the library and looked at the student artwork. I went down the pictures one by one until I came to the ugliest watercolor painting of a little girl that I've ever seen. Her eyes were lopsided and her nostrils huge and muddy. I looked down at the artist tag hanging off the mat and I'm not completely sure why, but I wasn't really that surprised that the painting was Ainsley's.

I was kind of excited to talk with her about it because I thought that maybe we'd end up in a conversation where we discovered we have a lot in common. I don't know why I want to have something in common with her, but I do. Anyway, when I went to the art room during sixth period and looked over by the window, her stool was empty and she wasn't near the sink, either. I sat down in the same seat I used yesterday and bit off my nails for the rest of the school day.

Six

The first thing I heard when I became somewhat conscious this morning was, "It's a man." But I was in that half-asleep, half-awake state where the outside world mixed with my brain's independent ideas, so I started hallucinating that I was in a hospital bed giving birth. I sleep with my knees up and bent, so I actually saw them in front of me in that position and woozily believed that there was a doctor at the head of the bed announcing that I was bringing a thirty-year-old guy into the world. I remember thinking to myself, "They were all wrong. This doesn't hurt a bit."

Then I heard, "Stella" and snapped out of my waking dream. I rolled over on my side and saw Shana there, holding out our cordless phone like she was trying to pass off a hot potato.

She whispered, "There's someone on the phone. It's a man."

I looked at the clock and saw it was six in the morning. I took the phone from her and said, "Hello?"

I heard Donald on the line. "I'm in the hospital."

I told him, "I know. Hold on." Shana was still there, hovering next to the bed, so I said, "It's all right. I know him."

She looked at me with suspicion and made a face that seemed to indicate she was sizing me up. It was a very small difference — the corners of her mouth came down a little and her eyes seemed a little bit more knowing, like she thought I was stealing alcohol from her liquor cabinet. I wasn't, obviously, but it was that kind of look. I had never seen it before, and in one instant she became someone that I thought might miss me once I was gone. I guess she just seemed that much more aware and of sound mind.

"I'm up now," she said, and then took a seat at the edge of the bed. I was pretty close to being in shock at that move.

I said, "Well, I have to take this phone call. It's somewhat important." It was such a weird moment. I had no idea what to do.

"That's fine," she told me. "Take the phone call." In the middle of "fine" Donald started yelling into the phone and his voice buzzed in the air, all tinny and thin. He was saying, "Stella! Where are you? Stella!" I thought, "I've got one lunatic on the phone and another on my bed."

Shana didn't look like she was going anywhere, so I lifted the phone back up to my ear while watching her carefully.

"Hi. I'm back."

Donald said, "If you knew I was in the hospital, then why haven't you been here to see me?"

I wished Shana would leave. I didn't want to have this conversation in front of her. But she was staring at me so intensely that I had the impression if I asked her for privacy, I would never be the same to her. I mean, the whole time I've been living with her and Simon, I've been an amazingly good, uncomplicated kid. It's like they think I dream of bunnies and sugar and that's it.

I told Donald, "You've had my phone number here for years. Why haven't you called me?" Shana looked really interested at that comment.

"I'm calling you now," Donald said. "You should be here."

"I don't know if that's true."

He sounded incredibly mean when he told me, "You should come see me."

Just to piss him off, I put on a really naive tone and asked, "Why?"

"I need you to help me."

I asked, "Why?" again.

"I don't want to be here anymore."

I was feeling very amused by the word *why*. It seemed like the perfect response to everything. I asked him one more time, "Why?" Then I gave one of those phony halfhearted laughs that's a combination of breathing out and huffing.

He tried to put on an epic voice, stuffed with old-man grit. "Because we're related. We're all each other has."

I turned my face toward the window and said (as quietly as possible—I only wanted Shana to hear an indecipherable murmur), "You can't fool me and I know you don't mean any of that."

"Stella, here's a piece of grandfatherly advice:"—he breathed out—"Why don't you try rising above being a woman? You're so hurt by everything that you can't separate your duty from your emotions."

"Crap, that's a shame you've got to go," I told him. "Bye." And I hung up the phone. After a second I pressed the talk button again so the line would be tied up, and then I stuffed the phone under the pillow with the mouthpiece down so Shana wouldn't be able to hear the "Blee bloo blee...If you are trying to make a call" stuff.

I gave her a small patient smile and waited for her to leave.

About six seconds passed and then she asked, "That was your grandpa, wasn't it?"

"Yeah. Sorry he called so early."

"Is there something wrong?"

I told her, "He just had a question that he didn't want to forget to ask me later."

Shana tucked her bottom lip under her top one, making herself look vaguely insecure, and said, "It's okay if you don't want to tell me."

She looked like such a mess, with her hair uncombed and her shapeless universe-themed nightgown on, that whereas normally I'd just say okay, instead I said, "You know what? He told me that you sounded like a very nice woman."

Shana just looked at me again like I was holding something behind my back. The phone had started to make the busy signal from under my pillow and it was completely audible when we were both quiet.

Later I was in third-period French writing an essay on "les choses je ferai cet été" in preparation for our final when I got paged. Mrs. Green came on over the loudspeaker and said, "Stella Parrish, you have a phone call in the main office," which was definitely a first. When you get paged, all the other kids stop what they're doing and stare at you because if it's anything less than a family death, emergency, or illness, then one of the office aides will come with a yellow slip instead.

The fourth-year French students at my school (and I suspect other schools, too) are mostly soft AP girls or weird kids obsessed with the Renaissance. But the thing is, they all fall under the category of being the kind of kids who know how to handle tragedy appropriately. I think that kids who take French have parents who've instilled basic values in them, like respect for school and other cultures. They just know that when someone gets paged for a possibly sad reason, they should give that person empathetic eyes and immediately offer to take notes for her while she's gone. The real assholes and morally ambiguous kids are the ones who take Spanish. I could make a list of those types that runs for days.

After I got paged, Belinda Mannerra, one of the aforementioned Renaissance kids, turned around in front of me and said, "I'll take notes for you." She had dangling crystals of different sizes dropping down from one chain and two small braids running behind her head. Her and her friends do reenactments after school where they put on dresses with billowing sleeves (the guys do the shirt versions) and lament about all the dragons or whatever that have overtaken their village, aka the football field.

I walked all the way around the auto-shop building and around the front of the school so I could come in the front entrance of the office. I have absolutely no desire to pretend not to see Larome anymore.

When I thought about who could be calling me at eleven in the morning, my first instinct was that it was Shana. She would tell me that Simon had had a brain aneurysm while studying beta versions of a new cookie box that were designed to prevent crumbling, and that he had died immediately. Then, in midsentence she would succumb to shock, her body would fail, and I'd be an orphan again. The doctors' eyes would fill with tears for me.

The thing is, I didn't want that stuff to actually happen. Sometimes I feel absolutely crappy about the ideas that surface in my mind, but really, that was the first theory that came to me. Tomorrow I should research the rate of twice-orphaned kids in America. There should be a club for them.

When I got to Mrs. Green's desk, I had to remind her that I was Stella Parrish and that she had someone waiting on the phone for me.

"Oh yes," she said. "It's your grandfather on the phone and he's in the hospital."

I told her, "I know" while she was handing me the phone. Then I got on the line and said, "What."

Donald said, "You need to come visit me. I'll keep calling."

"I don't understand why it's suddenly so imperative for me to see you. I've been coming to see you for six years, Donald, and you never seemed to care much before."

"Come see me and bring me a bottle of Tylenol."

I said, "If you have a headache, you should tell your nurse."

"I need a whole bottle."

"Oh Jesus Christ," I said. I rubbed my forehead with my entire palm because the nausea was starting up. Sometimes if I just put enough pressure on a specific part, then my body will forget that it originally wanted to be sick.

"Think about it like this, Stella. If you visit me now, then you won't have to visit me later."

"This is an absolutely insane conversation. The truth is that I just don't feel like seeing you."

Mrs. Green tapped her pen against her cheek. I could tell that she was listening and that she thought I was a horrible person. I wished I could explain to her how Donald was, but I wouldn't even know how to if I tried. Because I think in words, people all sound exactly the same. You can describe them as smart or nice or funny or assholeish, but millions of other people in the world are those exact same things on paper. It's not until you're around them for a lot of time that you begin to see the nuances in their personalities—the way their sentence means something different coming from their mouth than from someone else's. Sure, Donald is assholeish, but if I told Mrs. Green that, I probably wouldn't bring her closer to any understanding of his nature and, also, I'd probably get detention for cussing.

Anyway, Donald had been quiet on the line for a while and I could hear the machines in the background. I'm so glad I'll never be like that, resting there alone. Beeping.

I said, "Hello? You're not...gone, are you?"

Donald gasped back, "I'll tell you stories."

"What?"

"If you come, I'll tell you stories."

"What are you talking about?" I asked.

Donald asked back, "Aren't grandfathers supposed to tell their grandchildren stories?"

Mrs. Green cut in, "Is that really your grandfather, Stella?"

I kind of raised my voice and said, "What's with all the questions?"

Mrs. Green shot back, "I only asked you one."

I said, "Never mind," which didn't do much to calm her.

At the same time Donald was saying, "Who are you talking to? Who's there?" The phone was a few inches from my ear, but I could still hear him.

I was almost feeling as sick as I did on the boat to Catalina at the start of sixth-grade outdoor ed. The waves hadn't really been that bad and most of the other kids were playing cards and eating, but I stood on the top deck looking at the miles and miles of water and I think that's what made me queasy. The so-muchness of it. Now it was the two voices coming at me from both sides like two woodpeckers on each of my eardrums. And my nipples were popping up again because they keep that office so ridiculously cold. When I looked down to check just how obscene they looked, I got a chill on the back of my neck from my hair falling forward off it. It was the kind of chill that reminded me how it is when you get the flu, when your body is a hundred and something degrees so everything outside it seems like it's being blown through the peaks of two mountains in the middle of nowhere.

I put one elbow on the counter and then rested my forehead in my palm. I leaned against it as much as I could.

Mrs. Green was telling me, "I think I'll need to speak to your grandfather now, Stella."

At the same time Donald was saying, "Your mother would have come to the hospital. She hated me, but she still would have come."

I said, "Fine!" Mrs. Green held out her hand because she thought I was talking to her.

Donald told me, "I'll see you this evening then. Bring a bottle. Bring two!"

"Not tonight!" I said. "I've had enough of you today." I handed the phone to Mrs. Green and she got on it and said, "Hello? Hello?" but that was all the conversation she got through, so I guess Donald had already hung up.

I started toward the front door of the office again. I was going to stop in the bathroom in the math building because no one's ever in there during class. It sounded really good to just splash some water on my face and sit on the floor for a while. But then as I was pushing the door open, Mr. Frankel came out of his office from the left and said, "Stella?"

Today he was in a pink shirt with an embroidered alligator on it, but it had a big stain on it, right on the chest. It looked like it might be barbecue sauce or some kind of thick marinade (I think it was too brown to be ketchup). Also, the bottom of his hair was shooting out from his head at awkward angles, like every ten strands had decided they hated the ten strands hanging out next to them. One group wanted to kiss the sky, and another group was praying toward Mecca, and I don't have to tell you about another because you get the idea. He looked horrible. He looked very, very dirty. What I mean is he didn't just look dirty and downtrodden on the outside, but in his eyes and skin, too, like the stain had seeped inside of him and put its guck all over his bones and muscles. Not that he looked fantastic on Friday, but he looked nightmarishly craptacular today.

"Hi," I said. "I was just taking a phone call."

He told me, "Come have a seat in my office."

I followed him inside and took a seat in the chair opposite his desk again. He had the blinds drawn over his window and over the glass separating the far side of his office from Mrs. Green's eyes. The place had the lethargic quality of a room that's just been napped in. The air was so warm and stuffy. Also, it had a little bit of a salty smell to it, the way that everybody's sheets have when they (the people, not the sheets) wake up in the summer. Mr. Frankel sat down across from me and picked up a piece of notebook paper off a pile in his to-do tray.

While reading off it, he said, "I received a voice mail from Mr. Nichols this morning. He says you haven't been to sixth-period drama for the past two days."

"Well, that's true," I replied.

Mr. Frankel touched the tips of his fingers on one hand to the tips on the other and asked, "So, Stella, tell me: What's going on here?"

I said, "I've decided to stop attending drama class."

"I'm afraid that's a decision that isn't yours to make."

"Well," I said, "but I kind of think it is mine to make. Sorry, but who says I have to go to drama?"

After I told him that, Mr. Frankel's tongue went into the

pocket of his cheek, right above his jaw. You know the face that doing that makes—it's the one a lot of adults use when something's come back to bite them in the ass and they need a few seconds to weigh the impact. It was like that bulge in the side of his mouth was saying, "Oh man. You really don't have to go to drama, do you." I can't be too righteous about his cud chewing because the same idea only struck me a few days ago. It's not like I've been this clear about things since I was in diapers.

When he had had his few luxury seconds, he took his tongue back and said, "I think the health of your transcript says you have to attend class."

"Well, I've also decided that I'm personally okay with taking an F."

The corners of his mouth pulled back. "You don't know what you're talking about." He opened my folder and held it out facing me, like it was some kind of talisman that would blow me away with the sheer force of its magic. He said, "Let me remind you that you're headed to Princeton, Stella. Princeton University."

"Yeah," I said, "We talked about that last time I was here."

He blinked rapidly at me. "Do you think the admissions committee will shrug off a failing grade because you suddenly lost interest in the dramatic arts? They don't tolerate this kind of last-minute apathy."

I thought about this and said, "Well, not that I care anymore, but I feel like I need to point out that for years teachers have been telling me a single bad grade will ruin my entire life. And really, I seriously doubt that. Give me a break." I actually threw my hands up in the air. I don't think I've ever done that before.

He responded, "Seems you've given yourself a break. Let me tell you about Bri—"

I told him, "Please don't lie to me and make up a story about a former student who got a last-minute F and ended up homeless. Not that it matters or anything, but I just don't want to sit here and just let you believe I believe everything you guys are saying."

Mr. Frankel threw his hands up in the air, too. "What am I supposed to do? Stop being a principal because you've suddenly got a chip on your shoulder? If I had a dollar for every kid that gets a pre-graduation chip on his shoulder, I could quit this job!"

"A chip?" I asked. "I'm sort of insulted by that."

"There's one of you every year. The good kid that suddenly goes bad because it's the middle of June."

"Are you saying I'm bad because I don't want to go to drama?"

"You're not bad. 'Bad' was a wrong word choice. However, you're being difficult, arguing with me when you should be completing your last few days of class."

"Sorry," I told him, "but I just thought we were having a discussion."

His phone rang and he said, "Hold on a second" like he really didn't want me to hold on and would totally like to see me gone by the time he hung up. He picked it up. "Hello?"

From the way he sounded, I couldn't believe I did that to his voice. I thought, "Did I wear him down that much?"

Two seconds later there was a look of complete panic and

fury on his face and he was opening and shutting his left hand continually like the doctors make you do when you give blood. After that he started a pattern where his fingers would straighten halfway, bend, and grasp his thumb. His palm was facing me and when he'd first take hold of the thumb, a giant blue vein under the skin of his wrist would pop out and define itself.

I used to have a Childcraft dictionary about human anatomy that had a pull-out poster of a guy stripped of his skin, and I was always so freaked out by the way he looked without something solid and even covering his body. The drawing had these ridiculously bright colors, so that his muscle tissue was hot pink and the veins running all over were pretty much fluorescent blue. I always hated knowing that that's what I looked like underneath everything, that I was such a bloody mess. And I'm not saying "bloody" like the English throw around "bloody," but as in literally bloody. The body looks so dirty and hectic when you see it for what it really is.

And that's exactly it. His wrist looked so dirty and hectic.

Mr. Frankel spun his chair around toward the blinds and tried to lower his voice. But I still heard him say, "Today? Today?" From the way he was talking I could tell he was gritting his teeth. I mean, he was gritting them so hard that he barely got the last syllable out. The "day" sounded a lot like a growl.

He kind of hissed, "Yes, I know what you said, but I didn't think you meant it!" He caved over a little and the cord coming from the phone yanked the base toward the end of his desk. "Why do you have to be such a bitch!"

All of a sudden he jerked up and whipped his chair back around with this crazy, urgent look on his face, like someone had just called him and told him that unless he spun around his chair in under a second, he'd die. He still gripped the phone with one hand, but he reached out with the other and started dialing. Then I guess I came back into his periphery and he realized I was watching him.

As he rapidly punched in numbers, he said, "I haven't forgotten about you, but she's leaving now and I need to call her back." He reminded me of one of the actors on *Law & Order* who you just know is the murderer because of the way he says normal things in a weirdly aggressive tone that comes out of nowhere. Yesterday, the guy's like a grocer or something, and then forty minutes into the episode you realize he's not all there when you hear him talk about a pushy customer a certain way.

He made one of those "I can't believe this" cry-laugh hiccups. "She's not answering."

I offered, "Maybe she already went out the door?"

Without warning he slammed his fist down on his desk and yelled, "Bitch!" His pencil cup jumped and then spilled.

His fist came down three more times. "Whore! Whore! Whore!" It was kind of amazing because each "whore" he said had a slightly different inflection. I mean, one of them was angry, one was incredulous, and the last was sad. He pressed the hang-up button and started to dial her number again, while mumbling something about, "You think this shit only happens on soap operas, and my brother's a very ugly man." But as he clutched the phone and listened to the line ringing, I saw a change come over his face (mostly marked by the wrinkles straightening on his forehead and his eyes widening) and posture, and suddenly he looked a little embarrassed. Then he slowly hung up the phone.

"Sorry about that."

I told him, "Okay."

"Can you believe she would…" He stopped.

"Would what, Mr. Frankel?"

For three seconds he looked me over. Then he said, "I shouldn't be talking to you like this. But you're leaving, and I won't have to see you anymore past next week, will I? So this shouldn't be so shameful for me." He put all his fingers into the teepee configuration and straightened up some. "You've got to understand that I only spoke that way because of heightened circumstances, and that it in no way reflects my attitudes as the principal of this school."

I said, "I'm sure that's true."

"Then let's forget about this. Let's do that, Stella."

I asked, "Can we forget about my not going to sixth-period drama anymore, too?" I wasn't being a smart ass. I was genuinely asking.

Mr. Frankel didn't say a word after that, but I could tell we had an agreement by the way he was sulking. I walked out of his office thinking about his wife—I had seen her before at some of the Warrior awards. She looked just like a principal's wife, which means that she had a completely asexual dress on and the pores around her nose struck me as being pretty large while I was shaking her hand. That impressed me that she was doing something dangerous, leaving him and his awards ceremonies for someone supposedly very ugly. I hoped that she was madly in love now.

At 1:56 the bell rang for sixth period, and I speed-walked out of English. Mr. Muthler had been ignoring me and didn't call on me once. I couldn't wait to get out of that class.

I can't really put my finger on why I cared if Ainsley would be in art or not, but when I came into the room she was at her regular stool and I have to say that I was weirdly happy about that. She had her hair pulled back today, but she still hasn't figured out that it's tank top weather. She was wearing one of those shapeless boys' hooded sweatshirts with the sleeves pushed up.

The front door of the room was wide open along with the windows, and since today was breezy, the kids who were trying to paint and draw were having a tough time. One girl who looked too young to be in high school was trying to weigh down her paper with one of her shoes. The papers on the drying rack were rustling around, and on my way to the far window I stepped on a pencil that was rolling across the floor.

I took the seat next to Ainsley and said, "Hi, Ainsley."

She was painting watercolor stripes on her paper and looked at me sideways. I might have seen an eyebrow lift in acknowledgment.

"I was here yesterday, but I don't think I saw you. Drawing." I ventured.

She said, "I was with Ashley." She said that in the lowest, raspiest voice ever.

Those two do everything together. I mean, I kind of wish I had a best friend, but I'd make sure we didn't have to hold hands every second. We definitely wouldn't do that annoying going to the bathroom at the same time thing.

Anyway, Ms. Silver clapped and came out from her corner (which was pretty surprising and all the kids in the class looked up, majorly confused) and said, "How many of you want to do final projects for the next day or so? Then we can have a party during our Monday review time next week? Raise your hands."

Of course, we all raised our hands (me, too, even though I'm not even getting a grade in there). So Ms. Silver told us that we had to work with a partner and draw portraits of each other. Then she came around the room and started organizing the pairs by putting her arms around two kids and squeezing them together like two pieces of bread. The first pair she made was with Nina Comanche and this one small guy (I think his name is Todd). After they'd been slammed together they stole very intense and kinky glances at one another. Once they had that initial taste of shoulder bumping, I could tell they were telepathically making plans to stick their tongues down each other's throats in the parking lot after school. When Ms. Silver came around to the window area, me and Ainsley were the only ones sitting there, so we got pushed together.

"So I guess we're partners," I said.

Ainsley wadded up her watercolor drawing (it was still wet) and tossed it in the trash can, then told me, "Okay, let's get this over with." She got up and got us both fresh pieces of paper, which I thought was sort of nice and friendly.

When she sat back down she didn't say anything else, but instead picked up a black pen and started staring at me and drawing me at the same time. She quickly made an oval head, drew some long straight lines for my hair, and started filling in my facial features. She was making me look like some psychotic rag doll.

I was disappointed, so I tentatively asked, "Can't you please try at least putting a little effort into my portrait?"

She said, "I told you. I can't draw."

I took her paper and flipped it over. "But I think you could make that look a little more like me. Here, I know you can do it better and if you just try this time, I'm sure you'll surprise yourself." I took a pencil out of my backpack and handed it to her. She looked at me blankly and then started drawing my eyes. She was drawing my eyes as rectangles.

I couldn't help but say, "Jesus Christ, my eyes look nothing like that." I took the paper from her, flipped it around, and erased the corners of the eyes. Then I made them rounder and filled in my pupils and some eyelashes. I saw the eyes didn't look as real as they should, so I took the eraser and made spots of light right outside of the pupils. After that I passed her back the paper. Ainsley didn't say anything or get mad like I thought she might, but instead she got out a sheet of notebook paper, traced the eyes that I drew, and actually copied them onto the other side of her paper. Then she leaned back and looked at what she had done.

Almost in awe, she said, "Wow. Those are so good."

I asked, "Are you kidding me?"

She shook her head. "No, they're really good."

"Hmm," I said. "I haven't drawn for a long time. Maybe I'm better at it than I thought."

And then Ainsley really blew me away when she told me, "This is what I imagined the eyes of T. J. Eckleberg looked like."

I said, "I didn't know you were in AP English."

"I'm not. Ashley is though. T. J. Eckleberg was on one of her flashcards. We spent last night going over *The Great Gatsby* cards and we got halfway through *The Sound and the Fury* ones." She picked up my drawing and held it up in the window. "I loved the idea of those eyes though. I should read the book." Ainsley put the paper back down in front of me and told me I should finish my own portrait. She said she would do her own.

"You sit and do Ashley's flashcards all night?" I asked. There's nothing more boring than making flashcards except making flashcards for someone else.

"It's not a big deal though." Ainsley drew an oval on her paper, but pressed so hard that the tip of her pencil tore the paper. "We're next-door neighbors. She just comes over after dinner."

"Oh." I hadn't known this, but it made perfect sense. Just another way they were cemented together. "You know," I said, "you should have taken English with us, since you're memorizing flashcards anyway."

Ainsley was shading what (I guess) was supposed to be her hair. It looked like a five-year-old boy's random scribbling. She sighed, "That's funny because I can't even pull a D in regular English. The problem is, I can't make myself get interested."

I was thinking, "Well, this is pretty amazing. I've gotten Ainsley Cleveland to have a conversation with me." And it was even better than that because it was all really easy. Just us drawing and talking like I imagine normal friends do on a regular basis. I think I could have talked to her for the entire period. I could have told her all about the rest of *The Great Gatsby*. (I think she'd like the whole part about Tom's mistress getting run over and the whole irony that came with that situation— unless it was already on a flashcard.) And if it's just an eye thing she's into, I could tell her about Stephen Dedalus's eyeglass crushing incident from *Portrait of the Artist,* and I think I could tell it in a tighter way than Joyce does. I haven't really felt so excited to tell something about stuff in a long time.

I used to like to run home and tell my mom about every dumb thing that happened during the day, and then I'd repeat it all for my dad at night when he got home from work. He'd look at people's zits and moles all day (he had his own dermatology practice), but he'd still seem intrigued that I had caught a bee in a cup at recess.

Anyway, I was having a pretty good time sitting with Ainsley when Mrs. Green came over the loudspeaker and said, "Attention, student body. Good afternoon. I have a very important announcement." No one in the room got any quieter and no one turned the radio down, but Ainsley and I stopped talking and listened anyway.

Mrs. Green kept on going with a smile in her voice. "I am happy to announce the winner of the speech contest for this year's graduation commencement ceremony. We received many entries and the choice was particularly difficult, since there were so many wonderful speeches to make our selection from."

Our school refuses to have a valedictorian because once all the smack kids start getting GPAs toward the 5.0s (you get extra points for every AP class you take), it gets really tough to definitively say who has the highest average of them all. I guess there were a lot of arguments about it in the past. Like I heard one kid argued that an A in AP physics is more difficult to get than an A in AP chemistry, blah blah blah. And a full-out academic brawl ensued, complete with electricity contests and alphabetic periodic table name-offs. Anyway, this year everyone assumed that Ashley would win the speech contest, since the principal and his committee always pick the most beloved kid out of all the applicants.

Mrs. Green went on, "So after hours of deliberation, we have decided that the senior who will be giving the speech at our ceremony will be…Ainsley Cleveland." And, seriously, I suddenly felt like I was sitting next to a total stranger. Because the Ainsley I kind of know has never even strung together a sentence in front of more than one person. I mean, I don't even know if the Ainsley I kind of know can bang out a cohesive paragraph.

Mrs. Green said, "Thank you to all of the participants, and *goooooo* seniors!" There was no visible sign that Ainsley had heard the announcement. She just kept shading like a lunatic.

"Ainsley," I said, "you're giving the speech at graduation! That's phenomenal."

She said, "Looks like it."

I was absolutely dying to find out what her speech is all about. Tons of kids enter every year so they'll be the last word the other kids hear on the subject of high school, and Ainsley wins? That speech must be incredible. Some of the previous winners have made pretty impressive speeches. I know because I've been to our school's graduation ceremonies before. Last year Megan Chatworth (former president of ASB) based hers around an extended metaphor where she intricately described her family's last summer vacation at a resort in Mammoth. By the time she was done, everyone was convinced she had just made some kind of profound statement about the truth of friendship, the state of public education, and the intangibility of the future. Someone's grandma was sitting next to me and she said, "You know, baby, I feel changed for having heard that young woman talk" ("baby" was one of her grandkids who was sitting on her left side, not me), and the rest of the audience was clapping wholeheartedly. They were actually making the bleachers shake and I think there was even foot stomping.

By the way, graduation takes place on a football field, and it's not even ours. It's our rival school's field. We use it because ours is so small and crappy.

I'm trying to imagine Ainsley standing on the stage, giving a speech so moving that all the parents and relatives forget they're sitting in ninety-degree weather, watching a bunch of kids in square hats getting blank rolls of paper. I can't even picture how her voice will sound coming out of the microphone. Usually they pick someone with the kind of voice that inspires confidence.

Anyway, finally, after a huge pause, I just asked Ainsley, "What'd you write in that thing?"

She shrugged and then suddenly Ashley was standing behind us. She was blocking some of the light coming in from the door, so that's how I noticed her before she even opened her mouth.

"I had no idea you were even trying to write a speech," she said.

Ainsley immediately put down her pencil and looked up at her. "Ashley! Aren't you supposed to be in student government?" Believe it or not, that's actually an elective. Not fun.

After checking her hair for split ends, Ashley said, "I still am. I just had to come and talk to you." She looked at the wall, giving us a really photogenic view of her profile. Then she turned back and looked at Ainsley like she was looking at a mother who had left her kid in the middle of the street. It was kind of a mix of bewilderment and sheer horror. "You think you would have said something during one of the three million times you listened to me revising my speech."

"I swear," Ainsley promised, "I thought your speech was a lot better than mine."

Ashley blinked, her face frozen now, and then uttered a troubled, "Thanks." Then she spun around on her heels, walked out, and didn't look back. A whole bunch of guys watched her and one intentionally dropped his ruler under the table so he could look up her jean skirt.

But right in the middle of Ashley walking out, Ainsley made eye contact with me for what couldn't have been longer than a second, and I saw something there that looked a lot like happy unhappiness. It's like when you're smiling through your tears, except you completely mean both expressions. Today's the first time I've seen it on someone who wasn't acting in a movie.

Ainsley worked on her drawing for the rest of the period and didn't say a thing about her speech. When the bell rang, she held up what is now the ugliest portrait in the world (it usurped the title from her drawing in the library), and said, "It's me."

Seven

When I got up this morning (the crows again), the first thing I thought was, "Oh crap, I should really go see Donald." Since our final exams start tomorrow, today was the day unofficially designated as "Senior Ditch Day." You're supposed to come to school, but no one does except for the quiet Asians. And that's not me being culturally insensitive — it's just a fact.

Most of the kids plan a big trip to the beach or Tijuana, so the teachers just have review sessions during all the classes and lead the kids in totally useless multiple-choice and fill-in-the-blank games. Yesterday Mr. Muthler announced that we all should really think about attending his class since he was going to provide exam clues for those loyal enough to show up. I saw Ashley flinch because she already had plans to go to

Malibu. Then she turned to me and asked, "You're not going to come tomorrow, are you?"

I said I didn't know, which was the truth.

When I went to bed last night, I think I was actually planning on going to all my classes. I know I'm supposed to be slacking off and showing signs of being seriously troubled, but you've also got to fill your days up in the meantime, you know? I mean, in theory it sounded great a couple of days ago to blow everything off and freak my teachers out, but what am I supposed to do all day if I'm not doing the stuff handed out in class? I guess I could carve something into the desk or take a nap or whatever. But lately I'm figuring, is it really worth it to force myself to be someone different when I only have a few days left? And really, a few days. It hasn't entirely hit me yet. It's like when you have a few days left of winter vacation, except it's so cold (for California) outside and all the malls have such bright lights up and the songs on the radio are so serene that you can't imagine that Christmas isn't a month long.

At any rate, I also realized that I'd rather not be remembered as something worse than I actually was. I'm an A student. I just am. And I think I can have an A finish without compromising that, even if I don't set it all up like I'm supposed to.

I also decided that I should finish up my other responsibility, which is Donald. My mom always invited him to everything no matter what, even though I don't know if anyone ever benefited from having him there. At this block Fourth of July barbecue ages ago (I was maybe nine) he looked so bored in his plastic beach chair that I handed him a lit sparkler. That's kind of cute when you picture it in your head—me as a little girl, passing off this amazing thing that I probably loved a lot. And it was this act of innocent, heartfelt charity. Seriously, that's like the nine-year-old version of Meals-on-Wheels.

While Donald was holding the sparkler, one of the neighborhood kids waddled over and started shyly smiling at it. Donald held the sparkler out a little toward him with this totally troublesome look on his face, and the kid got scared of it (the sparkler, not the look) and began to back away. I got distracted for a second because the DJ announced the cakewalk, but all of a sudden I heard wailing and turned back around. I only caught the tail end of it, but Donald had taken the kid's hand and put the sparkler in it and then let go. The little boy was completely panicked with his arm outstretched. His eyes were so wide and he was looking at the sparkler like Satan had launched Armageddon at the end of his wrist.

I ran over to the kid and took my sparkler back, and the little boy sprinted across the street and into his garage. Donald watched him, squinting into the sunset, and said, "That kid has no balls."

This was before I even understood basic male anatomy, but at my tender age, I still knew Donald was being an asshole. I said, "Donald, that was mean."

Donald shaded his eyes. "I was going to help him get over his fear. Where'd he go?" But Donald wasn't really asking, so I didn't answer. He does that all the time. Poses questions that he knows you'll refuse to deal with. My mom came over at that point to give him a plate with food on it, and I took a walk up the hill and watched some birds get ready for the dark. After the nightcap fireworks, I saw Donald getting into a cab under our street sign and no one was seeing him off. He would never let my parents drive him back to the home, and he never tried to slip five bucks into my hand like I've heard other grandparents like to do.

Regardless, this morning at six I was up and dressed, so I walked to the bus stop near Culver and took the 53 toward Orange and then switched over and took the 71 to Newport Beach. Of all the hospitals to be taken to, I think Donald was lucky that he ended up at Hoag. It's right on the coast, so even though his room is depressing and sterile, he can look out the window and see the waves crashing and people who ride their bikes around all day. There's something very relaxing about the people who cruise around like that, and I think it has something do with childhood. Anyway, the sun was already out when I got to the intensive-care reception and asked to see Donald. And even though I was in a hospital, I had a general sense of well-being just because of how pleasant land near the beach is.

After asking me if I was a relative, the nurse said, "Actually, your grandfather was moved to a new room yesterday afternoon. I'll call his doctor for you." I thanked her very much.

A few minutes later a guy appeared and introduced himself as Dr. Barham and told me that he'd walk me to Donald's room. My first impression of him was that he seemed unrealistically tall. I've read that tall people are usually more benevolent than average because they see the world from a more flattering perspective. Like the daily act of looking down (literally, not figuratively) on others provides them with a kind of godlike love for humanity. It makes complete sense that Dr. Barham decided to become a doctor. When he looks down on his patients the first thing he must see is their eyes looking back up at him, and from that angle their heads must look proportionately larger than their bodies. So it's like he's probably more struck by people's expressions than anything else, whereas the rest of us kind of encounter their bodies and their heads at the same time, in one visual sweep. When we do that, I think we can't help but subconsciously get that people are clunky and a complete mess. But to him, everybody looks the way kids look when they stand at your feet and hold up their arms for you to pick them up. They look so little and poetic, if you know what I mean.

Anyway, after we got in the elevator, Dr. Barham looked upon me with this sort of loving, fatherly gaze and put one hand in his coat pocket. He told me that somehow Donald had gotten pneumonia, so I shouldn't be alarmed when I saw him hooked up to some tubes and monitors. He was strong and fully expected to make a total recovery.

I said, "That's good."

The elevator doors opened and Dr. Barham watched me exit safely first before he told me, "If you don't mind, I'd like to talk to you about Donald's attempt to end his life."

"Oh, sure," I said. "That's fine."

"We had a psychologist evaluate him at the beginning of the week, and it was his feeling that Donald isn't so much concerned with completing the act as he is with getting attention."

I didn't know if I should take that as some sort of accusation.

Dr. Barham made me feel better when he added, "I think your visit is going to do a world of good for him."

After our talk I went into Donald's room and he had the blinds shut and the TV set on one of the morning news shows. He looked bored out of his mind. I saw his eyes light up a little when I came in the room and there's a part of me that hopes that he was excited to see me specifically.

"Did you bring me something?" he asked.

I said, "Yeah, I brought you a car. I'm going to sneak you out of the hospital and drive you to Vegas like that guy in the Volkswagen commercial."

Donald bristled. "I had a feeling you wouldn't come through. You don't have much character."

I don't know why everyone thinks it's so funny when old people act all ornery in movies and on TV. It's not funny in person. Why do people get a kick out of old people talking back and being completely bitter? I'll never understand it. Like it's so great that they've gotten so wimpy that they can't even be mean in a convincing way.

Anyway, I took a seat on the Aztec-patterned chair next to the bed and said, "I've got an hour before I have to go to school, so why don't you tell me some of those stories you were talking about."

Donald sighed. "This is the tragedy of man." He held out his wrist, and there was a tube taped to it. "The end."

"No, I'm bored by that one."

Donald took back his wrist and said, "Me, too."

"So tell me something new and interesting."

I heard a humming and then Donald's mechanical bed

folded itself into a sitting position. Donald said, "Well, I'm not even sure if I'm related to you."

"What the hell are you talking about?"

He let his head drop back on the pillow and coughed. The skin on his neck sagged, but a vein running up the side stretched. "Katherine and I honeymooned in Hawaii. On Maui only…I didn't see the point in hopping from island to island when the first one we got to was perfectly fine. We never left each other's sides for two weeks. She liked to swim more than I did, so I would sit on the beach and wait for her for hours. I didn't like to get a suntan, so I rested under an umbrella." His voice was slurred by lots of heavy, noisy breaths. I had never heard him say this much in such a short time and vaguely started to worry about him dying right in front of me. "There were other women in the ocean, but I could pick her out in a glance. Once I remember seeing a tip of a head coming out of the water, just a tip, and instantly knowing it was hers. That was a big surprise to me. There's something incredible about that, isn't there?"

I nodded. I found it impossible to imagine him ever being in love, but I still knew what he was talking about.

"You wouldn't know. I bet you couldn't pick out your own forehead from a photograph."

I rested my cheek in my palm and gave him a look like, "Would you just let up?" He studied the look for a few seconds, and then decided not to fight with me.

He coughed and said, "We came home and stepped into our new house, and there were still boxes everywhere and nothing on the windows. She was tired from the trip and was worried about the sun coming in the next morning. She liked to sleep late. I suggested that we should get a dark sheet and pin it up over the window. I went into the living room to go through the trunk with the bedding. I found a thick blanket that was hers...I didn't recognize it...and I went back to the bedroom. When I entered, I saw that Katherine wasn't in there. I called for her. She didn't answer, so I walked in and out of the rooms of the house looking for her. It became clear to me that she wasn't there. I went into our front yard and she wasn't there, either. I looked up and down the street and didn't see anyone. At midnight I hammered the blanket to the wall right above the window. Then I went to lie down, but I didn't shut my eyes."

Right as Donald was finishing his sentence, Dr. Barham walked briskly into the room (his legs take him far with one stride) and said, "It must be wonderful to have a visit from your beautiful granddaughter, Donald." But I didn't look up at Dr. Barham and smile at him, because I couldn't take my eyes off of Donald. He was facing straight ahead, but his eyes darted to the side for one second and it was like as soon as they hit mine, we were automatically locked into this conspiracy together. Like he was sending me a silent signal we were going to play grandpa and granddaughter together for the doctor and under no circumstances were we going to continue our real conversation until we were alone again. And I felt like shutting up for him.

In response to the question, Donald said, "Sure."

Dr. Barham looked at his chart and listened to his chest and his cough, all the while asking me about school and boyfriends. I said school was great and I didn't have any boyfriends.

After he left, I told Donald, "Go on."

"With what."

I said, "I'll leave."

So he coughed and started again. "I was still in bed at four o'clock the next afternoon when Katherine came back home. I heard the front door open, so I sat up in bed and waited for her. She came into the bedroom, looked at me, and then looked at the window and sighed. Then she said, 'Oh lovely, you've gotten the sheet up.' I asked her where she had been. She wouldn't answer. After that, she pretended like it never happened. Her dismissal ate at me. I imagined that she had a lover somewhere. We had spent every moment together in Hawaii, but now I wondered if she hadn't been mine all along. I felt betrayed. We had taken vows to always be honest with each other, but she wouldn't even speak about where she'd been."

Donald's brows collapsed in a really troubled expression as he was remembering all this. I don't have memories half as old as that one and they still knock me upside the head with a kind of overwhelming depression because they can't be fixed. The important things I remember, I can always think of a way I could have done them better. Donald's memories must just build and build until it's like his old house is actually lodged within his brain, and he can walk around it and see everything as it was.

"Did she ever tell you about where she was?" I asked. "I mean, later in life?"

Donald looked crushed. "No." His eyes darted to mine again. And then they went away. He coughed. "She tried to make small talk with me. She asked me about the gifts from the wedding and whether or not I had become acquainted with the next-door neighbors. I answered her curtly as I continued to put our belongings away. I had never felt so angry and distraught at the same time before."

"At dinnertime, she said she needed to go to the store to get some food, since we didn't have anything in the house. I sat in our guest chair in the living room, believing that she would disappear again. I didn't try to stop her. You know the saying about the caged bird."

I said, "Yeah, I know that one."

"The thing about that saying is that it doesn't take into account how angry you'll be when the bird comes back."

I told him, "You should fix the cliché every time it comes out of someone's mouth."

He said, "I don't care enough."

I shrugged. "Oh well."

Donald wheezed for a second. I leaned forward a little, in case he needed something, even though I don't know what you can even do for someone who's wheezing. After he stopped and got his breath, he started talking right away.

"When she left for the store I was still sitting in the chair. I figured that I shouldn't bother putting more belongings away if she didn't come back this time. I didn't think I'd stay in that house if I had to live there alone.

"About ten minutes after she left, I heard the doorbell and I got up to answer it. One of the teachers from my mother's school, Evelyn, was standing on the doorstep. She taught first grade and had come over to our house for Christmas since she had no family of her own. I welcomed her into the house and we stood in the middle of the living room. She apologized for having missed the wedding, and handed me a wrapped box. Instead of taking the gift from her, I put my hand on the inside of her thigh…"

My jaw dropped. "I think you're really terrible."

Donald pounded his blanket and said through his teeth, "Then you haven't been listening to a thing I said."

"I thought you loved Katherine!"

"Yes, and I thought she loved me. Didn't I."

"Oh Jesus," I said, "what happened?"

"At first Evelyn didn't move my hand, but asked how I could be so heartless since I was newly married. I told her that Katherine had left me last night and never come back. She sympathized with me. Then I kissed her and she kissed me back, and soon we were in the bedroom."

I thought to myself, "Holy crap, I'm about to hear a sex story from Donald."

He went on, "While we were in bed I heard the front door open and Evelyn heard it, too, so she gasped and said that Katherine must have returned. I told her that we had to be quiet and held her close. Evelyn tried to pull out of my arms, saying that she had to get dressed and find someplace to hide, but I held her there. I smoothed down her hair and told her to wait. A few seconds later Katherine opened the door to the bedroom, calling for me, and I looked up at her with Evelyn still in our bed. We stared at each other while Evelyn announced how awkward she felt and asked if I could retrieve her clothes from the floor.

"While Evelyn was dressing under the covers, Katherine grabbed the fingers on my left hand and squeezed them so tight that she hurt me." Donald demonstrated by grasping his right hand with his left, but his hands were now so arthritic and shaky that I didn't think it was a very powerful demonstration. When he was done showing me, he threw his hands back at his sides and they landed with a thud on the blanket. I looked at his peeling nails and cracking skin and felt nauseous because I was hit with how old he's gotten. Not that I knew him when he was younger, but his story kept putting these pictures of a long-lost distant version of him in my head, giving me something to compare him to and making me queasy.

Donald said, "Then Katherine told me that she would do the same to me. That's what she said: 'I'll do the same to you.' And she left the house. She came home the next morning with mussed hair and her brassiere in her purse, which she made sure I saw when she placed her bag open on the nightstand. Again, I asked her where she had been. I had slept for no more than two hours, and I was frantic and wild. She only came over, kissed me, and said, 'Now we can start again.' I didn't feel quite that way, but over the next weeks we didn't argue once and we always slept in the same bed. About a month and a half later I came home from the office and she told me she had been to the doctor and that he had told her she was pregnant. That child obviously was your mother. I've never been sure that she's mine."

"Did you ever do a test of your features?" I asked. "Like did you look and see if she had your nose or your mouth?"

He said, "You tell me. Do you think we shared anything?"

"No offense, but I've only seen you as an old man and all old men look identical to me."

"All women look the same when they remove their makeup."

"Shut up, Donald."

"Didn't your mother keep a picture of me in the house? From when I was younger?"

"I don't think so," I said.

"I don't think I ever gave her one." He lowered his bed back into a reclining position. "So you got your story."

I stood up and looked down on him. "You didn't tell me anything. Do you think I'm your granddaughter? Does it make a difference to you if I am or if I'm not?"

"Of course, it makes a difference. However, I'm going to pretend that you are no matter what, for the time being."

"Why?" I asked.

Donald shut his eyes. "Because it's better for me that way. I'm going to go to sleep. I'm exhausted."

I took my thumb and my forefinger and propped one of his eyes back open. I knew he was just bored with me and our discussion and not even close to being on the verge of sleep. He opened the other eye and swatted my hand away. "What do you want?"

"Why's it better for you?"

Donald snorted and half joked, "Because then you'll be obligated to speak at my funeral."

Right in his face I said, "Ha. That's priceless." I picked my backpack up off the floor and told him, "Go to sleep, Donald." Then I walked out of the room. The nurses all smiled at me as I walked by them and when I passed by a room at the end of the hall, I heard crackling music coming out of an open door. The voice that was singing was one of those types from the past, where you can't imagine anybody singing like that now—so moony with all that shaky vibrato at the end of the lines. The words to the song were something along the lines of "The clothes you're wearing are the clothes you wore…But I can't remember where or when." The song was actually playing pretty loud so I slowed down and peeked in the room. There was an old woman lying in the bed, older than Donald, and she had a record player set up on the floor. She was singing along softly to the song and she couldn't reach the highest notes, so sometimes her voice would break and go silent. I suddenly could picture her dancing to that song in her room while clutching her breast, and then I could see her kissing Donald in his empty living room decades ago. She broke my heart and I had to get out of there immediately.

Oh Jesus, she made me sad.

A half hour later I got off the bus and walked north on the Yale Loop. I started out on the sidewalk but the grass next to me was sparkling and wet, and all I wanted to do was step on it. So I just went ahead and did that. Each time I put my foot down, the grass would stay squashed, and I only cut this out when I saw a city gardener ahead with his ear protectors on. After that I got back on the sidewalk and, when I came to it, stepped over a pile of his leaves.

Today it was easier to enter campus near the stairs that connect the math and English buildings, so I went ahead and did that, too. There's a whole culture that flourishes on the side wall there. Kids sit along that big hunk of whiteness and they strew their books and their things around like I've seen catalogs tell you to do with decorative pillows. They come early to school, and then they return to their spot during all major breaks between classes. And then they stay back there until at least four o'clock (unless they're in band, drama, or choir, in which case they hang out in their respective head-quarters until at least five). The side-wall kids are pretty much known as the loners of the school, except I guess I would consider myself more of a loner than them because those kids have a constant group of friends. They sit there during lunch and listen to their headphones alone together. I do my homework at the tables at the shopping center across the street. Which is fine, since I've always found it really peaceful.

Anyway, when I walked past that area this morning, Karen Baronsen was the only one sitting there. We have science together, so she called out, "Hey, Stella, did you finish the review packet?"

"Most of it," I said.

She asked if she could take a look at the section on circuits because she was having trouble with a particular word problem. I told her yeah, and got the packet out of my backpack for her. While she was looking at my calculations, I asked, "Karen, why are you here? Did you know it's senior ditch day?"

"Yeah," she said. "I knew. My family's Jehovah's Witnesses. We're not supposed to celebrate pagan holidays, but my parents take it to an extreme and don't let us celebrate anything at all. So they called Principal Frankel and asked him to make sure that I attended school today."

"Oh. That's really crappy."

"Yeah, it is," she said, "but I guess I could use the review time. I've been going clubbing in L.A. on weeknights, and there has been many a night when I've shirked my reading." Karen's going to Northwestern. "So why are you here?"

I looked around, hoping to seem like I was searching for an answer. "Oh, I don't know. Just am."

"Well, you don't need to be here. You don't need to review at all."

"Of course I do," I said. "Everybody on the planet could use a little reviewing."

"No, not you. You don't need the review." Karen flipped through my science packet. "Look at this. I bet you didn't even use the book." She handed it back to me.

"I have a photographic memory. I got it from my dad." The five-minute warning bell rang and kids started moving around.

She said, "You're like a genius."

"No," I told her, "no I'm not." And then we stared at each other for maybe three seconds, having run out of useful things to falsely debate about.

"Okay," I told her, "I'm going to my locker."

My locker area was weird and empty since it's the one they assign all the seniors to. I appreciated not having to lean over Tricia Rosen for once (she has the locker under me and has the nerve to bend over and snack from a bag of Skittles between every period, every day. She refuses to pick up the bag and eat away from her locker for no apparent reason).

I had about a minute left until I had to be in poli sci, and I just wanted to put all my other books in my locker. But when I opened my locker, a folded piece of paper fell out.

I picked it up from the ground and saw it had my name on it and thought, "Oh my god, a note." Because I've never gotten a note before in my locker. I've always wanted to get one. I see the other girls reading their notes secretively during class, and sometimes laughing out loud. I don't want to say that it makes me jealous exactly, but it must be a little comforting to know that someone thinks about you regularly enough to sit down and write a letter.

I opened it, and all it said was, "I miss you." There aren't words enough to describe the jolt that went up my spine and all around my skull. I can't even write about it. Just like I said you can recognize the nose hairs of your ex-boyfriend in an instant, you can recognize his writing, too. I looked at every single letter for at least a minute, so I was late to first period. And, you know, maybe it's stupid, but I did that press-the-paper-to-my breast thing, too.

Today I've almost screamed ten times. I keep taking that letter out of my backpack and looking at it, and it keeps getting more and more interesting each time. All this emotion just wells up from inside my stomach and almost explodes out of my head.

For the rest of the day I went to my locker twice during every period (I told my teachers I had to go to the bathroom), but there weren't any more notes. I think I kept expecting him to be there. I imagined we'd kind of smile at each other and he'd put his hand around the back of my neck and squeeze the roots of my hair.

Then, after school, I was walking home and I saw him everywhere. Some guy would drive by and he was forty, but I'd peer in through his windshield and get ready to run into his passenger seat and beam at him. You know what I was thinking this afternoon? Of all the times to decide he misses me, he has to do it now.

I won't get sucked in. Tomorrow starts the first day of finals. So, Daniel misses me.

Eight

I'd like to say that I woke up fully intending to go to my first day of finals. Last night I went to my room around seven and stayed up until three flipping through my books. I was having some trouble concentrating because I kept taking Daniel's note out and studying it for clues. I held it up to the lamp to see if there were any hidden messages in lemon juice. I ran my fingers over it to see if I could feel any erasure marks where he had written something incredibly intimate, and then been too embarrassed to leave it. I also thought about how he had ended, "I miss you" with a period and not an ellipsis, and wondered if that meant he was happy with that statement as a complete entity and not intending anything further. Because an ellipsis would have been more appropriate to indicate that there was more to the story, that I should be waiting for something.

But anyway, I was mostly using my time to study. The only time I truly took a break was when Simon and Shana stopped in at eleven to say good night. Shana came in and put a banana down on the edge of my bed in the same manner I imagine zookeepers use when feeding dangerous apes at the zoo. Afterward, she retreated toward the doorway and said, "Brain food." I thanked her and picked up the banana, even though I wasn't planning on eating it. I don't like bananas. Simon appeared behind her.

"Lights out at one. Remember, the neighbors get nervous." The kindergartener next door, Leo, had supposedly been crying because the light from my room made lines on his ceiling when it went through his blinds. He thought the lines were trying to eat him or something. So Simon got a phone call from Mr. Gornick, and I got my first house rule last year.

"Sure," I said.

Simon knocked on the wall and finished off with, "Don't let the bedbugs bite. If they're termites, they'll chew through your books. And then you'll flunk all of your subjects." He winked at me without smiling, which was creepy as usual, but then he left. Shana lingered longer, then finally burst out, "I have a surprise for you."

I said, "You do?"

Shana stepped inside the room again and leaned up against the wall. "I volunteered Simon and myself. To be chaperones at the Grad Night dance event. You don't have to worry because we're not going to be standing around, watching you. We're going to be dancing." She had bright, dewy eyes as she was saying this, and I realized she was actually excited.

I hadn't planned on being around for Grad Night.

I told her, "Oh, that's really exciting. That'll be a great day and night." Inside I was feeling a kind of fog come over my spirits. I asked myself, "Will it crush her if I don't attend the first event she's volunteered for during the entire time I've been living here?" I have no idea if I have that kind of power over her. I mean, I don't even have a clue what I mean to her.

"You and I should go shopping for dresses," Shana said. "For the dance."

What can you say, "No, Shana, we shouldn't? Save your money for a rainy day?"

I could only think to ask, "When?"

"Tuesday afternoon?"

I wanted to tell her to please, please, please not care about this stuff, and not to care suddenly. We could have gone looking for dresses three years ago, last winter, whatever. I understood why it was now too clearly though. I wished she would understand it in the same way and surprise me again with a "never mind" in three minutes. Then we could save each other the heartache of pretending. I got nauseous, just sitting there in bed. My saliva seemed to start coming more frequently from the back of my mouth to the point where I felt like I was having to swallow every second. I dropped my head on my pillow, and I could smell my skin in it.

But I told her, "Okay. That sounds great."

Shana kind of rolled once along the wall, and then she was gone.

I had to put down my poli sci book because my head was

spinning. That didn't seem to help too much and I felt like my room was very, very hot, so I went outside around midnight and took a walk to the lake. They keep the lights along the path on all night over there, and the tennis courts look sort of eerie when they're empty. Anyway, in the middle of the bridge you can go down these steps that lead to what is officially called "the island," except that it's really just a small block of concrete with rocks on it. There's a sign that says you're not supposed to go down the stairs after sundown or before sunrise, but I went down anyway and sat on the metal bench on the side that faces East Yale Loop.

There was a crow that wouldn't stop squawking, even though everything else in the world was quiet. I wondered if it was one of the birds that wakes me up every morning. Maybe it follows me everywhere I go, and I just don't know it.

When I went back to the house at one, I went straight upstairs. First I got my perfume out of the bathroom and sprayed it into my pillow, and then I got into bed and looked through my books for the next two hours with a flashlight. When I finally turned it off, I felt really good about taking my exams.

Then, this morning I put on one of my finals outfits, which is essentially just a combination of clothes that allows me to sit in many positions. Those desk-chair combinations are absolute hell. Today I wore this shirt I found on sale at a uniform store. It's a Girl Scout blouse for the girls who've actually stayed in the program until they're my age. Which is kind of mind-blowing, since I don't think I've actually ever met anyone who can confirm this happens. I also wore my loosest navy slacks and my incredibly old saddle shoes that have soles worn so thin they're pretty much like slippers. I only pull them out during this time of the year. I was so serious about test taking.

I got to school at 7:48 and the sun was out. The day was already pretty warm. The thing is, Daniel was standing outside my locker, looking like one of those orange-juice-ad kids who glows in the wondrousness of the morning (except he was that kid twelve years later). I saw him as soon as I came around the corner. He was leaning against the locker in profile and the light was coming through the row and outlining his nose and lips in a really heartbreaking way. I stopped and just stared.

He looked too different from everything else around him to be there. He looked like someone was making a movie about him standing against a locker, and that was the entire plot. Seeing him, the first thing that went through my mind was, "Jesus Christ, I've missed him." I wanted to cry, and I'm a person who doesn't really cry that often. I don't know if I was exceptionally happy or exceptionally sad, since I haven't been either for kind of a long time. I breathed deep, and hoped that soon, knowing he was standing thirty feet away wouldn't seem like that much to deal with.

I breathed for thirty-five seconds. I stood there and watched the second hand of my watch go around, and it was so boring and tedious that I could finally look up and walk.

I came up in front of Daniel, breathed, and said, "You know, today's the first day of exams." The last syllable of "exams" sort of trembled, and when I inhaled again, my lungs took the air in like it first had to jog down a hundred steps in my throat.

As soon as I said that, I saw the bad association creeping into various parts on his face. The last time we saw each other was the day of my junior year AP U.S. history midterm, when Daniel showed up outside the social studies building and told me he wanted to go to Del Mar. That's how we would get to-gether—he would always come find me at school. The strange thing about us was that neither had the other's phone number. But since Daniel went to S.E.L.F. and got out at one o'clock, he'd meet me after fifth period every day.

That day he wanted to go to Del Mar really badly for some reason, and he wanted to go right then. He was very upset and kept cupping his hand in back of his neck and looking up at the sky like the beach was that way. I told him if he would give me an hour to take my test, I would meet him in the parking lot and we could go to Laguna after school. He said no, "I have to go to Del Mar." I said, "I can't go to Del Mar. I have school tomorrow. We should aim for something closer." And then the bell rang, and I hugged him and pulled his head to mine so that our cheeks touched, and I went inside. After my test I went and waited at the curb. He wasn't there, but I actually didn't expect him to be. I know when I've been a complete asshole.

It wasn't like I could call him or go to his house and check on him, because I had no idea where he lived. The next day at school I felt terrible, really crappy, and couldn't wait to see him. But he obviously didn't show up. And I was starting to get nervous that he was dead, which is maybe something that happens when you've had people die on you. I don't know. When I was in P.E., I started to look for him on the other side of the fake ravine that divides our schools. I'm serious. There's really a man-made sewage tunnel that runs between the good and bad schools. I doubt the city's original intent was to make a romantic statement about the chasm between our academic abilities, but still. It's a pretty weird symbol.

Later I found out from gossip at the mini-market that Daniel had actually gone to Del Mar and was staying for a while.

I was in love with him. I know I was, but I was just too much of a smack to love him successfully.

So that was why standing outside my locker, Daniel looked at me for a split second like I had gotten on top of his chest and started jumping. But then he straightened up in a very sexy way because without seeming to make a very significant move-ment, he was suddenly very close to me. "I didn't know about exams," he said. "But I don't care about them, either."

I wanted to tuck my face inside his neck. But instead I stayed where I was.

"Screw them," he said. "How much are they worth?"

I told him, "Well, today my tests are both twenty percent of my grade."

"What do you have going in?" I knew that he knew the ballpark already.

"I guess I have a high ninety in each class."

"If you don't take your tests today, you'll get Cs.

I corrected him, "Well, C pluses."

Daniel reached for my hand without taking his eyes away from mine, and I let him take it. "So," he asked, "do you think you could you ever take a C? That's just average."

I nodded slowly, just a little hypnotized by him. "Yeah, actually I'm going to take some Cs."

"So now"—he paused—"you're willing to take a C for me?"

"Well no," I said, "not for you. I just can do that kind of thing now."

Then I slid both my hands into his hair. He slid both his hands behind my neck and we kissed while trying not to smile at the same time. His breath was hot on my upper lip. I knew I still loved him because all I wanted to do was breathe it in. And at the time I didn't think about that breath as a function of his body, but instead as something just simmering around us.

When I opened my eyes, I felt like I had to put my head on Daniel's chest. Then I saw that Annabelle Salinger (who's in pre-calculus with me) was pretending to open her locker but really was staring at us out of the corner of her eye. People make out all the time in the halls, practically lifting each other's shirts off, and no one gives them so much as a glance. I think there's maybe the perception that I wouldn't ever be involved with anyone, like it's beneath me or something.

Daniel and I headed toward the parking lot together, and I kept looking at him and he kept looking at me. He's so abstract to me, and it's not that he doesn't have all the normal features a guy should have. He has brown hair and brown eyes and a chicken pox mark on his forehead. I can tell you that much. It's just that as a whole, my mind makes it so that he's too much for me to process visually. When I look at him, it's like I get a concussion and my brain swells to the point where it makes everything having to do with him slightly blurry around the edges. I mean, what else can I say but that he's magical to me.

Even when Daniel and I met, I hate to say it, but that night was magical, too. I mean, as magical as an SAT prep class gets, really, but I remember feeling like I could jump out of my body and become one with the universe by the time I went home. The night was already strange because Simon let me take his car to the class, and I had been trying to imagine what it's like to be him while I was behind the wheel.

So the class was held in an industrial office complex, and Daniel and I ended up in the same room because Princeton Review splits the kids up by practice scores. But I didn't notice him at first. I sat in the front and he sat in the back, and I didn't look around when roll was called because I've always thought that looks desperate, like you're searching to make a friend.

At the hour-and-a-half mark we got a break. Everyone headed for the candy machines in the lobby, so I went outside and stood on the sidewalk. The area was all deserted buildings and businesses at that time. No cars were going by and it was very, very quiet out, and quiet in a cold way. As far as when there's a chill out in the winter, everything seems that much stiller. After twenty minutes I walked back toward our building and suddenly Daniel reached out and grabbed my wrist and my first thought was, "I'm being kidnapped." He seemed to come out of nowhere, but really, I guess he had been walking parallel to me for a few seconds. I just hadn't noticed I wasn't alone.

He asked, "What's your name?" He was still holding on to my wrist, but I liked it. I could feel the pressure from every single one of his fingers on my bone.

"Stella," I said.

"That's one of those names that no one has anymore."

"My mom named me after the title character in the movie *Stella Dallas*. She told me it was the saddest thing she had ever seen."

"My name's Daniel. I wasn't named after anything." He seemed disappointed about that, like he wished he had a better story to tell. Then he took his thumb and massaged the crease under his bottom lip. He went back and forth with the surface of his nail. "Do you want to go somewhere with me?"

"Like back inside?" I asked.

"No, like on a drive. I can tell you're bored in there, you don't raise your head. We could go to San Clemente."

I asked, "Why?"

"Why would we stay here?"

"Because we want to go from 1400 to 1500."

Daniel cocked his head and said, "I am at 1500." He was still holding my wrist. I gently flipped my hand around until I was the one with a hold on his wrist and my fingers could take his pulse.

I said, "Say that again."

"Are you kidding? What are you doing, giving me a homemade lie detector test?"

"Yeah," I said. "Say it again."

Daniel looked me dead in the eye. "I got a 1520 on my PSATs." I focused on the ground so I could pay better attention to the beat of his veins. It stayed steady. Really, I had no idea if that proved anything, but I liked standing there silent with him and there was something very sharp and new about that moment.

I thought I had never instantly loved a face more, and I also felt that I wanted to live in his bed, next to him. I wasn't as worried about what we'd do while awake, but I had this definite fantasy of just sleeping and waking occasionally, looking over at him, and then sleeping some more. So I told him, "I heard your score goes up at least fifty points between junior and senior year." I put my hand into his and we ambled (the best way I can describe it is we were drunk on finding each other) to his car, which is an old white Pontiac.

I found out that he was only taking the class to appease his mom since she loved him so much. He was flunking every single one of his classes (at S.E.L.F, no less), but his mom had heard that kids with perfect SATs can get into Harvard and MIT in spite of having horrible grades, so she signed him up for help.

But while he was telling me all this, he was about an inch away from my face. We were having this intense conversation, but we kept looking at each other's lips and it was pretty obvious that something was going on. Then as he segued into a story about how the phone in his room crosses with his neighbor's line and allows him to hear everything that's going on over there, he moved into my seat. And I suddenly got brave and climbed into his lap.

I leaned in and kissed his neck because I was too intimidated to kiss his lips, but he ducked his head down and kissed me as he inhaled in this incredibly sexy way. I had one of my plaid skirts on, and he put both hands on my hips underneath it and pulled me up against him. I had never been involved in something so sexy in my entire life.

It was my first time seriously making out, and it was my

first time having sex. I had been warned by sex-ed videos and had overheard girls talking about how it would hurt, but it didn't at all. I didn't bleed and I didn't walk home like I had just gotten off a horse. And I definitely felt different when I went home that night, but I don't think it was because of the sex. Because it wasn't like I was stroking my hair slowly in front of a vanity mirror that night and looking for a change on my face. I just felt sort of better about getting up the next morning, which was new. I remember thinking I couldn't remember the last time I had a night end with a bang…and I know how bad that sounds but, seriously, I wasn't aiming for a pun.

Today we also had sex within twenty minutes of meeting each other, and it was car sex again. There's a group of CPA offices that sit on the edge of the North Lake, and we stopped in the dead parking lot and lay across the back floor. Daniel had his back weirdly arched because of that bump that goes between the two floor mats. I sat on top of his hips and he pulled off my shirt while I unzipped his jeans. We were so turned on that neither of us waited for my underwear to come off. Daniel just kind of pulled it over to the side of my thigh. Everything felt so amazing and the morning light was coming in through the car windows, and it made Daniel's skin kind of glow.

But this time I couldn't ignore how hot the car was and for a second, couldn't shake the horrible awareness that we were both just animals, and not animals in the "Come here, you tiger" sense. I felt like we were just fish with limbs or deer with rounder heads, and what we were doing was nothing more than smashing ourselves together physically and pretending that it was emotionally instead. At one point he held on to me tighter, and losing my breath I thought, "It's because he presses on my lungs. It's because he presses on my lungs." And then it dawned on me that that phrase had become a rhythm, and I realized we were thrusting to the very same rhythm in my head. So I tried to think of that rhythm in terms of grammar, as far as my language translating into an action through my own will. But I ended up thinking of birds flying south because they just can't help it and the process of giving birth, too. I shut my eyes and wished that I could see the two of us as something ethereal, and we could even just be lips and loving thoughts and that would be perfect.

When I felt the start of nausea coming on, I forced myself to open my eyes and look at Daniel. I said to myself, "I love him like I've never loved anyone before, and he is magic." And I kept on going until it didn't occur to me that we were bodies anymore, but best friends and in love. Then I felt a surge of awe and commitment to and for Daniel. And my previous thoughts began to pass and I was incredibly relieved.

After we put our clothes back on, we sat in the backseat together. I leaned back between Daniel's spread legs and put all my weight onto his chest, and it felt amazing. When I'd say something, he'd bend down to hear me better and the tips of his hair would touch my cheek and I'd get the shivers.

We had the windows rolled down and listened to The Coast, which is this love song station around here. I guess it's supposed to be the audio equivalent of walking through foaming surf, so the DJs play waves crashing before and after commercial breaks. On the first night we met, we found out that we both really like 103.5 FM because it still plays the songs we remember from our childhood. It's really weird how the songs that were considered rock during our youth are now on the soft station. And even I have to admit, they do sound totally wimpier these days.

I can remember my mom pounding the dashboard slowly with her fist to the chorus of "Don't Dream It's Over" one time when we were all going out to dinner on a summer weeknight. And back then it didn't sound like a love ballad, but like this seriously powerful anthem instead.

She said to my dad, "This song is the most incredible thing I've ever heard in my life! Lance, it's the most sad thing I've ever heard in my life!" And if you've listened to it before, you know how true that is.

My dad nodded in agreement. He reached over and turned up the song, but I had speakers in back of my head and felt like my eardrums were going to get blown out. I could feel the blood stirring up inside of them like it was boiling in a pot.

But my parents were all wrapped up in the song, and they put their hands together and pumped their conjoined fist in the air. They looked so happy that I didn't want to ruin their fun, but after about thirty seconds I really couldn't take the volume. "Can we turn down the music?" I asked, but I couldn't even hear myself in my own head over the music. So I took off my seat belt and squeezed through the space between their seats and turned it down.

I said something like, "Jesus Christ! I'll go deaf!" and my mom said, "If you have to go deaf because of one song, then this is the one."

We ended up going to Bullwinkle's for dinner and in the main dining area (I use "dining" lightly) there was a water fountain show every fifteen minutes. Before it started, a mechanical Rocky and Bullwinkle would come out and do a jokey routine (sometimes a wooden Boris and Natasha would join in from the top of the stage), and then the water danced and the lights beneath the spouts changed colors. "Don't Dream It's Over" came on in the middle of the show, and my mom made us all put our pizza down and listen quietly.

Anyway, so Daniel and I were hanging out when "The Longest Time" by Billy Joel came on, and I said, "You know what my mom used to say about this song? That it was a ghost song."

Daniel asked, "What's a ghost song?"

"Like a ghost story, but to music. She thought this song was really spooky. The line about the voice in the hall and the emphasis on eternity. She thought that it was the song of a man who's going to murder his wife so she'll never change on him. Because the way it sounds, it's like he's so hung up on what the woman is doing for him right then that he won't be able to bear it when she disappoints him."

"That's so morbid," Daniel said. "When I used to listen to this song as a kid, I pictured a surfer and this girl he meets on the beach, and they spend the nights together at barbecues."

I asked, "Like, grilling hamburgers?"

Daniel said, "Sure."

"That's horrible."

"That's not horrible."

"Did you picture a picnic table?" I asked. "Were there condiments on it?"

"What does that matter?"

"It matters."

Then Daniel's pocket started to shake and he took out his pager and I sighed. He's a drug dealer, and when I'm capable of it, I like to pretend he isn't.

It isn't that I see his current job as a slap in the face because of my parents and everything. Because he was doing this long before he met me. And he felt really terrible when I finally told him about my parents the week before he disappeared to Del Mar. He put his head on my shoulder for about a half hour and refused to look at me.

But the whole idea of drugs kind of depresses me. Originally, I started feeling so crappy around Daniel's customers because when I'd sit and watch them smoke out, it was like I was watching this group admission that the world is less than gripping. It was really sad for me to watch them breathe in the smoke and shut their eyes. When they reopened their lids, it was with this strange eagerness that told me they just couldn't wait to see if anything (and I mean *anything*) was better than what was there before.

What's really strange is that even though now I understand how stark and bare things actually get, I still feel the same way about the drugs. If I could go through my days in an altered state of mind, but not know how I got to feeling so altered, then I would be much better off. Tim Sharpner, who is definitely the biggest druggie at Woodbridge (and one of Daniel's regulars), gets happy every time he sees, like, colors. One time I was watching his face when his old girlfriend, Jenna Portini, gave him a psychedelic birdhouse she made in woodshop. He almost looked like he was about to burst from the joy of her paint choices, but he was high.

I mean, can it really be better to love a birdhouse because you're not completely clearheaded than to see it for the piece of crap it really is? Why does that question make me more sad than just dealing with the fact that the birdhouse is a piece of crap? The topic exhausts me.

But really, it's the knowing that makes pretending so impossible. I'd snap out of my drug-induced haze over the next few hours and my heart would drop to the floor like it does after I realize I'm dreaming in the morning. One time I was dreaming that I won a gigantic stuffed panda bear at a carnival and seconds before I woke up, I realized that I hadn't won anything at all. I was so weirdly crushed, even though I had never had the thing in the first place.

Anyway, I found out the reason that Daniel had come to English last week was to tell Jeff Mahoney about a deal going down at a house on Golden Star. That's right around the corner from where I live, but he has no idea.

Anyway, again, Daniel looked at the number on his pager and said, "Man, I have to go to this guy's house."

"What for?" I asked.

He brushed a piece of hair out of my eyes, even though I wasn't facing him. "To pick up some stuff. It'll only take ten minutes, but I've got to go now because he's cruising in an hour. He's literally right across the lake."

I asked, "Am I going to have to watch you smoke out? Because then I'd really prefer to just go home and study for my exams on Monday."

"Nah, we'll just pick up the stuff from this guy and go."

The guy, Lenny Ansen, lives in one of the white planked condos on the North Lake with his mom and goes to Irvine Valley College (which is community) part-time. Daniel had me punch in a code at the front gate and then the first thing I saw was the fountain shooting off in front of the lake, and then we made a right at one of the cul-de-sacs branching off from it.

When Lenny opened the front door I recognized him from Woodbridge. I think he was a senior when I was a freshman. He used to always have one of those Mexican ponchos on every day in the winter and was voted "Most Likely to Never Leave Irvine" in his graduating yearbook. I think that's a pretty incredible prophecy because he still shows no sign of taking off. Today Lenny was wearing a gray Batman pajama top made for a little kid, but he's so tall and skinny that it pretty much fit.

Lenny said, "Hey, you guys." And then he paused and made eye contact with me as I stepped inside. From behind me he asked, "Do I know you?"

"No," I told him. "I don't think so."

Then he said, "Ehhhhhhh. You were the girl that walked by South Lake in the little skirts! I used to do business under the Alton bridge back in the day. One of my clients pointed you out. He said he liked to cheat off you during tests because you're really smart."

"Oh. Really." I couldn't figure out anything better to do than just nod slowly.

We followed Lenny into his house as he told us that his mom wasn't home. His living room had a definite Spanish influence, since all the furniture was in turquoise and orange fabrics and there were maracas and those nesting dolls on top of the piano. I asked Lenny if he had some kind of Spanish heritage and he just said, "Ehhhhhh," like he was thinking, but never finished the thought. Daniel didn't seem to think that was weird.

We went through these giant glass doors that opened onto his back deck, and Lenny lay down on a plastic lounge chair. Daniel and I shared the cushioned lounge chair closest to the water. I could hear the lake water sloshing against the bottom of the building, and there were also clay and bell wind chimes hanging from the beams overhead. The mix of the two sounds made me feel sentimental about something I couldn't put my finger on.

Lenny squinted up at the sky while pulling a bag out of his pocket. Then he slid it over to Daniel along the ground. Daniel picked it up and turned inward toward me, making a protected cave in between our two bodies where he could safely look at his prospective drug purchase. I looked down and saw that whatever was in the bag was white and not green.

Seeing that whiteness just instantly brought all this pressure behind my eyes and above my cheeks, even though I wasn't entirely sure what the white was. I felt like my skin was getting sucked against the muscle.

Daniel cupped his hand over the bag and rolled over on his back.

"Have you, ehhh, talked to Jeremy this week?" Lenny asked.

Daniel said, "Nah. Why?" He slipped his hand in back of my neck and started spelling out "I (heart) u" with his finger.

"He's been trying to come up with a weed lemonade brew

to sell at what do you call them? Ehh, stands. Like neighbor-hood lemonade stands that you put on street corners."

"Man, Lenny, he's not all there."

Lenny took sunglasses out of his pocket. "Ehh, I don't know. If it works, we could set something up over by Rancho. Like back in those split-level town homes there, and it could be a word-of-mouth thing."

"Why doesn't he just have a bake sale?"

"He wants to do something new."

"You know," I said, "I think I have to go to the bathroom."

Daniel looked at me. "Oh. Okay. Go inside past the kitchen and it's the door before you hit the laundry room."

"Thanks."

"Don't steal anything," Lenny called out.

I went inside the house and passed by these gigantic oil paintings of empty Spanish towns on the walls next to the kitchen. They didn't have any people in them—just bright houses and big suns in the right-hand corners. I looked over my shoulder at Daniel, but his back was to me, so I went through the door that connects to the living room.

First I picked up one of the maracas and shook it very softly, and then I went out the front door.

I got outside and there were kids riding on their bikes around the cul-de-sac, screaming, "The pirate is coming! The pirate is coming!" Then three seconds later, a kid with an eye patch actually sped by on a black bike. He was yelling, "I'm coming!" from this completely low place and his head was thrown back so far that it seemed like he couldn't see where he was going. He was zigzagging all over the place. I watched him as he furiously peddled by (my hair even flew up a little when he went past), and he was doing it with such intensity that I had a gut feeling that that wasn't a play patch, and that he really might be missing an eye. I felt horrible for him.

Daniel's car was unlocked, so I was able to get my backpack and after I put it on, I started to run down the street. I tried to steady the backpack by holding down the arm loops, but every time one of my feet hit the ground my stuff would thump against the back of my body. My breasts were killing me and my knees felt like they were almost arthritic, like they couldn't move in as fluid a way as they probably should. It was just so hot out and I couldn't take all the bouncing and moving, so I fell into a quick walk toward the middle of the street.

But then, when I hit the lamppost, I realized that Daniel would think I bailed on him again. I could see his face in my head, the way it would look.

As I walked back to the house I wondered what the hell I was doing on that street. I was thinking, "I should just go home. I really should just go home. He may make me feel better today, but I'll never feel exactly right. I have to remember that."

I mean, really, what am I supposed to do? Hope that he'll make the rest of the world fall away? Jesus Christ, I feel stupid even asking.

Last summer I went to the L.A. County Fair alone and there was a ride there called Lover's Lagoon, and you actually got into a swan and entered the cave underneath fake weeping willows. And basically, there wasn't a lot to see in there except some glowing plastic hearts, cardboard cutouts of people kissing, and even more fake weeping willows inside. But none of that mattered because the whole point of the ride was that it was dark. Because really, in order for people to fall in love, things only have to be dark. To see the world romantically, you've got to find a way to make it invisible (unconsciously, because once you figure out what you've been doing, everything just turns way too depressing). You can have the world made dark for you literally, by going through a pitch-black cave or by flipping off the bedroom lights. Or, if you're really good, you can keep your eyes open and pretend that everything else is falling away naturally.

And the most difficult thing is that we have to be in the dark about each other a little, too. You have to stop yourself from thinking about how you're on some rickety ride with a rickety human being next to you.

You have to say to yourself, "I'm in a lagoon. I'm in a lagoon. I'm in a lagoon." The water underneath you isn't in a tank and the tarp overhead isn't a tarp, but nothingness, and it wasn't put up by a bunch of guys who travel from county to county, hating the people they put on the swans.

So I'm upset. Not that I should let it matter, but when the world started to crack in today in the car with Daniel, it was a kick to the stomach. It was like the last thing that I knew I shouldn't believe in, but wanted to anyway, removed itself as an option. Like it decided on its own that it was untrue.

I wanted to be dragged into a present that feels like it could just go and go and go. I wanted to know exactly what that's like. What if every day could stand still in just the right places and the leftover time could eat itself?

By the time I reached the walkway, the door opened and Daniel was there. I ran to him and pressed my mouth against his like I could transfer some of myself into him if I would just put everything I had into the action of pressing.

I cried into his open mouth, "I love you."

"Hey, don't go," he said. "I'm sorry. Man, I shouldn't have been doing that around you."

I pulled back from the kiss and put my lips to his forehead. Now I talked into his skin. "I feel sick. I need to go home."

He reached around my back and unzipped the front pocket of my backpack. I didn't move from within an inch of him.

He pulled out a pen and then he pulled my arm to him and started writing on it. I didn't look at what he was writing. I kept my eyes shut and I rested my cheek on his.

He said, "That's my pager number. You call me later and I'll come to wherever you are." When he talked, an actual tear came out of my eye and ran down my face into that gap between his cheekbone and jaw, and since my face was pressed in there it made a sort of wet pocket.

He slowly unstuck himself from me. "What's wrong?" he asked. "Why are you crying, my baby?"

I said, "I'll call." I turned around and walked away from Lenny's house. Then I walked around the Loop for awhile until I finally went home and told Shana I was feeling sick.

Nine

I rolled out of bed at 1:06 P.M. to a very dim room. I looked out the window and saw damp streets and realized that's why the crows probably let me sleep. It had been drizzling all morning. June gloom.

I went to my door and listened quietly, trying to see if I could hear Shana and Simon making sounds in the house. Sometimes I get up on Saturdays and everything's so still that it feels like I live in a really boring museum. But today I heard the TV on in the family room, so I knew they hadn't gone out to run errands yet.

I pulled on a pair of slacks (I sleep in my underwear) and a little-boy's undershirt that I got at Target. As I came down the stairs barefooted, I could make out the Janet Jackson song with the video where her artistic boyfriend reaches down into her pants and pulls out a chain. I always thought it looked like he was extracting an enchanted silver pubic hair.

I heard Simon say, "Who am I?"

That made me pause on the step. My mind raced ahead with an imaginary conversation in which Simon and Shana questioned who they were and what it meant to be my guardians.

Simon would say, "Who am I? Who am I to this young girl? Does she love me? What does she think of me?"

Shana would say, "I know. Heavens, I know. Simon, do you realize she's leaving in two months? And that after she's gone to Princeton, we've given her no reason to want to keep in contact with us?"

Simon would look like he had been staked in the heart. "Do you really think she wouldn't come home during her breaks?"

Shana, in a whisper, would answer, "Would you consider it home if two strangers lived there?"

I snapped out of it when I heard Simon ask, "Am I famous?"

"Yes," Shana said.

"Am I...a rock musician?"

"No."

I heard an actual snap. Simon, I guess. "I was already picturing myself in leather pants, having sex with jailbait."

Shana said, "Simon!" in the loudest voice I've ever heard come out of her, and then she actually laughed. So that's how I found out she does think he's funny.

"I'll try again," he said. "Am I an actor?"

"Yes."

"Am I still alive?"

"Yes."

"Am I older?"

At this point I sat down on the second to last step, pretty amazed.

Shana said, "Yes."

"Am I in blockbuster movies?"

"Yes."

"Was I in *Working Girl*?"

Shana said, "You were!"

Simon sighed, "Ah, I'm Harrison Ford today."

"Yes."

"All right. So it is, Doris."

I had to look around the corner. I propped myself up on my fingertips and leaned forward very, very slowly because I was scared they would even hear my slacks crinkling. First I saw a sliver of Simon's leg and there was a pant over it, so I breathed a silent sigh of relief and just hoped Shana wasn't topless.

I leaned forward farther until they came into view, and I saw they were slow-dancing. They weren't even holding each other very close. It was more like they were dancing at a fancy wedding and Simon was holding Shana's hand so lightly because he didn't want to get palm sweat on her white glove. Their backs were straight and they were keeping the beat perfectly, but the weirdest thing of all was that they both had their eyes shut. Simon's chin was tipped down toward Shana's and she had hers tipped up toward his and they were holding their heads as a couple would if they wanted to gaze in each other's eyes while dancing. But their eyelids were closed completely. I mean, I've seen people dance together with shut eyes, but they've always had their heads resting on each other's shoulders.

I watched as Shana's eyelids began to scrunch up, creating deep folds around her crow's-feet and along the sides of her nose. By the time she was done, she looked like a little kid protecting herself from danger through the sheer force of her squint.

I leaned back again and slumped against the step. The fake names, the closed eyes, the ballroom waltz. The two of them were pretending that they weren't each other, and that means they were pretending that I wasn't in their lives. What did I tell you before? That's how you fall in love again. You shut your eyes.

Sometimes I have a recurring dream where I walk into the house and there's two unrecognizable people sitting on the couch. I apologize for being in the wrong place, but they ignore me and start asking about random things. As they talk, I always hear the blood rushing through my head like when you hold a shell to your ear, but the worst part is that phlegm begins to build in my mouth and the back of my nose. I can taste it and feel it (I always wonder if it's happening in real life). I feel so disgusting and want to get out of the house badly, but I either find out that my legs don't work or the door isn't the same place it was when I came in. I tell the people in the house that I hate them, and they tell me that I don't mean it. Then I tell them that I know this is a dream. To prove it I start to rattle off the people they resemble, to show that they're a composite of others in my life. I tell the strange dad that he looks just like a cross between the Asian guy who exercises by the lake and this one teller at my World Savings bank. The dad proceeds to pull a spoon out of his pocket and he runs it up along his neck and chin, scooping phlegm off of himself. He's made out of it. I gag. He holds out the spoon toward my face. Sometimes I try to punch him and sometimes I wake up.

I looked at Shana and Simon, and they were just such strangers. Watching them dance was like when I look out the window in the bus and stare at people in the car below me. I always have to remind myself that to someone, those people are familiar. Those people have jobs and relatives and their picture sits on somebody's desk at work somewhere. Somebody is able to recognize their writing just by picking up a grocery list, and somebody thinks those people are special, even though there's a ninety-nine percent chance that they're really not. When I look down at people in their cars I have to remind myself that they have lives once I can't see them anymore.

In a split second I understood why Donald wanted to insist that we're blood. Then I decided that I insist we're blood, too. And I had to get out of that house.

I got up from the step and tiptoed into the front hallway. I held my breath and I unlocked the door and stepped outside. And then as I was shutting it I heard Simon call, "Stella?" from the other room.

I felt like a robber who had broken into a house and the owners came home while I was stuffing jewelry into a pillowcase. Panic set in. Suddenly I was scared of being discovered near the house and started to run. The path under the breezeway was dry so I only realized I didn't have shoes when I hit the wet cement on the driveway. Blossoms and wood and stained glass flew by. The water made small pebbles stick in the cracks between my toes when I pressed down on the cement, and every few seconds I would feel a sharp prick in my skin. But I didn't stop. I went diagonally across asphalt, my feet pounding the ground and my eyes trained up on a long cloud because it was dark and still and there.

After running for a few seconds, my body instantly got very warm inside, even though the drizzle was cold on the outside of my skin. I physically felt like two different girls at once.

I was deathly scared that if I turned around, I would see Simon and Shana standing at the camphor tree in front of the house. I could hear Shana's stammering in my head. "Where, Simon? Where is she going? What? What is she doing?" So that's why I ran for a long while even though my legs felt so much like rubber. And so I wouldn't think about them or the pain in my sides, I thought about Donald instead.

I realized that the greatest thing about me and Donald right now is that we don't even know the truth. I mean, it's absolutely impossible for us to lie to ourselves right now. We don't even know what's real and if you held a knife to our throats, we still couldn't tell you. I think that's kind of amazing. To be able to look at each other and say, "Hey, I can kind of see how our noses slope at the same angle," and even if we're full of crap, we won't be able to tell. Somewhere deep in our blood and our cells and our atoms there either is or isn't something that matches up, but it's hidden from us. And unless we go seeking it out, it'll stay a secret, literally buried inside of our bodies.

And I know school isn't important unless I make it, and I know that love isn't as pretty as I want it to be, but Donald and I are a real mystery. After all, something's been keeping us together all these years, right? It can't be time, because I've spent more with Shana and Simon. It can't be genuine affection, because like I said, he's a complete asshole. All I could come up with is there's just something about him that isn't strange to me. And when he told me he was going to believe I was his granddaughter, he must have thought there was something about me that wasn't strange to him.

I was jerked out of this thought when I stepped on a nail. The tip was the only part that went into the ball of my foot, so I just pulled it out and tossed it in the gutter and then I looked up.

I was standing on someone else's street. The houses looked familiar, the colors the same ones in a handful of sand. Wide shutters divided up bay windows and chiseled panels divided up front doors. Nothing different there except the black Rabbit parked against the curb in front of me. I went forward and looked in it and a tiny California license plate was affixed to the glove box and in capital yellow letters it said "Ashley." But I already knew the car was hers. I just didn't know that she lived right on the other side of Wood-flower pool.

Half of the car was parked in front of a house with short stone light pillars on both sides of the walkway, and the other half was parked in front of a house with brick ones. A metal-lic banner with graduation hats and confetti went from a stone pillar to a brick pillar, dipping across the mutual property line. I stood there looking back and forth at the two houses like I was watching a tennis game.

"Stella!" someone called. A car door slammed behind me. I looked over my shoulder and saw Darren Pinsky from AP English crossing the street and ducking from the rain. He was holding a huge bag of potato chips and a two-liter bottle of Dr. Pepper.

"Oh. Darren." I felt something sticking to my forehead and cheeks and when I went to brush it away I found out it was strings of wet hair.

Darren said, "You don't have shoes on!" Then he looked at me like I was a doe who had come down from the hills to eat leaves from his backyard. All starry-eyed and awed, and worried about scaring me off. "And…listen, I feel like I need to tell you that I can see through your shirt."

I looked down and saw that my shirt had been dampened in the drizzle. The white cotton was clinging to my breasts like I had inadvertently entered a wet T-shirt contest in San Felipe, and my nipples looked darker through the material than they actually do when I'm naked in the bathroom mirror. While looking down I saw a rise starting in Darren's shorts, so I said, "I can't see through your shorts, but…" and that was all it took. It was like his penis tapped him on the leg. His hands flew over his crotch and he turned away from me.

Darren asked, "Why don't you just go inside and I'll be there in a minute?"

"Why am I going inside?"

"Just please…go inside."

"Why are you here?"

"The same reason you're here."

"I don't think so," I said.

"What?" he asked, facing a house with a rose garden.

I said, "I guess I'll come inside."

After a few seconds Darren turned back around (the front of his pants flattened now), seeming very wary of me when he saw that my shirt was still transparent. I didn't care at all. For the first time I felt very strongly the sensation of soon never having to see someone ever again.

He averted his eyes and said, "I feel like you're not acting like yourself today." He put the chips and the soda on the ground and then he peeled off his shirt, revealing maybe the skinniest chest I've ever seen in my life. His ribs were poking out through his skin and I felt like I could see his lungs swelling and deflating underneath it. He wrapped one arm around his stomach and held his shirt out toward me with the other. "Please take my shirt." He gave me a pleading, insecure smile.

I looked at the printed insignia on it (Cornell, that's where Darren's going) and asked, "That one day we were in the hall you told me you don't really know me. Do you remember?"

"I said that?" Darren asked.

"Yeah. I was wondering how I could be acting unlike myself when last week you said that you didn't know who I was."

"Oh, I don't remember saying that. I have a bad memory." He looked incredibly self-conscious.

"Never mind, I was being too literal anyway."

Darren nervously ran a hand through the wave he makes with his bangs, except the wave had collapsed from the damp weather and the action of taking off his shirt. "Are you going to put on my shirt?"

"Sure," I told him. I slipped it over my head and while my face was inside it, I was overwhelmed by the smell of detergent and cookies. I could picture his mom hiding a letter in his suitcase before his flight to New York and then mailing him a care package a week after he got there. She'd call every other day and ask him if it was getting cold yet (even though it was September), and she'd say she couldn't imagine how he was going to get through the winter with only four pairs of long pants. For a second I thought about leaving my face inside for a little bit longer, just because together the smell and the darkness made their own fascinating world. Really, I never knew a shirt could work almost like a movie. I guess I haven't really ever spent time in someone else's clothes. But instead I pulled my head through and said, "Okay, well, let's go inside."

We started walking toward number nine together, the house with the brick pillars. Darren kept looking at me like he'd find something to talk about there.

At the door Darren simultaneously knocked the brass knocker and said, "You really shouldn't be walking around without shoes. You should take mine."

"Whatever," I said. He pulled off his tennis shoes and they were so big that I could slip them right on. I told him, "I just forgot to put mine on this morning."

"How do you forget something like that?"

"I don't know." I did know.

Darren said, "My dad has a theory that some people are so smart that they can't get the smallest everyday things done. That must be you."

A kid so angelic and fair that he nearly looked albino opened the door. "Hi, please wipe your feet." We did. "They're all in the family room.

A giant circle skylight above the staircase brought green light into the entryway, but the sunken dining room was so dark I could only make out furniture outlines. The golden boy had us follow him past the staircase and around the corner and then we came into the family room. I saw the gigantic built-in fish tank before I saw the people.

Ashley was reclining on the couch lit by a banker's lamp. She held a hardback version of the *Picture of Dorian Gray* with both hands and kept her feet resting seductively on Mark Nelson's lap. Matt Taketano was slouching on the couch on the other side of the mahogany coffee table, and Jeff Mahoney was sitting next to him with a whole bunch of pillows behind his back. Toby Marcus, who's on the school's junior league of psychologists (he does conflict management for students when they get in fights), was lying on the floor holding a copy of the *Sound and the Fury* at arm's length.

The whole lot of them reminded me of those drawings I've seen of Victorian people in a state of leisure, where they're all lounging in the drawing room or parlour (with a *u*) or whatever and looking like it's painful to be so relaxed. Ashley only snapped out of her tortured ennui (vocab word last week) when she realized it was me standing in her family room. I looked kind of haggard I guess, so it didn't register for a few seconds. But when it did, she got very concerned and propped herself up onto her elbows.

"Stella?"

Toby said, "Look, it's Diane Court."

"Who?" I asked.

Ashley said, "Oh my god, Stella! I thought you were dead!"

"What?" I asked.

Ashley sat all the way up. "Karen Baronsen told me you didn't show up for your coordinated science final yesterday. Then Susan Allen told me you didn't show up for your poli sci final, either. Wait, what are you doing here?"

"You didn't show up to your finals?" Matt asked. "Fuck. Do you have a sick note?"

"Didn't you invite her?" Darren asked from behind me.

I said, "Yeah. I have a note. Because I had the twenty-four-hour flu."

I saw Ashley's shoulders come down a few inches, but she didn't look any more calmed. "So how does it work? Do you get to take your finals after school next week?"

"I heard when you're sick you get to take them at home," Toby said.

Ashley asked, "Who times you then?"

Toby told her, "Your parents."

"That could be unfair. Also, don't you think that gives people extra time to study?"

"I heard that's why you can't get anything higher than a B plus when you do a retake. Even if you really get an A, the teacher has to give you a B plus anyway."

Ashley, feeling better herself, looked back toward me and asked, "But Stella, you're feeling better now? But wait, how'd you know where I was going to be today?"

"Didn't you invite her?" Darren asked again as he took a seat in an armchair and suddenly everyone saw he was shirtless.

"What, Darren, too sexy for your shirt?" Jeff asked.

"Actually," I said, "I don't think I'm better yet." At that point I was already turning around. "I don't think I'm better yet. I think I'm still sick."

"Sick? Again?" Ashley asked.

I was moving.

"My shoes! Nikes!" Darren called, and I didn't know if he was just requesting that I not puke on them or if he knew I was leaving. I slipped out of the shoes in the entryway without slowing down. While I was passing out of the house, Ashley's presence loomed so large that I swear I actually felt her mouth opening to yell something, even though I was already gone.

At Ainsley's door I heard faint rustling against the other side, the whisper of clothes brushing against its surface. This is the sound of someone pressing up against the peephole, trying to decide if she's not going to be home. But finally the door opened and the thin strawberry blond woman behind it already seemed bored with me because I think she expected a candy bar pitch line or a request to get my Frisbee from her backyard.

"Yes?" she asked.

"Is Ainsley home?" I asked as she looked me up and down. She got to my feet. "I left my shoes next door. I was over at this study session and just wanted to come by to see her."

"Oh, Ashley's study session?" she asked, and let me in as I was confirming this.

From the second I stepped into the house I saw how very, very white it was, with white tiles on the floor, white walls, and white leather furniture in the den off to the right. There was even a white pen sitting on the white desk in there. The only deviations from the color scheme were a few lamps with silver bases, and a gigantic frame hanging above the couch in some kind of pearly paint that had flecks of pink and blue in it.

What really blew me away was the picture inside the frame. In a white rose garden a fairly handsome man had his strawberry blond wife on his knee, and two kids sat on a white bench in front of them—Ashley and Ainsley when they were younger. Ashley and Ainsley aren't related.

"I'm Elizabeth," Ainsley's mom said, pausing in the hall-way. Her hair touched below her shoulder blades, exactly the same color as Ashley's. "Were there enough brownies over there?"

"What?"

"There's still enough brownies for everyone over there? I have another plateful in the kitchen if you kids need them."

"Oh, there's plenty left," I said, not remembering having seen any baked goods.

I followed her up the stairs. She moved like fishing wire ran from her shoulder blades to the ceiling, lifting her along. When we got to the first landing I saw a wall full of family pictures, and Ashley, not family, was in all of them.

It wasn't like they were all pictures of her alone (there were only two of her yearbook photos), but she was present in every single one. There was an eight-by-ten of Ashley pool-side with two preteen guys (cousins, maybe) and they were all wearing matching sunglasses. There was also a large picture from some kind of picnic, where Ashley was laughing on a blanket and Ainsley was hanging out in the background by a tree. There was even one of those faux-saloon pictures you get done at Knott's Berry Farm of Ashley and Elizabeth in old-time showgirl wear, and Ainsley was hanging in a stock (I think that's the right terminology) and her eyes were shut. Not funny shut, like she was mugging for the camera, but nonchalant shut, like the picture was taken just as she blinked.

The things that really killed me were two disks of plaster with small handprints at the top of the stairs. At this point in my life I have to just assume that someone took my hands when I put down my doll or something and pressed them into wet plaster because my mom had her own disk, too. And she also had one of my feet. Anyway, like I said, there were two disks when only one kid lived there.

I pointed to the one with "Ashley" written on it in pencil. "You have Ashley's hand?"

Elizabeth put her hand in the plaster's sunken print. "The girls have grown up together. Very, very close. Ashley's a part of the family." Her attention snapped and she went back to the thumb indentation. "But look how tiny it was. Things are so precious when they're this tiny."

I put my hand into Ainsley's palm. "This one's Ainsley's?"

Elizabeth nodded, "Yes, that's hers." She gave me a wistful grin without teeth. "Sometimes when people ask me how many kids I have, I accidentally tell them I have two daughters. That's how close we all are."

We stood there for another moment, pondering the disks

like we were studying clumps of pure wisdom that had hardened on the wall.

Elizabeth showed me Ainsley's door and then floated toward her winter wonderland of a bedroom down the hall. I knocked softly, but the sound of the wood against my knuckles seemed much louder than I intended anyway.

I heard a muffled, "Come in," like she was inviting me over from a make-believe land inside the walls.

All I saw when I entered the room was a white dog sitting on a chair at a desk and a huge pile of stuff on the floor. The dog cocked his head and looked at me with extremely knowing eyes. For a second I had the crazy thought that Ainsley had transformed herself into a dog and only I would be able to hear her talk. Her voice had sounded so distant because she was actually trapped inside the body of the animal, and her words were coming not out of its mouth, but its heart. We'd walk everywhere together and people would say, "There goes that girl and her dog. It's like they can talk to each other." Together we'd look like the cover of a young adult novel, like *Island of the Blue Dolphins* or *Where the Red Fern Grows*.

But then I heard a husky, "What" from behind the left door of the closet and I realized what weird and horrible fantasies I have sometimes.

I called out, "It's Stella. From art." Ainsley appeared in the open middle section wearing a sweatshirt from Disneyland and her hair in a bun. Her forehead shone from perspiration and the whole effect reminded me of all the kid ballerinas that start appearing in family restaurants in June. After year-end recitals parents make their daughters put sweatshirts over their costumes, and then the whole family goes to Denny's to have cheeseburgers and ice cream. I didn't feel like eating at the house one night a couple weeks ago, so I told Shana and Simon I had a school project. I went to Denny's to have grilled cheese and there was a whole swarm of tiny ballerinas there in sweatshirts. I've seen the same thing lots of times, always at the beginning of summer.

And all the little girls always have the same look on their faces. I can only describe it as them wanting to be looked at badly, but pretending like they aren't aware that anyone's looking.

But anyway, Ainsley looked very aware of being looked at and very confused that I was standing in her room. She wrinkled her forehead and said, "I don't get it."

I tugged on the bottom of Darren's shirt, pulling it away from my body. "I was studying at Ashley's and you told me in class that you lived next door." It was only then that I noticed the rain had started outside again because in Ainsley's room, the water actually sounded like it was dripping inside of the house.

"Oh," she said. "So, you're just coming by?"

"Well, yeah." I kind of shrugged. "Just coming by."

"Your shirt's wet though."

"I was outside before and I had to borrow Darren's. I lost my shoes and it's a long story."

"Do you want to wear something of mine?"

I did. Badly for some reason. I said, "Sure."

"I don't have anything very good." Ainsley shrugged without looking me in the eye.

In a pile on the floor I spotted the thermal shirt she wore

the other day in art, so I pointed to it and asked, "Can I wear that?"

"You can have it," she said.

"I can have it?"

"Sure."

When she let me have that shirt I guess I instantly felt that some kind of intimacy had been achieved between us. I didn't think twice about pulling off Darren's shirt while standing there. And she looked at my breasts, but she looked at them like they were knees.

"So can I hang out in here?" I asked.

"Aren't you going to study with Ashley?"

"The thing is, I don't feel like it."

"I wouldn't either," she said.

She was sitting in the midst of the pile on the floor, sorting through all the stuff. There were some clothes, some plastic figurines, a hula skirt, a jewelry box, and a few stuffed animals. I sat down next to her and I began to sort and fold, too.

For a while neither of us looked at each other, and we just kept on moving things in the pile around. I felt completely at ease.

I asked, "Ainsley?"

"Hmm?"

"Will you tell me what you put in your speech?"

I looked at her and she kind of grinned in spite of herself, like she didn't want to reveal how funny the coming idea was but couldn't really help it. "Not a word of truth." She opened the jewelry box, which resembled a miniature armoire, and began sorting through the mess inside.

"What does that mean?" I asked.

"You really want to know?"

I nodded.

"I called my speech 'The Observer.' It's all about how lucky I am because I'm an outsider. I don't use that word though. I talk about how I get to take the time to watch everyone around me, and the good things I've seen of them. It's all lies." Her voice was like the hum of a machine. It's the kind of a voice that could put you to sleep because it's so solid and scratchy. In fact, it kind of has a similar quality to the record (the record itself, not the singer) I heard in the hospital. "Ashley's really mad about it though."

I said, "You know what? Good."

Ainsley looked at me. "That's what I've been thinking lately. Good. Last week I was doing her English flashcards for her and going through *Catcher in the Rye*. I was looking for names and places. I ended up reading a lot of whole pages though. I thought the guy who was telling the story seemed really interesting. I told Ashley he sounded like someone I'd want to know. Ashley said, 'That's just because he's in a book. Everybody loves an underdog when he's in writing. But if you really had to deal with a Holden Caulfield, you'd think he was very annoying and a real mess. Harry Mendel's a lot like Holden. Everybody hates him.'" (Harry's a kid who's kind of on the edge of the popular crowd and he's always screaming about how real he is compared to everyone else, and I had to admit that Ashley had a point.)

Ainsley continued, "She gave me an idea though. I thought if everybody loves an underdog when he's in writing,

I should write an underdog speech. Do you want to hear my opening paragraph?"

"Yeah."

She concentrated wholeheartedly on the carpet. "Some of you out there may wonder why I was chosen to give this speech. I wasn't the homecoming queen. I wasn't your class president. When you flip to the index at the back of the year-book, I'm only listed on one page." She shrugged to let me know she was finished.

"And where does it go from there?"

"I lie about a time when I saw a teacher staying until five o'clock at night to help his student study. I say I was so lucky to see that because I was walking through the school alone and looked in a window."

"And that never happened?" I asked.

"No."

"Every male teacher's going to be wracking his brain, trying to remember if he could have been the one in the window."

"I think that's why I won though. The only thing I'm good at is making people feel special. I also told a story about a student that came early to school to bury her parakeet on the football field. I made up that story to show how much we think of Woodbridge as our home."

I said, "Jesus Christ!"

"I know. When Mr. Frankel called me into his office he said he loved it all though. He said I got down the spirit of our high school. So that's about it. At the end I say that I've been in the shadows, waiting for my moment. The last sentence is, "And by giving this speech, it's finally come.""

"That's a big finish."

"It's the only true part."

"The speech means that much to you?"

"You don't think it's stupid?"

"No."

I was playing with a string of small pearls that Ainsley had detangled from a gold chain, and I held them up to my neck. I remembered what Elizabeth said about small things being precious, and they really were.

Ainsley asked, "You want those?"

"I can have them? Really?"

"Have them. I haven't touched them since my grandma gave them to me. She said that every lady should have a good set of pearls, and she gave me the necklace and Ashley a pair of black pearl earrings."

I studied Ainsley to see if there was any sign of her being annoyed at Ashley's inclusion at what seemed to be every single thing in her life, but she just stuffed the bulk of her plastic figurines into a garbage bag. Her face stayed totally blank, empty of emotion. And forget about her voice. It just rasped on, telling me to take the pearls again.

They were on a short string and I had trouble doing the clasp by myself, so I lifted up my hair and Ainsley put the necklace on for me. Since I was facing away from her, I decided to just finally ask, "Do you even like Ashley?"

"I'm not always sure. But yes. Deep down."

"I want to tell you something," I said.

I felt her hands release the clasp, and the necklace stayed. "Okay."

"The thing is, I used to wonder why Ashley liked you. And now I feel like I'm wondering why you like her."

"Jeez."

It was then that we both gave up on the sorting of the pile and leaned back against her bed with our knees bent. Her dog, whose name I never asked about, stayed on the chair the whole time and put his head between his paws.

Ainsley slumped and said, "We've been friends forever. She's like family."

"That's what your mom said."

"Yeah, that's the saying around here."

"But what does she bring to your life?" I asked. "I'm not trying to be an asshole, I'm just curious."

"I'll tell you something. You can't think I'm dumb though."

"I swear I won't."

"I like that she's great at everything and I'm not. When she first started calling me a lot in third grade, I felt really needed. All the boys in class liked her. The girls, too. My parents really loved her and said she was socially great for me. When the house next door to hers got put up for sale in fifth grade, they put an offer down right away so we could be neighbors." I thought about that graduation banner out front, hanging there like an umbilical cord sending love and nourishment to Ashley.

"Nothing's changed, though. People still like her." Ainsley paused. "I've put some thought into it, and I don't think you can have two friends who are both great at everything."

"Why not?"

"You just can't. It works out the best when they're opposites. Like I think I've helped Ashley through a lot of things, and I couldn't do that if I was going through the same things. I can look at things different than she can. Like, imagine if you were her best friend. You wouldn't be able to bring out the best in her. You two are so much alike."

I said, "No we're not."

"I think so."

I thought about that for a second, but decided I was definitely right. "If you're only trying to bring out the best in her, then why are you the one giving the speech at graduation?"

She smiled with only one side of her mouth like she was embarrassed at herself. She cupped her hands on top of her knees in a way that made her seem like she was holding two counterbalanced weights in her palms. "It's true. I want to be important and talked about for a few minutes. Ashley's leaving for Harvard in three months. I'm not doing anything. Maybe going to Irvine Valley College." She exhaled and looked to the ceiling. "I'm embarrassed that you're listening to all this."

There was much more that was said, but too much to remember and too much to write down here. We talked until six in the evening, until she was called down to the dinner table. I thought about paging Daniel and seeing if he wanted to go somewhere, but I guess the rain and all the changing had rubbed the number off of my arm. And I even thought about writing it down last night, too.

Anyway, Ainsley gave me a pair of thongs and an umbrella from her closet and I slipped out of her house and started to walk home. But as I was heading along the back side of the South Lake, where the tennis courts are, I thought, "Ainsley gave me thongs. And an umbrella. And a string of pearls. And the shirt off her own back. And a whale figurine." (I said I thought it was funny looking, and she pushed it toward me after rubbing its tail between her thumb and forefinger.) And then a realization came up in my gut and I said to myself, "Jesus Christ. Is Ainsley going to kill herself, or is she just a really generous person?"

Ten

I found myself in temple this morning, and I'm not especially proud of it. I had a wimpy morning, a spineless morning. And to be completely honest, a wimpy night last night, too. When I came home from Ainsley's it was around six-thirty and Shana and Simon were out, so I made myself chicken and had a pretty good time being downstairs and alone. When I heard the garage door go up at eleven, I ran upstairs and turned out my lights and pretended to go to bed. I was still wearing the thermal and the pearls. Really, I just lay there and thought about all the things I could be doing with the lights on, but oh well. Car headlights kept going up my walls and across my ceiling to the sound of tires on wet pavement, and I guess I eventually fell asleep watching them and listening.

Then, this morning, I heard the garage door go up and down again at 7:40, so I figured the coast was clear. I went downstairs to get a glass of orange juice, and as I passed the front door it opened and Shana came in wearing a baggy lace dress.

Her initial reaction was almost to step back outside and shut the door, like she had to protect herself from a grizzly bear that had broken a downstairs window and climbed into the house. I even put up my hands a little like I was calling a truce. I mean, Jesus, she's got me involved in the whole scenario. Sometimes it's like I can't help but play along.

And I think that's why I said, "Wait!"

Shana stepped inside, remembering that that was her intention in the first place. "Wait?" she asked.

"I...wanted to go to temple with you guys." As soon as it was out of my mouth, I regretted it immensely because of the feeling it brought on, like I was suddenly being dragged toward temple behind a horse that I'd tied myself to. Again, there was the nausea of imagining myself someplace I didn't want to be, and the double nausea of actually being in a place I didn't want to be at the very same time. It's weird how one second the house can seem harmless and in certain lights even border on pleasant, and then the next seem like it just breeds nausea. Like there's just natural sickness in the air. Like when a whole family has the flu and they all stay home together.

But then, at the same time, I felt a wave of relief when Shana's eyes stopped being wide from alarm and started being wide from her interest at having me come to temple. And then, after that, her constant sense of nervousness seemed to completely change into something that (I thought) looked more like subdued excitement.

She checked her watch, which is so small that you'd hardly believe it could be checked, and said, "It's 7:41. You're not dressed yet. How?"

I thought, "Oh well, I think I did a good job here," but out loud I said, "Sorry, I meant to get up earlier. I really did."

Shana just stared at me for a few seconds in the same way she'd looked at me that morning Donald called when I tried to hide what we were talking about from her. It was like she was just waiting for me to unzip my skin. Like a full-grown devious woman would step out and laugh at her for thinking she was raising a kid.

Finally, she said, "That's fine. We'll wait."

And then thirty minutes later she was seriously holding her breath as the three of us walked through the lobby area outside the sanctuary. We could hear the rabbi's voice droning from inside. An usher outside the door offered Simon one of the blue beanies that some men in the temple wear and handed us Xeroxed sheets of special songs. He flared his nostrils and I saw lots of hairs inside and they reminded me of the hairs you can see on bugs' legs when they're magnified. That nostril flare was to show that he disapproved, so once he took care of that he held his pointer finger up and put his ear to the giant wooden door. When he heard a pause that he thought was appropriate, he pushed the door open with his right arm and we passed in front of him.

Shana looked completely terrified to be entering in the middle of services (or I guess I should say, more terrified than usual). Like she was going into the Temple of Doom and not Temple Ba Hoff. She let Simon lead the way in as she looked around bewildered, but really, very few people were looking at us. It wasn't that big a deal because the rabbi had just told the audience to flip to a certain page in the prayer book, so there were pages rustling and legs uncrossing and I didn't feel like I had walked into a silent, awkward room.

We took a seat toward the back, and Shana swiftly picked up a prayer book from the pocket in the back of the pew in front of us. I saw her trying to peek off the lady's book next to her to see what page she was supposed to be on. I wanted to yell, "Jesus Christ, just ask her and she'll tell you!" Simon put a book on my lap and whispered, "Better pick it up before your legs start to smoke." Thanks.

Despite the air conditioners whirring on all sides, the room was stuffy with the same wash of perfumes that you run into when you go through the fragrance department at Nordstrom's. There are lots of women at the temple who make their hair blonder, and a pretty big handful who've gotten nose jobs. Sometimes you'll catch one in profile like I did today, and practically shudder when you see the angle the thing slopes at. When you look at a nose like that, all you can think of is the doctor sawing on the bone with a file and then taking whatever tool he uses and breaking it (the nose, not the tool).

Anyway, so the room was pretty airless and I had trouble getting comfortable. I think you can always smell summer inside of places, no matter how well they're ventilated and cooled.

I opened my prayer book, too, and pretended like I was following along. The prayers all have phonetic translations next to the Hebrew, so I moved my lips silently and went through the motions of praying. With the luxury of something like a half an hour more on my side, my mind went to Ainsley. My first thought was that if she's planning on doing anything, she's not going to do it before the graduation ceremony. Giving the speech means too much to her. My second thought was that I don't think I'd try to stop her.

Back in February my poli sci class took a trip to see an African American arts and politics exhibit at a gallery in Laguna Beach for Black History Month. Around three, Mrs. Sylviani got completely exhausted from trying to keep everyone quiet and trying to maintain her authority. (Jared Delaney kept cracking really lame "yo momma" jokes to her about the artwork, and for whatever reason, she couldn't stop herself from laughing. He'd point to a wall-length painting of a heavyset black woman and say, "Mrs. Sylviani, yo momma's so fat this painting's of one of her toes.") So I think mostly to save face, she announced that we all had an hour of free time to explore the shops and the area since the bus wasn't coming back until four.

Turning away from the beach and heading up Broadway, I went into an ice-cream shop and got a scoop of mint chocolate chip in a cup. At the time I was the only one in there (except for the totally lost guy behind the counter who immediately tried to hand me back my dime when I gave him three dollars and ten cents for a two-sixty ice cream). I seated myself on the stool at the far counter so I could look out the window, but I started to regret it when I could just feel the guy staring a hole through my skirt. When I sit it gets shorter, so I couldn't even tuck it under me. The skin on the back of my thighs stuck to the stool.

The bells over the door jingled and a woman came in holding a dog that looked like a greyhound, only reduced to a quarter of the size, and it was like she was talking from the second she entered. She said, "Breezy today, huh?" to the guy behind the counter, and then started rattling through her feelings on each flavor of ice cream. She wondered who ate the bubble gum flavor because it seemed impossible to do. She asked, "Is it the kids?" I was able to look at her out of the corner of my eye, and I saw that she was barefoot and wearing long pants made out of some kind of gauzy material. She looked exactly like the kind of woman who lives in a one-story house near the beach and who never puts on shoes unless it's raining (and then she puts on sandals). Her hair was a complete mess, half wavy and half straight, and I could see her freckles starting to peel above the neckline at the back of her shirt.

She eventually settled on something brown (she had pointed to it through the glass). I don't know if it was chocolate or peanut butter or what. I was hoping she wouldn't take the stool next to mine, and of course she took the stool next to mine. She put her dog on her lap. Then she just started talking like she couldn't tell the difference between me and the guy, and was only continuing her conversation.

She said, "It's a great day, isn't it? Kind of has a zip to it. You'd think eating ice cream would make you colder when you go back outside, but it doesn't. I think what happens is that it makes the temperature of your body more similar to the temperature outside, and then you become much less sensitive to the chill." As she talked she held the plastic spoon between her thumb and pointer finger and kept rocking the thing like she was about to throw a dart.

I thought about getting up and leaving, but I really just wanted to sit there and watch the people walk by. And I wanted to do it in silence. Still, I nodded.

She asked me, "Are you in high school?"

I nodded again.

"I thought so. You looked about that age. When I was in high school I used to go to the beach almost every day after school. Even if it was raining, we'd all get in Tony's car, park in the sand, and watch the water." She stared off longingly out the window. "Those were the best days. The most fun."

Stupidly, I said, "Oh, really."

Then she turned to me very intensely, and aside from being annoyed that she wasn't done talking yet, I found what she said very interesting and thought about it for weeks. She told me, "You know when you've had the best days of your life. Not when you're done with them and going through later days, realizing they're not quite as good, but right when you're in the midst of them. I call it your peak of happiness. Everyone has it."

It occurred to me later that week that the beach woman might be right, that everyone has it, but the really difficult thing is that everyone has it at a different time. My mom used to have all those magazines like *Redbook* and *Cosmopolitan* lying around the house, and sometimes I would pick them up and flip through them. I liked the articles on aging best. There were always tons of stories from women who said their thirties were even better than their twenties, and that they couldn't wait for their forties because they heard those were going to be the best years of their lives. One woman wrote a first-person article about how, since thirty, her sex drive had been increasing and increasing until at the point of being published, she felt just like a sixteen-year-old boy. That idea really stuck with me. I was definitely really surprised at the having-to-wait-twenty-five-years thing to feel the best I could about it. I wasn't even sure how sex worked, I think, but I imagined that when you hit thirty something either got bigger or smaller on or inside of your body. I hoped it didn't stick out when you wore tight pants.

But now I wonder if those magazines don't just keep on pushing the best age back and back, so that people will still keep thinking there's more to come. Because when you're thirty you read beauty magazines and try to get excited about being forty, and then I guess when you're forty you switch over to travel magazines or whatever, and get excited about taking vacations to islands when you're fifty and can finally wear those huge floppy hats.

On that day in February it definitely crossed my mind (after I finished my ice cream and told the woman that "No, I don't have a boyfriend" and she said that I was lovely and should) that I had reached my peak of happiness a long time ago. It had happened somewhere in between fifth and sixth grades, when every day I went to bed kicking my feet under the covers because I felt excited about nothing in particular and had to get it out. I think that's when my body realized that things were at their peak, and it almost couldn't handle the happiness. So it would suddenly shake or twitch because

I was reaching the point of being overloaded. And one day I must have reached it, and I don't want to make a big deal out it, but maybe it was that afternoon of my birthday party before everything happened. Because I remember that quick jump as my mom curled my hair and it sticks out in my mind, and then, you know, everything else happened. But during the year before that I remember walking into my house after school at three and just having a general sense of well-being. And also being curious about certain things, like if anything good had come in the mail or what we were having for dinner.

There's no way that I could even say to Ainsley, "The best is yet to come." Because even if I wanted to, that promise could never be true. And I can't remember the first time I heard that everyone in the world is supposed to have someone that looks just like them, but what if everyone in the world has someone that thinks just like them? There are bodies timed to give out at the very same second. Thousands. I don't see why there can't be minds also, a group of minds ready for death at a moment when their bodies are fine.

The rabbi said "death" just as I was thinking it, and my attention returned to him and the squeal his microphone made every time he took a deep breath. He was saying, "Death, for children of Israel, is not an opportunity." (His finger went up in the air, pointing toward the flame-looking light fixture.) "Nor is it a threat. We do not hope that God will surround us with the greatest riches and shower us with our greatest fantasies if only we are good people in this life. We do not expect that if we have sinned, we will be thrown into a deep, scorching blackness, where the Devil has posses-

sion of our souls and we must spend eternity in torment."
The rabbi sighed (mike squeal) and when he swallowed, I
could actually hear it. He's a man that's forty going on eighty.
Anyway, he continued, "Because the heaven we should look
to is the heaven on this earth. This earth, where we have the
power to do mitzvahs and watch ourselves as we create the
greatest of chain reactions. Our good deeds are like a wave.
The water gathers itself as we join together, growing stronger
and stronger in force, until our efforts become so large and
wondrous that the rest of the world will see them clearly and
smile. Ah, but once our mitzvah has been completed and the
wave breaks on the shore and turns to foam, the ocean recalls
the water to itself again so that it may begin the cycle anew,
and that good shall never cease to regenerate itself."

All in all, I was pretty impressed with the speech. Not so
much the part about banding together and doing good deeds
because—please. But I thought the Jews were very smart for
figuring out that this world is all we have to go on. It's not like
when I go I'll float up above the clouds and open a door to
an exact replica of my childhood house, where inside my
mom and dad are in their bedroom doing rounds of heavenly
coke (the kind that's blessed by angels, right). Or even that I'll
just enter a mist where everything is so hazy and beautiful
that I can't differentiate between people, objects, and the en-
vironment, because I've heard that one, too. If anybody tried
to sell me on those stories now, I would ask them why, if I can
see the inner workings down here and they've exhausted me
in seventeen years, why would I ever want to have an eternity
to become a million times more clear about the trappings?
One day I'd see the pattern to it all through the mist (the mist

194

would have a pattern, too), and then I'd have to reenact that pattern forever, and you can't even get rid of yourself in heaven.

The rabbi said, "We should not wait until a tragedy befalls us or our loved ones to turn to God. Because God... God is not a last-minute resort. He is not someone we can apologize to when he becomes the last one around to hear our voice. He is not a secret resource when we discover we've exhausted all others. He is a way of life, and that means he must not only be internalized and lived with, but lived in as well." The rabbi placed both hands on the outside of the podium and looked like he was holding on for dear life. Like God was the podium itself and he was demonstrating how we should cling to him. Behind him the man who sings rose from his chair, and went to his own microphone. A guitar was already hanging around his neck and after he took one chord strum, he launched into "Yesterday" by the Beatles. He sang it with such vibrato and seriousness that it failed to sound like anything that I had ever heard on the radio.

At the end of the service, everybody stood up and stretched and brushed out the wrinkles from their suits and dresses. I had thrown on a flared black skirt and a blue button-down blouse with puffy sleeves. I looked like I was going to a party.

We all filed out the giant doors and into the big room next door that's three-quarters reception space and one-quarter stage. Lots of long wooden tables had been put together to make a giant plank, and a huge white tablecloth completed the seamlessness of the thing. There were paper platters with brownies, cookies, strawberries, croissants, miniature bagels, and those long braided breads, but the silver tray with the small plastic glasses of red wine was the first to empty last time I came to temple. I remember watching as tons of little kids came up to the table and walked away with what are essentially disposable shot glasses. And when I asked Simon why they served such small portions of grape juice he said, "That's wine, and it's so the babies can drive home safely."

After loading up their plates, all the kids went and sat with their legs crossed on the edge of the stage, and the adults mingled in small circles around the fake plants and tables that no one was using.

Shana said, "That fruit looks delicious" and Simon said, "It's the gloss from the pesticides," and they moved off toward the table together, either forgetting they had brought me or assuming I was following along. Hoping to prevent them from finding me either way, I moved off toward the back corner next to the stage-right stairs. There was nothing keeping me from going backstage — no velvet rope, no handwritten sign asking nicely — so I went up the stairs and behind the heavy blue curtain. Once my eyes adjusted to the dark I began to see the plywood cutouts of things like warriors and trees, and when I leaned in very close I could make out the painted details, which were actually done nicely.

Toward the back of the stage there was a beat-up couch, and happy to see it, I went and lay down. The curtains muffled the sounds of the congregation asking each other what the kids were doing during summer vacation and what vacations were being planned, so the voices came to me like they were coming out of those electronic boxes in the stomachs of stuffed animals. They reminded me of a teddy bear I had when I was six. When I squeezed his paw he would spout sayings about friendship and love, and while I could pick up words here and there, I could never grasp his full sentences.

A few minutes later I heard feet coming up the steps on the opposite side, and I lay as still as possible and tried to meld with the furniture. A shadowy figure appeared near the grove of stiff trees clustered on stage left, and I watched as it slowly made its way closer and closer to me. I held my breath and tensed up every muscle that I could locate, rolling my toes in and pushing my fingers into the fabric to steady myself.

I saw the silhouette of a turtle-man approaching, his head poking out from the larger curve of his shoulders and back. Still hunched, the figure came within three feet and then two feet and then he was bending over me and studying my legs from about a foot away. Now that he was up close I could roughly make out the features of John Steiner, and his acne was actually looking pretty soothed by the dark. He gingerly stuck out a finger and poked me in the knee. Then, not sure of what he had just felt, he took the tips of his fingers and ran them across my right thigh.

I said, "John" and he jumped, flipping his hands around in the way that I've seen hysterical Southern women do in movies when they've got the vapors. I whispered, "It's Stella, from drama."

He smiled an idiot smile. "Stella! I thought you were a mannequin! I didn't know you were Jewish."

"My family usually goes to another temple," I lied. "What are you doing back here?"

He gestured toward the trees. "I'm doing a scene with Tina Lubbitz from *Desire Under the Elms* for the final performance on Tuesday. I remembered that the temple had some trees from a performance way, way, way, back. Do you know what an elm looks like? Do those look like elms?"

I looked over at the fluffy shape of the backstage trees, which couldn't be described as belonging to any particular tree family except the kind that five-year-olds learn how to draw first. "I'm sure if you use those, no one will know the difference."

"Because I want the performance to be authentic," John said. At the last syllable of "authentic" his tongue sent a drop of spit flying over onto my leg. I wanted to peel the skin off of that calf and leave it lying on the floor. John whined, "I want it to look professional. I want it to be goooood."

I rose and told him, "I hear my mom calling me."

"What?"

"Yeah, I hear her."

I turned and stumbled a little through the props and a treasure chest on the ground and John didn't seem to get that I was leaving. Maybe he thought I was looking for more things to help him create a proper milieu for his performance. He asked, "So where have you been lately? Mr. Nichols is angry and wants to know." And when I was already back at the stairs he called, "I can tell him I saw you here today." I thought about yelling, "You're talking to yourself, John," but instead I picked up a bouquet of silk flowers at the top step and chucked it in his general direction. And then I was back out in the reception area before I could find out if it connected with his head.

Simon and Shana were standing near the far trash can, and Simon was talking with a couple while Shana stared in the general direction of his midsection. On my way to them I passed the long table and saw two little girls giggling as they took wine cups in both fists and quickly downed them with their backs to the room.

When I came up to the group, I heard Simon saying, "Ridged cookies and crackers are at the height of their popularity. In the past couple of years, the American public has realized the importance of texture and left us no choice. We have to listen."

The thick man he was talking to cocked his head and stroked the rim of his eyeglasses. The buttons on his white shirt looked like they were about to burst from the enormous pressure of his chest. "Do you think that points toward a certain boredom in the country? After all, in my industry, we're experiencing the same trend in box design."

Noticing me, the other couple turned and gave empty smiles, expectantly waiting for the introduction.

Shana almost looked pleased when she offered, "This is Stella." And my mind began to race. What will she say— their daughter? Their charge? Their tenant? During the past six years, I couldn't remember ever having the need for Simon and Shana to introduce me. If neighboring housewives stopped by to borrow detergent, they would already somehow know my story. They would nod gently to me and say, "Hello, Stella. How's school?" And if a couple came over on Saturday night to pick up Shana and Simon for a restaurant date, the husband would clap me on the shoulder while the wife gazed at me intently. He'd ask, "Big plans tonight, Stella?" even though I would never have any idea what his name was.

But instead of elaborating on the nature of our relationship, Shana finished off with, "She came with us today."

The woman said, "Oh! Shana was telling me the other day how you're headed to Princeton in the fall. Isn't that right?"

"Fantastic, great, Princeton," murmured the man.

"That's right."

I shook hands and told the couple (Mitch and Barbara Diamond) that it was very nice to meet them, but then I turned to Shana and said, "Sorry, but I've really got to be going because I'm supposed to visit my grandpa. Don't worry about me. I'll take the bus."

"Right now?" she asked.

I said, "I think he thought I was coming earlier. I just spoke to him on the phone."

Simon asked, "Will we see you at home by dinner? Or are you running off to Vegas?" Simon's delivery was so flat, so horrible, that Barbara and Mitch actually leaned in a little toward me like they were seriously interested in my response.

I ignored him. "Okay, well, see you later," I said. But right before I left I felt Shana raising her arm next to my body, and then I suddenly felt a pinch on the upper part of my arm. It was hard and cruel and more than deliberate. I jumped, and then began to back away. Shana didn't turn her head. I couldn't see what was happening on her face.

I stared at her wash of hair, which didn't have the energy to be curly and didn't have the conviction to be straight. I thought about running up and pulling some of it out. I was still moving away and she wasn't turning. I mouthed, "Fuck you" and left the temple and was met outside by glaring sunlight.

At the end of the street I waited under the bus sign and twenty minutes later the 57 came. I found a seat by myself and put my ear against the window on the ride over and listened to the loud hum the glass made. And it was so loud that I could count the vibrations per minute, and all that distracted me for a while. Then I switched to the 71 and did the same.

Like an old pro, I marched inside the hospital and went up to the third floor in the patients' tower. I walked straight past the nurses' station and into Donald's room. There I found a completely strange, haggard man lying in the bed. After studying his face for a few seconds, just to make sure he wasn't an incredibly sick, deteriorated version of Donald (who knows what can happen in a few days?), I returned to the nurses and asked, "What happened to Donald Moonan?"

A youngish nurse with a pencil through her hair looked up and answered, "He went home."

I said, "But he's sick. He has pneumonia."

She corrected me, "Walking pneumonia. And this morning"—she made a face like she clearly recalled attending to Hitler earlier—"he said some unpleasant things to some of the girls here and then he walked."

Eleven

In my sleep I felt butterflies in my stomach, except the strange thing was I could actually hear them bouncing against my insides. They were making such an unbelievable racket. Like they had lead wings and were trying to break through the lining. Half awake, I slid my hand down my front and pressed, trying to get them to calm the hell down, and I snapped out of my confusion when I ended up pressing too hard and causing some pain. Crows again. That's what I was hearing—them picking on the roof.

I got up with the uncanny feeling I get every other year, entering into the very last week of school. You wake up on a Monday, and it hits you that it's your last Monday. Next Monday, you'll be doing something entirely different, and you won't be wearing shoes. You'll wake up at a different time.

Your day will have a completely different quality to it. Three o'clock will come way sooner than it normally does, and eight o'clock will seem more open and lazy.

I've never experienced the feeling as gigantically as I did this morning. And it was just like I had licked a few nine-volt batteries (I actually did this once) and was jolted with a huge surge of sad happiness through every nerve ending. And the sad happiness said, "You know precisely when you're going to finish."

I looked around at my bedroom. The printer was loaded with a thick stack of sharp paper. The blinds were tilted up a little. The floral comforter was folded back perfectly at the edge of the bed, since I had been too hot for anything other than a sheet last night.

Every summer my parents used to take me on a vacation, and we'd always stay in a high-rise hotel. My dad believed that if you were going to take a trip, why would you stay in a rented condo or cabin when after two days you'd feel like you hadn't gone anywhere at all? The new house would just start to seem like the old house, and then what would be the point of getting away? So we liked our accommodations sleek and impersonal and unnaturally clean, so that we always understood we were staying someplace that wasn't our own. Anyway, we would vote on our destinations based on the pictures of the rooms in the brochure (and sometimes based on the architecture of the building), and we'd favor hotels with balconies. On the last day of the vacation, ten minutes before check-out time, my parents and I would stand in a far corner and carefully study the room in its purest state (we'd make the beds and everything). I remember doing this for as long as I can remember, and the first explanation I remember being given was my dad saying, "It's a mysterious feeling to be able to look at a room, and to know this is the last time you'll be in it." Now I looked at my bedroom in the same way and had the same feeling. And even though I had something like over ninety hours to go, I still felt time very strongly.

I went out into the already sunlit hall and then into the bathroom, and straddled the toilet so that I faced the mirror. I stared at my face until it started to bunch in all the wrong places and I was on my way to the expression that tells you a person's about to cry. So I pulled my shirt up over my head and by the time I reappeared, I had wiped the look from my mouth, eyes, and whatever you call those lines that run from your nose to the bottom of your cheeks when they aren't actually from laughing.

At S.E.L.F. they have a marquee just like we do, except it's smaller and only has room for one sentence. Currently ours reads: first line, "Good luck on finals," second line, "Grad Night on Thurs at 8," third line, "Have a great summer," and fourth line, "Summer school starts July 7." But the sign at S.E.L.F. says, "Clean lockrs out b4 Tues." I got there around 7:30 and was worried that school had already let out for the summer since I didn't see any cars or kids in the front parking lot. But I cupped my hands to a window and peered inside a classroom, and I saw that "Last book report on book of your choice" was due on the twenty-third, today, so I sat down on the curb and waited. It was hot out already.

About ten minutes later, cars began to swerve into the parking lot, all filled with adults. When I could see in through their windshields, the teachers and administrators looked uniformly sleepy and bored. A woman sucking deeply on a cigarette pulled into a space, but missed it by a half so that she ended up occupying two. A man with an untucked shirt walked into the main office trying to tuck it with one hand, but soon became distracted when he saw me. It was like he had to stop tucking in order to have enough mental energy to put into studying me suspiciously.

When we were together last year, Daniel told me the greatest thing about S.E.L.F. is that its adults and kids are matched up perfectly. He explained that the two groups have a silent agreement that makes for barely any problems at school. If the students won't expect the teachers to get in early and make up complicated lesson plans, the teachers won't bitch at the students about "showing" the world and getting into an Ivy League college (in turn making the kids feel worse about themselves). And then everyone's happy, kind of. At least there's a basic understanding.

It's not necessarily that the kids at S.E.L.F. are delinquents in the exciting, dangerous way that they really should be, but they're mostly just more apathetic than normal and less likely to do homework. The few kids that started strolling into the school around 8:00 weren't scary or tough, but annoyed and stoned. The thing is, Irvine doesn't really have a wrong side of the tracks.

Daniel pulled into the parking lot about fifteen minutes late for school, and I got up and walked to his car. He was slumped way down in his seat, so far that his head was below the window line. I felt a disorienting sense of déjà vu until I realized that he was reminding me of James Taylor on the front of one of my dad's records. In the photograph James is reclining against a stone wall, wearing a dress shirt, and his hair comes down so far that it almost blocks out his eyes. You can see them just enough to understand that he's looking at the camera like he doesn't trust it one hundred percent and wants to know what it expects him to do. Daniel was looking up at me exactly like that. His hands were folding a small bag of whiteness into a tiny jeweler's envelope.

I opened Daniel's car door and said, "Your number washed off my arm."

He took my arm and I thought he was going to literally check, but instead he pulled me inside his car and onto his lap. After shutting the door and sealing us in, he took his hands and dug them both into the bottom of my hair and then ran them upward, and he pressed his forehead into my back. I loved the pressure of him between my shoulder blades.

Still up against my back, he asked, "Do you know what today is?" and I felt his lips moving through my shirt.

Happy in a way I could never sustain, I asked him back, "No, what is it?"

"It's supposed to be my last day of school."

He reached around me and turned on the ignition and I started to climb over into the passenger seat, but he held on to me by the waist. "No," he said. "Stay. I can drive like this."

"You'll get a ticket," I said, and slid myself down so that only my head was in his lap and the rest of my body was on the passenger seat. And he brushed my hair away from my forehead and I settled in and said, "There."

We drove to Woodflower pool. I asked for it because I didn't want Daniel to see my house, but I wanted him to be near it. Some of the community pools have better perks than others (Blue Lake has a high dive, and is kind of considered the crowning jewel of the whole group), but they're all guaranteed to be clean, temperature controlled, and painted turquoise on the bottom. Woodflower is smaller and its diving board is crappy, so it's less crowded than some of the others on weekdays.

Since we didn't have our community keys with us we used the lock on the gate to support our weight and we hopped the fence. My right ankle and leg stung a little when I landed, but it was more from the shock of the ground on my bones than from an actual sprain.

The pool was completely empty, which surprised me, since there's usually at least two mothers there with their diapered kids alternately soaking up and peeing in the baby pool. I looked at Daniel in his crisp white shirt with his rolled long sleeves, and then down at myself in my navy skirt and polo shirt. "We look like a preppy married couple," I said.

Daniel responded, "Maybe one day we'll be married."

"Maybe," I laughed, and my heart fell. I wanted to smash my face into his and cry for hours down into his throat. For being so lazy, for not having any viable dreams, for thinking in the back of my head that he could be enough and then not being willing to believe in that idea after all.

He pulled off my shirt and I unbuttoned his and that made me feel thirty. And then we held hands and ran and jumped into the pool and I felt five.

In the deep end Daniel came up from behind me and slid his hands onto my breasts, and when I looked down through the water I could hardly believe how white my skin looked.

My skin was transparent (I could see what were either veins or patterns of blood in my thighs) and my bra was transparent, and my underwear, which was navy, seemed completely out of place. My hands went to my pearls. And no, that's not some dirty euphemism. I'm talking about my pearls. When Daniel pressed himself into me from behind, the water made tiny lapping noises in between us. I got a shiver up my spine from that sound. It reminded me of the quiet click your lips make when they leave someone else's skin, but over and over and over again.

"You know what?" he asked. "I don't have a condom." I remember the first time we had sex I hadn't even noticed him pull one on. One second we were kissing and the next we were physically attached to each other and I marveled at when he could have found the time and why I didn't hear the package tearing. It was better for me that way. Because knowing there was a condom reminded me that we were things who secreted things and those things were often harmful and inconvenient. And also, those things didn't have anything to do with me alone, specifically. But now, with Thursday approaching, I felt relief as all those things were canceled out.

"That's okay," I told him.

He pulled my hair to the side so he could see my profile better from where he was floating. "What?"

My body was split into two temperatures. My hair, dry, was nearly burning up in the sun, especially at the small bald point at the top of my head where all the strands meet. Then my body, under the water, felt perfectly cool and invisible.

"I went on birth control," I lied.

"When'd you do that?"

"It kicked in a few days ago."

He said, "Unbelievable. Does that mean you're planning on being with me? For a while?" Even without looking at him I could tell he was kind of kidding, and kind of not.

I reached in back of me and slid my hands down into his shorts, just far enough until my fingers went past his pelvic bones. He was still, I heard him breathing, and my fingers continued to creep on in a diagonal until he reached around me and slipped my underwear down from my hips. The water instantly surrounded my skin, and I had the impression of still being clothed and thought, "This is the closest to wiping out sex that we could ever come."

I put my arms out toward the cement rim of the pool, and rested my cheek on its warmness. I heard a small splash and knew Daniel had gone under the water because his breathing disappeared from the air. Seconds later I felt his tongue going up my back, and I wondered if his eyes were open and what he saw.

I turned around as he surfaced, and I felt lust at the drops on his eyelashes and the chemical chlorine smell around both of us. I kissed him. I put myself around him. He exhaled and deeply, painfully groaned like I had kicked him in the stomach. I opened my eyes occasionally to make sure that one of the Woodbridge Association guys wasn't coming around to check our IDs, or the city gardeners weren't watching from behind the bushes lining the gate. I heard cars whizzing by and the ghostlike sounds of a few kids playing on the blacktop over at the elementary school, but no one came through the gate. The water made it kind of impossible to tell what we were responsible for from what millions of molecules were making us do, so we seemed to move together better than ever. And even though I turned around again and pressed up against the pool wall, it felt like we didn't even separate and he wasn't outside of me for a second.

Daniel put his head next to mine and whisper-talked, heavy breathing, "What are you doing this summer?"

"I don't know," I told him.

Slowly he said, "I talked my mom into renting a condo in Del Mar for the summer. With an ocean view. She has all that money from my dad taking off and she doesn't do anything with it, so finally she's going to start. I think it'll be cool for her. She's excited about, and I quote, meeting a kind gentle-man while having a margarita on a restaurant deck."

I was breathing rhythmically. I tried not to pay attention to the pattern, and instead listened diligently to Daniel.

"I've told her all about you. I asked her already about you coming to the condo, and she got excited about it. Really ex-cited, and just thought all in all, it was a cool idea. I know you're going away in the fall, but you have a whole summer now. Stella," (his talking became slower and slower, as he came closer and closer to losing it) "I know you hate it, but I have money from all the selling. I have a sizable bank ac-count. Man, I have so much money that I can fly to New Jer-sey every month if I wanted." He paused. "Sometimes I get the feeling you don't want to invest in things, because you're not sure what you'll get for your effort."

The last word came out with his last bit of energy, and knowing it, I turned myself around by circling my arms in the water and looked at him carefully, not wanting to look down. I wrapped myself around his body like I used to cling onto an inflatable giraffe I'd take to the pool when I was young, and we stayed like that.

The first to break the silence after a half hour, Daniel said, "You're going to think this is very funny, but I have to get back to school. They won't graduate me unless I take my cumulative test at ten."

"Did you study?" I asked.

Already turned around and swimming away from me, he said, "Nah, it's an essay test. Which means I can say anything, but I just have to be there."

I swam with my head above the water. "Daniel, what do you want to be when you grow up?"

"Nothing," he said. "Or, in other words, a dealer. I like people. I like the free time. Why, what do you want to be?"

I told him, "Dead."

"Right," Daniel said.

We pulled ourselves out of the pool. The sun reminded me it was out and hot the second my last toe left the water. I pulled my shirt and skirt on, making them wet in the process, and Daniel kneeled down and unzipped my backpack. Balancing one of my notebooks on his knee, he ripped out a sheet of paper and grabbed a fat black permanent marker from the front pocket. He held the piece of paper up to the back of a lounge chair for support, and the plastic bands underneath bulged outward from the pressure of his wrist.

"I'll put it down on paper for you this time, so it can't wash off," he said.

I sat on the chair and watched. Daniel wrote two lines, and then having finished, lifted up the paper. The address wasn't only on the sheet, but had also seeped through onto the plastic band. I thought about how certain women and families would be puzzling over that mysterious address for a few hours, at least until the association removed and replaced the chair the next morning. Tuesday's when they have men come around and clean the pools.

Daniel handed the paper to me and I read, "1103 Luneta" from the first line and "Del Mar, CA 92014" from the second. He put my pen back and zipped up my backpack and handed it to me. We walked through the gate (all we had to do was turn the knob now) and out toward his car.

"We're leaving tomorrow morning around ten, and I know you have graduation on Thursday, but you should drive down right away after that. Come Thursday night."

"I don't know," I said. Daniel wouldn't look at me. He was looking at the fence.

"I should really come Thursday night?" I asked.

He slipped his hand into mine and said, "Yes. Give in. Just give in."

"Okay," I told him. I felt like I was holding my own hand. Daniel squeezed it and tucked it under his shirt. Like if he just warmed up my hand, then the rest of me would be fine, too. I balled my fingers against his chest.

I had him drop me off at the 86 stop on Creek. But before I got out of the car I kissed him, sucking on his bottom lip, and stared and thanked him for the ride. He held me for at least a minute. He told me he'd see me on Thursday. As he drove away I collapsed on the bench and watched the car like it was him, actually him, moving down Alton faster than he should've been going. Then all I could do was study my watch and keep repeating silently, "Monday, 9:53. Monday, 9:53.

Monday, 9:53" until I felt sufficiently that it was Monday at 9:53 and that was all I knew.

Lupe put her hands over her eyes at the sight of me, shaking her head. Her elbows sank into a crooked stack of forms, carbon copies, phone numbers, prescriptions, whatever. That stuff is always on her desk. When she mails the papers out into the world, she says she sends a piece of proof that the people in the home still exist.

"Oh Stella, Stella, Stella."

I stood there with my arms to the side, waiting for the rest. After a few more head shakes she looked up with exasperated eyes and said, "He calls me yesterday and says, 'You must come get me. I'm done. If you don't, I'll walk.' And the doctor says that it's best for him to stay in the hospital, but your grandfather says no, he's leaving. So I go with Gumer and we get Chris to cover the office, and the doctor says that Donald won't do anything to himself, that we must give him attention and"—she gave a frustrated laugh—"love. When we get in the car I tell your grandfather, 'You're putting blood on my hands. I hope you know this.' He should be in the hospital. But he won't stay. He tells me that I have no idea what's best."

At that point she swung violently around in her swivel chair and bent over and her shirt crept up in the back, revealing a light strip of hair going down her spine. I crossed my arms and rested them on her counter, wondering if my face looked sympathetic. What facial moves combine to make a sympathetic look? Do eyes really smile or frown on their own? I mean, is there a physical change in your eyeballs alone (and I'm not including use of eyelids or the muscle under the eye here), like your pupils shrink or enlarge or twinkle? Or have people been imagining this forever?

Anyway, it wasn't that I didn't care that she was having a difficult time with Donald, but I felt like, "Lupe, wake up. Where have you been."

Straightening herself, Lupe presented a piece of construction paper to me. Peach. On it I saw a scribble of a man lying horizontally along the bottom edge, recognizable as a man because of his short hair, overly bushy crayoned eyebrows, and the bulge he had drawn for himself coming straight up from his pants. Next to him a woman (breasts, hips, a dress) with black shoulder-length hair stood with her palms toward me, and red watercolor paint pooled in her hands. I thought, "Oh Jesus Christ, Donald."

Passing the picture toward me like it was something I wanted to take home and put on the fridge, Lupe said, "He told me he thought I would find this funny. He said it's a token of affection. And he looked like he believed what he was saying, Stella!"

Up close I looked at the care that went into the drawing. "He was making an inside joke."

Lupe took my statement as an incredulous question, either not listening to the tone of my voice or hearing something different in it than I intended. And she told me, "I'm sorry that you have a man like this as your grandfather. I've bitten my tongue until now. I am very, very sorry, Stella." And she meant it. I felt like any minute she was going to start clucking at the shame of it. Me, my grandfather's granddaughter. She looked like I was the mother who had produced

the naughty asshole child. The child who was the first to introduce four-letter words to the other five-year-olds and the
child who kicked when she tried to take him into the bathroom before he finally went in his pants. It was like Lupe was
trying to comprehend how a girl like me could have brought a
nasty little boy like him into her world when, really, I had
nothing to do with it at all.

I didn't like that look, and I didn't want it. But you can't
just tell someone to knock off her look because she'll only
give you another. And if you happen to raise your voice too
much while asking her to stop looking, she'll hurry off to tell
a friend about your behavior the second you walk out of
earshot. And then that friend will come find you under some
kind of pretense, wanting to decipher what's up your ass
today. She'll open the door acting like she's checking for
something, and she'll give you the look, too (thinking you're
a much sadder case than either of them ever imagined).

I leaned over the counter with my arms outstretched so
Lupe would clearly understand what I was initiating, and I
embraced her. Close to her, I said, "Thank you for saying
that." (I paused.) "You've been like a mother to me." My
breath actually made the gold dangling chain (with hearts on
the end) hanging from her right ear sway. It was like a happy
concertgoer, swaying to the chorus of my thank you and
singing back to me, "No, thank you for making me happy."

When we separated, Lupe's eyes were aglow, attached by
some kind of membrane to the ears that had heard exactly
what they wanted to. I tried to think of something very sad to
make my eyes the same way. But as soon as the idea of something sad began to creep into my mind, I knew I didn't wel-

come it and like a boy who thinks about baseball so he doesn't come too early, I thought about the glass jar of paper clips that Lupe kept by the phone. I wondered who invented paper clips.

"Oh, honey," Lupe said.

I told her, "Don't worry about me."

"Give me that," she said, and reached her arm out for the picture I was holding. I gave it up. "I'll throw that away for you. We'll ignore it."

Nodding like I agreed and starting to feel like a horrible, patronizing asshole myself, I asked, "Is he in his room?"

"Yes. Don't let him say anything to you."

When I passed the kitchen I heard the staff busily preparing for lunch. The sink faucets were on at full blast, as someone cleaned whatever fruit was going in the home's small fruit dishes. (I was told that Donald once threw one directly above a ninety-two-year-old lady's head, missing the top of her scalp by maybe five inches. After the bowl crashed into the wall and fell down to the carpet, the woman sat there not knowing what to make of it. She never even saw the dish coming, and Gumer told me that the staff didn't, either. I mean, no one had even seen Donald raise his arm and by the time everyone figured out the direction the bowl came from, he was eating applesauce peacefully with a smile.)

When I came to 103 I knocked, knowing that Donald wasn't expecting me. I heard some kind of noise inside like a slow, low rumbling but there was officially no answer, so I turned the doorknob and went on in. After entering, I immediately looked toward the bathroom, which was dark and empty. Then I moved into the bedroom, which was light and empty. Next I got down on my knees and looked under the bed, but I only found a pair of leather slippers and a wooden box. So I got back up and went to the closet and slid the right door open and there was Donald, standing in the middle of two shelving units.

From the front, his white hair separated into four straw chunks, two sloping outward from above his ears and two diving toward the back of his head. He blinked at me, daring me, and his nostrils flared.

"You don't just act like a kid," I said. "You act like a re-tarded kid."

Not moving, Donald asked, "What are you doing here? I didn't call you."

"I felt like visiting. What are you doing in the closet?"

"I thought you were Gumer. She checks on me every half hour now. See these?" He gestured to the plastic shelves on either side of his body. "She took away my hangers and gave me these. What does she think I'm going to do with a hanger? Untwist it and abort my baby?"

I walked over to the dresser and picked myself up and sat on it. A minute or so passed and Donald came out of the closet. After gently sliding the door shut again, he sat on the bed. I was struck with the impression that this was essentially similar to how roommates probably position themselves when they talk late at night in college. One girl swigs from a Captain Morgan's bottle while perched on the dresser, and the other one sits and tells a story about how bad the party was and how incredibly drunk she got.

Donald exhaled and said, "I am very sick of seeing her face. I tell her that she looks heavier each time I see her so she'll stop coming. Soon it'll work, and she'll come less. All women are vain."

"You look older and more ugly each time I see you," I said.

Ignoring me, he put his hands behind his head and reclined on the bed. "Did you bring me anything today?"

"No."

"That's fine. I'm done begging things of you. I'll find a way." Suddenly he sat up and pretty much rolled off the bed and onto the floor. He got on his knees and bent over to look under the bed, and I couldn't help but think that I had done the same thing only a minute ago. Moms pick up the phones all the time to find that their daughters are waiting on the line, calling from another residence. The mom dials (the line already connected) and says, "Hello, hello?" Confused, the daughter says, "Hello? Mom?" The mom says, "I didn't even hear the call go through," and the daughter says back, "That's because I was calling you! At the same time! I was calling you!" The mom laughs and says, "Oh my god. This is so weird. I was calling you."

So what if I was in the mood to grasp at straws.

He sat up with the wooden box in his lap. "You may not have something for me," he said, "but I have something for you." That really blew me away. "Really?" I asked, and got off the dresser and came over and sat on the bed next to him. First he looked uncomfortable at my proximity. Then his look changed and he seemed like he had decided to accept it, and he tapped the lid of the box with his left hand. "Katherine gave this box to me."

He opened it. The box was filled with (I counted them

later in the park by Springbrook Elementary) sixty-three envelopes, and some lay flat and some were puffed out with objects inside. Donald said, "Take a look in the top one."

I picked up the designated envelope — it was one of the
flat ones. Inside I found a yellowing piece of paper and when
I unfolded it, all I saw was the word "Cross." I asked Donald,
"What does that mean?"

"That was the first one I ever got. I would find an envelope under my pillow each time I slept with another woman."

I pushed my hand into the box to get a feel for the bulk
of envelopes filling it. My jaw dropped a little. "You slept
with this many women? You are really just an unbelievable
asshole."

Donald took the next envelope in the pile out of the box
and lifted its flap, saying, "You could say this many women
slept with me. I never took my wedding ring off. They knew. I
didn't care a whip for a single one of them." He took a square
of wax paper out of this envelope, except it was really two
squares pressed together and in the middle of them was a
jagged chip of yellow paint, no bigger than a paper clip. Donald picked up the artifact with the nails on his right thumb and
forefinger, pinching it like two prongs of a tweezer.

"Yeah," I said, "you keep telling yourself that, Donald."

Snidely, he told me, "I have." I honestly felt like punching
him then. I don't know why. I never knew my grandmother,
and all this was in the past.

Staring at him, I asked, "How did she know when you
were with someone else?"

Donald handed me the wax square to look at up close.
He started in on the next envelope in the pile. "I made no at-

tempt to hide it. I took the women to restaurants. Even restaurants where I knew that certain people in our neighborhood might have been regulars. I took the women for ice cream, and we sat on park benches and ate our cones. I took them dancing, and strolling, and to the pictures. People talk."

"And you didn't care that they were talking? You were trying to hurt her on purpose."

He had moved on to the next envelope. Inside was a purple flower, also pressed between two pieces of wax paper. "I thought this one was somewhat pretty." His hand shook as he held each object.

"What does it mean?" I asked.

"I don't know."

"You never bothered to ask her?"

"She never bothered to ask me about what I had been doing. She obviously knew about it. She never said anything."

Next envelope: A business card for a San Francisco dentist. He handed both over to me. I was keeping a stack on my lap in the correct order that my grandmother had intended them to be received in.

"Why did you even stay married?" I asked. "If you were going to just have nonstop affairs, why didn't you get a divorce and have some legitimate girlfriends?"

Donald opened the next envelope, which contained a piece of paper with some kind of dried pink liquid on it. It looked like a smear of that really bright lemonade, or some kind of watery syrup. He held it up to the light coming in from the window and the smear was almost translucent. "I always wondered what this one was."

I repeated, "Why didn't you just have girlfriends?"

"I never liked any of them longer than five hours. What boring, shrill, insufferable women I've known in my life." He laughed, getting a kick out of jerking me around.

Inside the next envelope was a piece of paper with a rubbing of the letter "E" in what looked like pencil. I could see she had been patient with her shading. She wanted the image to come out perfectly clear.

"Would you open the envelopes in front of her?"

"I used to take them to the office and open them there. She would put the envelopes under my pillow while I was sleeping. I never felt her doing this. I would wake up and hear a crinkle. Or I would stretch my arms under the pillow and feel the paper. She always turned over and smiled at me, and I would pretend that I didn't know there was anything under the pillow. I only removed the envelopes once she went to wash her face."

"She smiled at you?"

"Yes."

"And you didn't feel like a horrible person when you got that smile?"

Donald jerked and went to get the next envelope, and he reminded me of one of those Small World dolls at Disneyland suddenly returning to action after its ride just broke down. There was a small chunk of red brick inside this envelope. To the box, Donald said, "I had been feeling horrible since the night we moved into that house. I couldn't tell you if her smile made me feel any different."

I looked at him sitting there and was surprised to notice that despite the normal signs of age (the thinning of his hair, the wrinkling of his skin, and the nonstop shaking of his hands), he didn't seem much like the other old men I've seen at his age. He seemed thicker and much more sturdy, almost muscular. Also, he doesn't keep his pants pulled halfway to his neck. They start at his hips and then his chest goes pretty broad, and even though I've never seen what he looked like when he was young, I'm guessing he was kind of a physically imposing man.

"And what was my mom doing during all this?"

Sarcastically, "That depends what year you're referring to."

"Shut up," I said. "You know what I mean."

"You'd be the one who would do better shutting up. I know what you mean, and that's an impossible question to answer. For the first few years of her life I'm sure she was unconscious of everything in the world except for her thumb. Then she was loved dearly by her mother, and spent the majority of her time with her mother, and I have no idea what they talked about. I would come home from the city at the end of the day, and they would be gone. They'd come back around seven without packages, without purses. Amelia came to me for her checkups for the first nine years of her life, so I knew her blood pressure and regular temperature, but aside from that…"

I had been listening to him, picturing my mother as a small girl with a stethoscope to her chest and a thermometer in her mouth, so I jumped a little when Donald put the latest envelope and its cold contents into my upturned hand. It was a shard of glass. The amber color reminded me of a beer bottle. Anyway, my jumpiness had caused the pile of envelopes to slide from my lap and land on the floor. Quickly bending over to pick them up, I said, "Don't worry, I have a good memory. I'll put them back in the right order.

Donald asked, "You think I don't know exactly what order they go in by now?"

I looked at him and shrugged, my silent way of saying, "Who knows what the hell you know?"

Donald took the envelopes from my hands as I was shuffling them and put them back in the box. Then he closed the lid and put the entire thing on my lap. "As I said before, this is a gift from me to you. I know that girls love to collect love letters from the past."

I reopened the lid, went straight to the eighth envelope, pulled out the shard of glass, and grabbed Donald's arm and quickly dragged the glass into the underside of his wrist. Blood sprang up from the cut immediately, even faster than it took Donald to realize that he had been cut.

The wound wasn't very deep. It was just meant to be an idea. I don't know. I guess I should have just hit him earlier.

Donald sucked a breath in and I heard a little of his voice whinnying in the back of his throat. He looked up at me. Straight in the eye for a change. And then he stuck out his other wrist and very seriously asked, "Was that you volunteering to kill me?"

I took the piece of glass and pressed it to his left wrist, but now the verve had gone out of me and I knew I wouldn't do anything. "I can't," I said. I looked back up at him from the bottom of my eyelids. "Why can't you do it for yourself?"

He took the shard from my hand and turned my arm upside down and ran the glass down it, his hand shaking the whole way. I could barely feel its edge. He was reminding me of a game I used to watch girls play during assemblies in elementary school. Girl One would tell Girl Two to shut her eyes, and then Girl One would run her pointer finger slowly up the underside of Girl Two's arm. When Girl Two felt that Girl One's finger had reached the crease between the bottom and top parts of her arm, Girl Two would say stop and open her eyes. The two of them would usually laugh because Girl One's finger ended up at least a few centimeters from the right spot.

But Donald wasn't pressing lightly because he was playing a game with me. He was really having trouble gripping the glass. He just sort of kept it propped between his fingers and scooted it along, but his fingers wouldn't lend him any additional force. And they wouldn't stop shaking, so he was zigzagging his way up my arm.

He sighed and raised his eyebrows, like he was saying, "See?"

"Oh," I said.

He dropped the piece of glass back into the envelope, but his wound was still bleeding a little. I took his wrist back and used my shirt to wipe it clean.

"I'll help you," I said.

"It's fine. It'll stop and I'll wash it in the sink."

We sat there, looking at the feathers on the wallpaper. He told me, "It'll happen one day. When they found out Katherine had cancer they only gave her a year. She lived for eight. Her doctor said it was because she had an abundance of faith and hope. I choose to believe that the same goes for people who are the opposite case. I will believe in nothing, and so I will cut my life expectancy accordingly."

I gave him a kiss on the shoulder and he let me without flinching.

Somewhere down the hall Gumer started to speak to

someone in a coaxing voice. I heard the words, "room," "okay," and "water," but the rest was just a jumble. As soon as he heard her, Donald got up from the bed. He bent over and dipped his fingers in a glass of water on the table next to the bed, and then suddenly his fingers were in my face and he was dabbing the water underneath my eyes. "I'm going to get back in the closet. Pretend like you're crying. Tell her I'm missing. She'll go away."

Gumer, louder, "Max, I've told you a million times today! You need to cut the carpet outside Mrs. Simonson's room. She's going to trip! It takes nothing to make her fall."

Meanwhile, Donald was backing up into the closet and shutting the door as quietly as possible, and I was just standing there completely thinking about what I had just done, what Donald had just done, and what was left of my family.

Gumer knocked on the door and called, "Donald! Pull your pants on. I'm coming in and I don't care what I see hanging out."

She opened the door, and seeing me, said, "Stella! I can't believe you're here." Shutting the door behind her, "You're a saint, baby girl." Getting closer she asked, "Are you crying?" She held her red nails to the bottom rim of her eyes, like she was mimicking eight gigantically bloody tears. "What's wrong? Where's Donald?"

"He's in the closet," I said.

Through the closet I heard, "You're no fun."

"I'll see you Thursday," I told him. "I'm going to go grab some lunch and study for my test tomorrow."

Twelve

When I arrived at school this morning, the first thing I saw was the gigantic Arabian palace facade erected in front of the library. It's at least thirty feet tall and painted purple, gold, and a very bright green. Since the makeshift stairs (leading to the slide leading into the quad) are specially reserved for Grad Night, they're taped off with yellow police tape. I just had to roll my eyes at the pointlessness. I'm sure at least half the student body has been down the slide since yesterday.

I walked through the cut-out doorway in the palace gate, going by a crappily painted guardsman with a golden spear. I guess the idea is that he's supposed to be beckoning you through, and you're supposed to feel special. Someone took the time to paint individual lashes on the tops and bottoms of his eyes, but the artist failed to keep him from going drastically cross-eyed. The parent volunteers have the best intentions, and really, they work all year on this, but all the kids show up to Grad Night completely wasted anyway. You could hang a flannel picnic blanket from the front tree with fishing line, tell the attendees it's a magic carpet, voilà, there's your Arabian Nights theme.

Next I entered the quad, which had been transformed into "a magical desert." I got this from the banner across the backside of the office that says, "The sultry air and garnet skies whisper in your ear, calling you to the magical desert." Plywood sand dunes run across the entire cafeteria wall and a gigantic moon was pneumatically stapled to the overhead beams. The man in the moon has semi-slanted eyes and a swarthy smile, and I know he's intended to look Middle Eastern. I imagine someone's dad painting him, standing back, calling over another parent to judge his work, and then getting a pat on the back for his unwavering dedication to the spirit of the event.

In front of the planters on the left side of the quad there's three harem women, also made of plywood, and they're supported by two-by-four planks nailed to their backs. One of the women sits on the ground with her feet tucked under her genie pants, and her veil is held in place by a crown of painted (I think) diamonds. But really, she just looks like she's wearing some kind of blotchy white tiara. So naturally, today Brendan Buckminster positioned himself right above her head and pretended to jerk off into her hair to the unending amusement of Ronnie Barlow, Seth Baumgarten, and Travis Ames.

Mrs. Green came over the loudspeaker announcing, "Those of you who haven't picked up your yearbooks should proceed ASAP to the library and collect them." And seriously, the yearbooks were everywhere. You never see open books in the quad except at the end of the school year. Beth Lash was composing a seemingly complicated message at one of the lunch tables with her curly hair hanging down, and you couldn't even see her face from the side. She was hunched over and gripping her pen like it was a joystick on a plane about to crash into the ground. Bianca Martinez, her best friend, was also writing feverishly. I guessed they were writing to each other and wondered what they could possibly have to say. They've been to all the same parties, and they've probably talked on the phone every night.

While I was watching them, Tiffany Wong shyly held her yearbook out to me and asked me to sign. Her real name is something like Hyong-Don, but her parents had her choose an American name when they moved here. We've had classes together over the years, but since she doesn't talk and doesn't raise her hand and wears lamb barrettes in her hair that make me really nervous (I know that behind closed doors, she can't possibly be that good and sweet and nice), I searched my brain for something to write.

I'm always surprised when random kids want me to sign their yearbooks. I really don't get it, because they've got to know I'm going to whip out the "It's pretty strange to think we're not freshmen anymore" or the "Wow, time really does fly." In return I usually get the "Wish I had gotten to know you better" or the "Call me over the summer [insert phone number I'm never going to call]."

In my head I got this image of Tiffany going home and looking in the back of her yearbook while lying on her bed, and so I wrote, "We've been through four years together, and now we're both off to the East Coast. New Jersey isn't that far from Maryland—we should meet up and have Thanksgiving together or something. Let's make sure that we keep in touch." She's going to Johns Hopkins.

When I got to the library there were only a few kids waiting for Mrs. Balsam to give them their yearbooks, and Larome was one of them.

He was bending over her checkout desk and she was telling him, "Larome. Grasp this. Fact. There's a red dot by your name."

He was laughing. "It's a mistake. Come on, come on."

"You need to talk to the office then," she said. "You owe money. I can't do anything."

More laughing. "Yeah, you can. You can give me my yearbook."

"Larome. Red. Dot. Go."

He lazily swung while beaming and checked out who was watching him. When he saw me, he looked even more amused, if that's humanly possible. "Oh shit! Twenty-one Jump Street! You're getting a yearbook? That's hilarious, girl."

Mrs. Balsam said, "Larome. Don't curse. Go pay."

Some small girls standing side by side in front of me (freshmen, I guess, but they didn't look a day over thirteen) turned to look at me. I felt their eyes, but I just shrugged at Larome. "The guys down at the station get a kick out of flipping through it," I said.

Larome nodded knowingly, like he really and seriously

thought he'd uncovered the truth about me. I've seen the same nod on Simon when he says there's going to be traffic. Then there's traffic and he resigns himself to it and seems to be glad that at least he knew it was coming.

Larome laughed, said, "See you at graduation," and winked, picturing me diligently delivering a four-year list of student drug deals and weapon possessions to the nearest precinct. Then he slapped the counter and yelled, "I'm gonna go clear this up, Mrs. Balsam," and I completely knew he would.

After I got my yearbook, I flipped to the back and found my picture for "Most Smart." Me and Matt Taketano were in the bottom left-hand corner, pretending to solve global warming (indicated by me pointing to the top of a globe and Matt working out an equation on the blackboard behind us). Ashley was in the middle of the page with Sam Richie's arm around her because it really is hard to come up with a fitting pose for "Most Most."

The bell rang, and I walked to my English final totally interested in the way that the yearbook people had airbrushed all the senior portraits so we all looked gentler. And we didn't even have to pay extra for that—I guess they just did it. Even John Steiner's complexion looked powdery soft, like he was one of those movie stars from the 1940s who'd been filmed through gauze.

I looked nicer than I've ever looked in my life. And by nicer I don't mean more attractive, but just way more accommodating. I wasn't smiling, because the photographer was a total idiot who put me in a bad mood, but I still looked pleasant.

When I got to English I sat down next to Ashley, who was taking the last minute before the final bell to scan a whole bunch of underlined details in the *Picture of Dorian Gray* with her pinky. Jeff Mahoney was standing behind her, loosely braiding her hair.

Today she was the absolute picture of summer, wearing a white halter top and a short yellow skirt and thongs discolored from a million trips to the pool. All in all, a really attractive outfit. As soon as Jeff said, "Hi, Stella," she looked up and closed her book and said, "You look fine to me."

"What?" I asked. I heard her, but the room was pretty noisy so I could kind of get away with pretending I didn't. Darren Pinsky and his crew were sitting on top of the desks and barking out possible test questions to each other. Tanya Morehead and Lauren McCarden were reciting facts in unison over and over together with their eyes shut. Pages of novels flipped from every direction, putting out their white noise into the air. Mr. Muthler sat at his desk and anxiously watched the clock on the wall while twisting back and forth in his grunting chair.

Jeff let his braid work go, patted the top of Ashley's head, and went to Darren, who was calling him. Ashley's hair fell to her shoulders, and while examining the tips of it, she said, "I said you look fine, Stella." Then she dropped the tips suddenly and flipped them over her shoulder. "I heard you missed your finals again yesterday. And I don't know what was going on Saturday, but you seemed fine to me. I don't know what the fuck you're up to."

I put an elbow on my desk and my chin in my hand and said, "Oh, I wasn't the one sick yesterday. It's my grandpa. He was in the hospital with pneumonia and the doctors were really worried about him. And even though he kept insisting he was going to be fine, that made me worry. I just knew I had to go be with him, and I couldn't take my tests so I didn't even try to come to school."

Ashley's face softened into something not exactly sympathetic but comforted, and then it turned into something stupid (which clearly made her miserable). I wanted to say, "Jesus Christ, Ashley, drop this competitive crap. It's such a colossal waste of time."

I mean, it's pretty much the modern equivalent of the one and only time Donald offered to play hide-and-go-seek when I was seven. My mom and dad had gone into the garage to look for an old poker set (aka, as I now know it, cocaine), and as soon as they stepped out, Donald asked, "Do you want to play a game?" And I was at the age where yes is the answer to everything a stranger asks you (which is pretty much why parents have to totally drill it into you over and over again that you can't go looking for puppies or getting into the backs of vans for candy). Of course Donald pulled the trick where he didn't even attempt to look for me while I was hiding upstairs in my parents' closet. I remember standing there, going through their clothes and their shoes and not really minding the forty-five minutes I spent in there, but still. The point is that you can't enter into something with someone who just isn't participating.

Anyway, I told her, "Don't feel sorry for me. He'll be fine." Meanwhile, Stephen Lee passed by on his way to Elijah Bregman's desk and gave Ashley's shoulder a quick massage as he did.

"Oh," she said. "Now I get why you weren't taking your finals. I thought you had, like, decided that you were above it all." Even though she was using the past tense, I could tell by the edge in her voice that she was still thoroughly convinced that I continued to consider myself better than her. "I guess this all explains why you left my study session."

I nodded, "Yeah."

"Well, so did you get time to study for this test?" she asked.

"A little bit," I said, "when I was in the hospital waiting room. But those chairs aren't really comfortable and someone's getting paged every two seconds on the loudspeaker system." The final bell rang when I was saying "two." Simultaneously, Elijah got up and rapped on Ashley's desk on his way to spit his gum out in the trash.

At the sound of the bell Mr. Muthler ejected himself from his chair like someone had just put pushpins under his ass, and I saw that he had been holding the Scantrons in his right hand the whole time. He looked like crap, like he had been up for the past two nights studying for this test instead of us. His shirt was wrinkled and untucked as usual, and the only thing fresh about him was that he has the kind of skin that doesn't show stubble until it's at least a few millimeters long. Everybody returned to their seats. Mr. Muthler said, "You've got to be quiet now" to all the kids as he began distributing the Scantrons to the front of the rows to pass back. I smelled suntan lotion all around me.

After Ashley pulled out two refillable number two pencils and one old traditional one, majorly sharpened, she whisper-talked to me, "This is the last test that matters for me. I have student government next period, and we're having a party."

"Yeah," I said, "this is the last test that matters for me, too."

She accepted her Scantron from Darren Pinsky, who gave me a darting glance when he turned around, and she said, "In college we'll just write papers." Then, seeing the pencil I had taken out, dull and without an eraser, she asked, "You're using that? You're crazy if you think you're not going to want to rethink any of your answers." I was immediately exhausted. Reza Sahpour handed me my Scantron. I slapped it down on my desk. Mr. Muthler said, "If the room isn't completely quiet by the time everyone has their answer sheets, I'm not going to hand out the tests themselves. Believe me, you don't want to cut into your time. Some of you will take the entire period to finish."

I picked up my pencil and said to Ashley, "Yeah," and then before she could talk, "You know what I've been thinking?"

Distracted by my pencil, she asked, "What?"

"It's much easier to get around between the states on the East Coast than it is around here. I'd be really curious to see what it's like at Harvard, and I could take the train up and stay with you and we could even do something like meet in New York for Thanksgiving."

Ashley looked at me like she'd just put a peanut butter and banana sandwich in my mouth, having told me for years it was a great combo, and I had just chewed, swallowed, and pronounced it, "The best thing I'd ever tasted." Like I was finally making sense, and like I was making her happy and sure of herself. She exclaimed, "You're so right, we should! I love that. For real, let's plan that. We're on the same path, and when you think about it, it makes so much sense for us to keep in touch. I've always thought we should be better friends." She shook me on the wrist, genuinely excited. "I'm excited," she excitedly whispered.

She was actually making a decent point with the same-path stuff because as I looked around the room, I realized that these kids would probably be bumping into each other in odd and expected places for the rest of their lives. In high school they mixed in with everybody, all forced to take P.E. (no AP P.E., obviously) and most of them having filled their lives with people from outside of these classes. A lot of long-standing friendships had been formed in the days before there were different levels of English.

But in the future some would end up at the same grad school and laugh at the coincidence. A fair number would run into each other at twenty-four-hour diners up in the Bay area, taking a break from Stanford or Berkeley. Even more would be surprised (but kind of not) when they ran into to each other on spring break in Florida, having driven down from Massachusetts, Rhode Island, Connecticut, New York, and Pennsylvania. And I figured a lot would end up at the same/competing consulting or I-banking firms when they graduated.

As Mr. Muthler passed out the last of the Xeroxed tests (still warm because he never makes copies until the last minute so kids can't steal them), Matt Taketano continued to quiz Jeff. He was busy mumbling *a, b, c,* and *d* answers for

"What are the name of the apartments where Lord Henry Wotton's uncle lives in *Dorian Gray*?" It took him a few seconds to grasp that he and Jeff were the only ones who hadn't been handed their tests yet.

Mr. Muthler, hairs practically standing up on the back of his neck, said, "Matt, you are one syllable away from taking a zero for your exam."

Matt rolled his eyes and burst out with a phrase often uttered during the past few months, but never audibly in a nearly silent room.

"Once a bitch always a bitch, what I say."

We read *The Sound and the Fury* in March. We'd been assigned pages 150–200 on a Wednesday night, and by Thursday morning, the saying had become as popular a greeting as "What's up?" among the guys in my class.

It was probably the first time Mr. Muthler had ever been called a bitch to his face. Matt grasped that he had said something out loud and too loud about a second and a half after he did it. His solution was to stare ahead at the blackboard while Mr. Muthler stared at him. Matt's friends made animated, silent "oooooh" faces to each other (puckered lips and scrunched up forehead—everybody's seen this one), and I just rubbed my right eyebrow.

Coming up with the lamest pseudo-apology ever, Matt finally said, "That's from one of our books."

I could sense that a number of factors were bearing down on Mr. Muthler's decision process: the desire to not actually look like a bitch, the seconds on the clock going by, the way Matt had shown that he was ready to bend. It also couldn't have helped that after Matt ignored his authority the other day, Jeff did also, and then Daniel, and then me, and I thought it pretty likely that he was wondering if he had any left.

Putting two fingers to his lips, Mr. Muthler said, "Save the quote IDs for the test." He put Matt's and Jeff's tests in front of them and told the rest of us, "You may begin." I got the feeling that he wasn't going to be teaching here next year.

Possibly taking inspiration from the "Dare to Soar" poster on the wall, which features a spread eagle flying in deep blue skies above some murky pine trees and the motto "Your attitude almost always determines your altitude in life," I began my test.

I have my dad's photographic memory, so I see answers appear on pages in my head. The first question. "In *Huck Finn,* which one of these sentences is NOT one of the inscriptions that Tom Sawyer creates for Jim to scratch into the rock?" Somewhere behind my eyes I searched and found words on the left-hand side of the book, italicized, indented, and clear. The false inscription, "*B.* Here a lonely old man met his demise, and thus entered and left captivity a stranger to the world." Very similar in phrasing and tone to the correct answers sitting around it, but just not actually found in the book. So I went on through the thing answering, "In *The Sound and the Fury,* how much do the flatirons the clerk *initially* presents to Quentin weigh?" "In *A Portrait of the Artist as a Young Man,* which poet does Stephen Dedalus think is 'only a rhymester'?" And my personal favorite, "In *The Catcher in the Rye,* what is the name of Holden Caulfield's regular elevator boy who isn't working the night Holden returns home?"

I worked fast mentally and chose my answers right away,

but I couldn't stop taking the time to completely blacken the dots on the Scantron. I just can't handle it when they look sloppy. Still, I didn't even try to change any of my answers after committing them to paper.

I finished a half hour early and looked around. Davis Carrasco was staring out the window, watching the gardener roll by on his lawn mower outside the building. Stephen was checking the stopwatch resting at the top of his desk every time he answered a question. Cara Quon seemed on the verge of tears while she scratched her head with one finger, like she was attempting to break open a hole in it and physically release the right answer. I wanted to leave all of them, but Mr. Muthler doesn't accept tests until the bell rings. So I put my head down on my desk and took a nap.

The bell and the shuffling woke me. Still in the process of regaining consciousness, the first thing I heard was Ashley saying that we were now unofficially college women. I was still pretty out of it when I dropped my Scantron on Mr. Muthler's desk and he asked me to stay.

He waited until everyone filed out and then said, "So, I read your brief meditation on the way my classroom smells." I had actually forgotten I wrote that during the pop quiz. I felt a little bad about it now. Before I could say anything, Mr. Muthler looked down at his desk, where he had the essay, and began to read aloud while keeping one hand behind his neck. "In the room of Mr. Muthler I am reminded of glue, ammonia, and kneepit." Yeah, I had totally forgot about all that. He tipped his neck and head back toward his hand, so that he was kind of tilted toward the ceiling. "Stella, what is kneepit?"

"Kneepit," I said. "You know, like armpit. If you've ever bent down to tie your shoes on a hot day and you're in shorts or whatever, it's just a really salty skin smell."

"Why did you write this?" He looked slightly pained, and it occurred to me that maybe he took the kneepit description as an insult to his own, like they were the ones fouling up the room. In reality I'm sure the smell just came from all those kids getting in from after lunch all hot and sweaty.

"I wanted to amuse you," I lied.

His gaze came down from the opposite corner. "You wanted to amuse me?"

I thought quickly, saying, "I imagined that you probably get bored reading essay after essay on the same subject, so I decided to do something different to break up your day."

Mr. Muthler picked up my Scantron and asked, "Did you take this test seriously today?"

"Very seriously."

For a second he had the eyes of someone who's been helped up from a fight after getting his ass kicked. Kind of embarrassed, kind of relieved, kind of grateful, and kind of worn. He put my Scantron back in the pile with the rest of the tests and then dumped the whole heap in his briefcase, snapping the clasps shut and turning the combination. He smiled in the smallest way. "I'm glad for that."

We walked toward the door, and he flipped off the lights to the room. "Look around since this is the last time you have to see this room." I did, and then we left together.

I stood and waited as he locked the door with a single key (not on a keychain), and I watched as some small kid (another freshman?) down the hall threw one of his folders in the air.

It opened and released tons of handouts and papers. While I was thinking, "That's going to be a pain for him to clean up and reorganize," the kid just left it all on the floor and walked away.

I heard Mr. Muthler say, "Well," and my attention returned to him. "I was beginning to think I had done something wrong, and I couldn't figure out what it was."

"No, no," I said. "It's just the end of the year. But in the future, you might want to ease up on your test questions. You know, have the kids write a final essay on the symbolism of eyes in *Gatsby* or whatever and let them have a little room with it."

Mr. Muthler shifted his weight from foot to foot, studying the vinyl floor. "In college a professor of mine concluded his lecture with the statement, 'A universal symptom of insanity is that one sees the entire world in terms of signs.' I didn't think with, with…the mix of hormones and the itch for rebellion, that signs would be a useful way to go in a high school English class. I thought it would be nice for kids to see things in a straightforward manner before they went out into the world and learned how gray things truly get."

Mr. Muthler had stopped shifting and had come to rest at a place that didn't look too pleasant for him. He was kind of slouched over to the right, putting all his weight on one hip and seeming pretty defeated.

Wanting to keep his year from ending with a whimper, I told him, "Well, if it counts for anything, you were my favorite teacher. I learned a lot from you."

I saw that tentative smile again. "You did?" he asked.

"Yes," I said, and then I put out my hand and he put out

his and we shook. I went one way and he went the other, and as I was on my way toward the south door, he called out, "Have a good summer, Stella." I waved and stepped out into ninety-something-degree weather.

As I went toward the art building's open door, I pictured myself walking in and finding Ainsley already gone. I don't think I really believed in this picture, but I felt myself moving faster anyway.

After passing between the planters and beyond the lingering band kids and their depressing band flirting, I came into the room and there she was, working in her usual spot by the window. It felt good to see her. Like one of my long-lost stuffed animals had resurfaced at a neighbor's garage sale for all of fifty cents.

Since her body was in the way of the light coming through the window, she only read as a dark spot against the stucco wall outside. All around the class, kids were on their knees on their stools, leaning across the tables as they pointed to each other's drawings and borrowed each other's pencils. And when I watched their busyness and her relative stillness side by side, she looked like a cactus in a room of tumbleweeds.

I walked over, careful to step over Tyler Allen (he was drawing really crappy mushrooms on a piece of butcher paper on the floor), and when I got closer I saw Ainsley was coloring like a madwoman with a bunch of oil pastels. Her right elbow vibrated as she filled in the entire area (and I mean entire area) around the eyes I'd drawn for her the other day. Her technique involved rotating colors of the cool spectrum and laying them on ridiculously thick in overlapping layers, and then taking a paper towel to smudge the whole mixture together. My eyes were looking like they had been sucked from my body and spit out in a tropical swamp.

I sat down on the stool next to her and said, "Hey."

Ainsley looked up. The corners of her mouth lifted by a nearly invisible increment and a stranger would have never noticed she was actually smiling, but I could tell. And I was pretty surprised by that because four days ago she was a blank. "Hey," she said, "you're wearing the pearls. I didn't think you would use them for everyday things."

I patted them and told her, "You know what? I like them a lot, and really, I think pearls are far more versatile than people give them credit for."

"You sound like my grandma." She went back to grinding the blue-green pastel into the paper. "I hope you don't care. I'm turning in your eyes so I can pass the class. I'm just trying to finish it up though. I noticed that Ms. Silver wears a lot of greens and blues, so I'm going to color this whole page green and blue."

I nodded. "I really think that's a pretty decent plan."

Ainsley shrugged. "It's the best I could come up with." She had about six square inches more to go until the entire sheet was so completely waxy that it would rival Margaret Banchoff's forehead for the oiliest surface in the school. "So what are you going to do this period? I'd draw you something to turn in. It would suck though."

"Don't worry about it," I said. "I'm actually going to go to drama." Ainsley looked up from her coloring, and then back down.

At the front of the room Ms. Silver was beginning to clip final projects on clothespins across the blackboard. The first was a charcoal portrait of a girl with immense eyes, and in the back of her head a delicately shaded horse galloped happily off into the sky. Right away I knew it came from one of the Asian girls in the corner by the flowerpots. All I have to say is those kids are either incredibly optimistic, or they've developed the most complicated sense of humor the world's ever seen.

Then there was a pen-and-ink drawing of an angular girl with spray-painted stars circling around her forehead like a lazy halo. I knew this one came from Todd, who had obviously totally fallen for Nina Comanche while doing the assignment. He drew her way prettier than she actually is.

Ainsley closed in on the last few remaining fibers of white on her paper and asked, "So, are you going on the trip tomorrow?"

I said, "I kind of figure that I should. I've never missed a single field trip during my entire academic career. You?"

Ainsley got up from her stool with her picture of me. "I wanted to skip it. Zoos make me sad. My mom volunteered to be a parent chaperone though, so I have to go." She stood there and stared at me, her eyes silently saying, "But really I could stay home or go to the park or drop off the face of the earth (should I?) if I wanted because she probably wouldn't notice anyway."

Ms. Silver called out, "Ainsley, do you have anything to hand in today?" And as Ainsley turned toward her to bring the drawing, I said, "Okay, then let's meet tomorrow in front of the office sign so we can be sure we'll get on the same bus."

She nodded and said, "Let's sit together" and headed toward the blackboard, balancing the plain side of the paper on her right palm. I slipped out of the room to the strains of "Freebird" crackling on the radio and went to my very last final.

The second I stepped into the theater I almost turned back around because of that smell. I had been dreading it and trying to prepare for it, but when we were finally reunited I realized my sensory memory hadn't even come close to pegging it down. My theory is this: the theater is the one building besides the gym (which is saved by the sterility of its sealed hardwood floors) where tons of glands on different bodies come to a fevered pitch at the exact same time. That kind of thing leaves its mark on a space. During some of those ensemble numbers there's thirty dripping kids onstage and the dancers are doing their stuff barefoot and they leave microscopic pieces of their feet in the carpet every time they do a turn. And after those pieces have been there for a semester, I'm pretty sure they grow their own toenails, dig themselves into the fibers, and rot.

John Steiner was onstage wearing overalls without a shirt, and while I think he was trying to capture the spirit of the character, he looked ten times as stiff as the wooden trees behind him (loaners from temple). Sitting on the stage with one knee tucked underneath his body and the other one bent, he wrung his hands and silently recited his lines. His partner, Tina Lubbitz, stood under an elm doing breathing exercises. These included circling her wrists and elbows round and round as she inhaled and exhaled.

The theater lights were dimmed to an almost painful point and were flickering a billion times a second. They also hummed softly, pathetically begging, "Jesus Christ, someone put us out of our misery and turn us off." The other kids from my class were seated in the audience area waiting for the start of the scene, but most of them were examining their own costumes or signing yearbooks. If only John could have realized that no one cared about his performance aside from the fact that once he finished the next person could go, then I think he could have put things in perspective.

As I neared Mr. Nichols's folding chair (just a generic metal one, not a director's model) he turned his head eagerly. He was probably expecting to find a student waiting to ask his opinion on her latest interpretation of a line. But when he saw my face he rose dramatically and stroked his chin once, sort of resembling the love child of Robert DeNiro and James Dean if that love child had just accepted an invitation to a game of chicken. Then he wimped out and pulled me toward the back of the room by holding on to my elbow and steering straight.

In a hushed yet dramatic voice, he said, "I believe you've found yourself in the wrong class, Ms. Parrish." His arms were crossed and he bent over as he spoke and he was obviously not trying to project. For once he talked in the direction of the ground so the carpet would swallow his words.

"I have?" I asked.

I saw his face redden like it did the last time I saw him. And I understood that he loved drama, just not when it happened away from stage and screen. "As those who are serious about theater are about to begin their final scenes, I cannot have you here. A receptive audience is everything to the actor."

"But I came here to give you something."

His shoulders relaxed some (but not much) and he nervously quipped with a slight English accent, "What is it? Have you brought me an apple in hopes of passing this course?"

Inwardly I sighed, but outwardly I said, "I brought you this" and tossed him an invisible beach ball. I'd describe its colors for you, but it was invisible.

He stood there kind of looking like something had just hit him in the face. "Did you just…"

"You didn't catch it," I said. "Now it's rolled all the way down by the water and I'm pretty sure it's gotten wet."

A smile spread from rosy cheek to cheek. "I missed it because I was watching a young girl and her puppy as they ran across the sand!" And then, dropping into a conspiratorial voice, he asked, "It's fun, isn't it? That's what I wanted you to see…the great fun it can be if you just open yourself up to the experience."

I told him, "Well, that's why I'm here today. To have fun."

He looked off toward the rest of the class and scanned the options for me, excitedly muttering about this being the last minute but the last minute being better than nothing. He muttered, "Well, you could be the nurse in that scene…only a few lines, but"—he shook his head—"no, not fair to Dana. Well, oh! Addison is performing the soliloquy from *Hamlet* and perhaps you could do some sort of interpretive dance behind him, communicating, say, the burden on him…"

I saw the humor in that, but I'm definitely not a dancer. "Do you need a stagehand?"

At first he was reluctant. "I suppose we do…"

So I reminded him, "There are no small parts."

And then he exclaimed, "You're absolutely right! That's brilliant."

Clapping as he walked to the front of the room, Mr. Nichols called for silence and respect. Yearbooks closed and everyone turned toward the stage. I went and sat next to Danielle Reinhardt, who was wearing a starched suit and a matching hat with one of those mini-veils. She tapped me on the knee and mouthed, "What happened?" but I whispered I'd tell her later.

Once everyone hushed, Tina picked up her fake baby from the ground and sashayed to the center of the stage. John, taking a deep breath, rose to join her. He took his first step. Immediately his left leg folded upon itself and he fell back to the carpet with a shriek of, "My leg! My leg!"

Mr. Nichols clumsily jumped onto the stage right away, freaking out and roaring, "What's wrong, John? What are you feeling?"

And John moaned and cried, "The leg I was sitting on fell asleep. I can't feel it! I can't feel my leg!" He was punching his ankle to demonstrate. Mr. Nichols bent down and slipped his arm around John's waist and helped him up, and after some more bitching John finally did his scene balancing on one leg, looking like an incredibly inflexible flamingo.

I moved trees. I handed Addison Collins his plastic skull. I watched the clock and said to myself, "This is your last hour of school" and then "This is your last half hour of school" and then "This is your last eight seconds of school." I counted those eight down, feeling like the second hand moved in tandem with something inside me.

As the bell rang, Mr. Nichols asked that we all get in a circle and join hands and squeeze once for a job well done and once for good luck in all future endeavors. On my right side were Nick Dalton's ridiculously cool hands (like he had been feeling up refrigerators) and on the left were Mr. Nichols's, sweaty and exhilarated.

I ambled toward the front of the school. Coming out of the theater, my eyes were sensitive to the light, so I shut them. I felt the wind off the bodies running past me as everyone spilled out of their classes. I heard happy yells from in back of my head and a girl screaming, "Fuck this place!" as she sprinted past. I listened to plans being made around me. Two guys (one had an amazingly deep voice) were going to go over to the house of someone named Kevin, and they were all going to watch satellite cable and play pool. I recognized Tim Sharpner's voice as he lazily invited a silent partner "to smoke some dank weed in back of Barnes & Noble." I wondered if he bought it from Daniel.

My eyelids finally stopped fluttering, and I got to the point where I was able to open them. I sauntered past the cluster of freshmen lockers and saw relief in the bodies who had just tucked a year under their belts. Then it was on to the math building, which was bizarrely calm and already emptied. As I walked down the concrete path splitting the southeast lawn, I followed behind a pair of twins wearing identical sundresses, and neither of them held books. Their backpacks hung like deflated balloons. Just like she said she would be, Shana was waiting in her sedan on the corner of Alton and Meadowbrook.

I opened the car door and ducked inside and gave her a

little scare. Not on purpose by shouting boo or anything, but just by getting in the car. She had been looking out the window toward the road. Her hair was pulled back with a tortoiseshell clip, and she was wearing a tank top featuring small daisies in all colors of the rainbow if you put the rainbow through the wash fifty times.

Ever since the day she pinched me, she hasn't been coming into my bedroom to say good night. We'll answer each other's questions and say good bye in the morning, but we don't say anything after eleven P.M. That's the time the murmur of her bedroom TV goes away.

I put on my seat belt, and we both said hi.

We were silent while she checked over her shoulder for traffic. But as she pulled away from the curb and faced forward again, my sheer presence in the corner of her eye seemed to have a visible effect. I had seen the same kind of mannerisms onstage less than ten minutes ago — the deliberate movements of those who are amazingly aware they're being watched. They begin to perform tiny busying actions based on the ones they think they'd perform if actually alone. Today in drama Nick Dalton pretended to make spaghetti while he was giving Oedipus's final speech. And there Shana was, scratching an itch on the side of her nose for too long and fingering the hem of her skirt.

I took my last glance at the school. It became obvious that something had to be said.

"So how was your day?" I asked.

Shana glanced toward me quickly and then back to the road, and then she tentatively ventured, "My day was on the stressful side."

"Oh yeah, why?"

"I got a call from Simon's boss this morning. Simon fainted in a meeting."

I studied her and asked, "What, he fainted? Is he okay?"

"Oh, we think he's fine. He's already back at work. I drove up and met him at the hospital and they did tests, so we'll know for sure tomorrow. The doctor was fairly sure that this was only a fluke incident. Simon thinks that he was simply tired. He hasn't taken a vacation in a long time. We haven't gone anywhere during the past summers."

I wanted to say, "I know. I live with you." We got on the 405 North and Shana started to repeatedly check over her left shoulder again, hoping that someone would let her enter their lane.

I said, "Oh, really?" instead.

"I think Simon needs a vacation. A few weeks in Florida could really make a difference. I told him that today, and at first he tried to dismiss me, but then he promised he's going to think about it."

"Well, that's good," I said. When Shana talked about her and Simon's life I somehow felt that she was the equivalent of a small-town girl trying to explain to me, the foreign city dweller, the kinds of things that happened around her parts.

On our way into Macy's I saw the two of us reflected in the dark double doors and didn't feel so hot for a second. A fifty-something saleswoman smoked and watched us, and I wondered what she thought about the two of us as a pair.

We rode the escalator to the second floor. After stepping off and only finding jewelry displays and makeup counters extending in all directions, Shana turned a half circle. I guessed she was trying to sense the direction of the dresses. Like a horse figures out the epicenter of an oncoming earthquake by using natural intuition. I turned to the incredibly bored Persian woman at the watch counter and asked her to point me in the direction of my department. When she spoke I saw one of her front teeth overlapped the other. Because the one was hogging the spotlight, the other had given up and let itself turn green. I winced.

Shana and I were shopping on a Tuesday at twelve-thirty and we were basically alone since other people obviously have better things to do. I felt like migrant workers in an orange grove. The racks and racks of dresses were just so hopeless and going through them seemed like one of those tasks we could never actually complete. Some of the dresses had ruffles and some had no straps and I really didn't care. I mean, Jesus Christ, put me in a bag today and I can pretend I'll wear that on Thursday, too.

I decided to just start grabbing things in my size that looked like someone might wear them to a party when Shana tapped me on the shoulder and asked, "Do you like this one?" Sunflowers beamed at me. I guess Shana saw something on my face because before I could answer, she jumped in and choked out, "Fine." And she hung it back up on the rack.

I retrieved it saying, "That one just didn't look my size. Let me find the right one—" and she cut me off with, "I don't care anymore." She took off down the aisle and I followed after her, taking the sunflower dress with me.

"Shana," I called out as many, many things inside of me snapped, "I'm trying it on! I'm fucking trying it on, okay?" As

I walked I slipped the dress over my head and over my clothes and since it was three sizes too big anyway, it fell on easy. I yelled, "Look how perfect it fits! Doesn't it look great?" I grasped below the hips of the dress and pulled the fabric out, and I spotted myself in a wall mirror on the opposite side of the space looking like I was about to curtsy. Shana, speed-walking, disappeared into a hole in the wall labeled as the fitting room. And I stormed in just as fast and knew immediately which stall she was in because its slatted door continued to bounce in and out of place.

I pushed it open and she was there facing me, and her eyes were small and narrow. When she's around me they're usually wide and glassy with constant alarm, so I was incredibly taken aback by the difference in her. Also, her shoulders were collapsed forward and whereas normally she's just kind of dainty, at that second the word that leaped into my mind was "hag." She was a youngish, clean copy of one of those ancient women who stand over their cauldrons and mix up potions, never standing up straight and always possessing the eye of the tiger while their hearts chant, "You'll pay, you'll pay, you'll pay." Suddenly she stepped forward and took hold of both of my wrists with both of her hands and pulled me closer to get some leverage. She shook me so hard that I got a quick ache in the small of my back.

I cried out, "What the hell is wrong with you?"

She gritted her teeth and said through them, "There is nothing wrong with me. Everything's wrong with you." As she said this she had to look up to me because I'm about six inches taller. I was staring down at her widow's peak and suddenly viewing it as a mark of intense vulnerability, just like how all babies have that soft spot in the back of their heads and you hear all those horror stories about pushing into it. I'm stronger than her so I knew that if I tried, I could twist my wrists away and take the hard part of the bottom of my hand and thrust it forward into her forehead if things got too bad.

She spit out, "The first time I set eyes on you my heart sank."

Now I yanked my wrists away, but did nothing else. She flinched.

"Why's that?" I felt myself sneering. "Were you hoping for someone who looked more like you? Were you hoping for a baby who wouldn't learn how to say anything for at least a few months so you could sit and be quiet with her and not be so goddamn scared all the time? Am I just too big for you?"

Her fists were clenching and I wondered if she was going to deck me. I had already started a fantasy in my head where I'd hit her back and then take her by the shoulders and turn her toward the mirror, showing her the red mound already blowing up on her cheekbone.

She shrieked, "At the very least I wanted someone who didn't give me the chills from the moment she set foot in my house!"

"Chills!" A one syllable laugh came out of me. "Really, what was so frightening about me, Shana? Was it my hair? Did I forget to wash it the night before I came? I can't remember. Did my knuckles crack and startle you? Was it the fact that I wasn't wearing fucking flowers and that just totally blew your mind?"

Her nostrils flared and the right corner of her lip lifted a little. "You came into our house and you looked at us, and I could tell everything you were thinking." She was taking shallow breaths although she didn't seem like she was about to cry. She was nearly barking at me. "They told us we were getting a girl and we cleared the upstairs office for you. The week before you came I thought about painting and putting up posters. Then I thought I should wait for you to come to me and tell me how you wanted to decorate the room."

She hadn't blinked for at least a minute when she finally delivered this one. "And then you show up and you're not a girl, but you're a wolf. You look around at us like you could eat us. You look at us like we're the stupid ones. We didn't ask for that. We took you in. Simon thought that it was a much better thing to take in someone who was already grown and that the rewards for our love would be greater. He said, 'She'll bring so much to our lives.' He told me you could be a companion for me. You would come home at three o'clock and we would do"—here she slammed the side of dressing room wall with her fist—"things!" And she did it again. "We would make dinner together!" She was now taking a step forward and a step back repeatedly, looking like a lazy boxer. "Instead, what have you brought? You've only brought the feeling I've had for the past six years that all of a sudden my walls have eyes and I'm involuntarily shamed for everything I do! Every day I live under your judgment! Every single day!"

"It wasn't my job to make you comfortable with me!" I yelled. "Jesus Christ! I was all of eleven years old!"

Grasping at her hair and making lumps in it, Shana said, "You didn't have to hate me from the second you stepped into my house! I gave you no reason to! I was nice to you!"

"If you wanted immediate, unconditional love, then maybe you and Simon should have looked into a puppy. Or having your own baby."

"We wanted to do something good, you bitch. We thought that having children is selfish when there are so many abandoned ones who need love." So they could have kids. "After you leave for college I would bet the house that we'll never see your face again. It will be like you never even existed. And the only thing you'll have left behind is this weight on me that comes from having spent years underneath your watch. I will never be able to look at myself the same way again. You can't begin to imagine what it's like to take in a daughter and find out that she's alien to you in every way."

I took a few seconds to consider what she had said. And then I told her, "What you've got to understand is I already had parents."

I turned and opened the door and walked down the hall of the dressing room, quickly getting nauseous. After passing back through the clothes and back through the nauseating racks of dresses, I walked out an exit without thinking. The security alarm went off. The electronic woman politely told me that a salesperson had forgotten to take the tag off my item and requested that I please go back and let the offender fix the error. I pulled the dress over my head and tossed it onto a display table and flew outside.

During my last summer with them, my parents and I went on a bike ride. The banana seat on my bike was my favorite part about it, even though it looked old and crappy. The three of us pedaled up Jamboree past the wildlife and bird reserve and my dad rode effortlessly without using his hands and my mom shouted things back to me that I couldn't hear, so I was constantly saying, "What?" And she'd repeat, "Tell us if you get tired" or "Check out the pants on this guy" as a fellow bicyclist in crotch suctioning shorts rode past us in the opposite direction.

We all stopped at a light up the hill and a woman in a convertible looked at us and yelled to my parents, "You should really put a helmet on your daughter. Should a car hit her"— she looked to the sky—"heaven forbid, you would never forgive yourselves." My dad solemnly saluted the woman, who was wearing a straw hat with fake sunflowers decorating the top of the brim.

The light turned green and after the woman sped off, I looked at my mom expectantly, waiting for her opinion. And she just told me, "Sunflower hat. Enough said."

I went back into Macy's and visited the rack where Shana's favorite dress hung. I got one in my right size.

When I came around the corner she was standing there with her arms crossed, watching one of the TVs that the store had mounted to hang down from the ceiling. A bright, blurry music video played in which bodies ground against each other to thumping techno, and Shana couldn't take her eyes off the screen, she was so entranced. I stood next to her and I knew she knew I was there, but she never looked away from the dancers.

After a good minute or so I said, "I'm going to get this dress."

Without changing the direction of her glance she took the dress out of my hands and hung it up on the nearest rack, where it stood out against a collection of black shirts. "Let's go." She abruptly turned and walked through the department.

For the past few hours I've had to keep reminding myself that today actually was a success, despite one unsuccessful endeavor.

Thirteen

It's true that it's easy to get sentimental about things from afar. I could fall into that trap myself if I started thinking about chunks of time as hazy pillows ahead of me (with soft edges calling me back into the bed at the end of each decade).

Obviously the seniors at Woodbridge don't need a whole lot of time to feel the effects of distance because the senior day trip is always famously well attended. Yesterday (and when I say this I'm referring literally to yesterday) the kids were spitting on the walls and flicking off people they couldn't wait to get away from, and today they're on the bus with the majority of their graduating class. Even the rebels show up, suddenly nostalgic for the company of the people they seriously never saw or knew before because they were so busy ditching. Essentially, the class trip is incredibly weak and avoidable and if you miss it, the absence doesn't even affect your final GPA. Our grades get turned in the night before because the administrators need a full twenty-four hours to make a final list of the kids they're holding back. But everybody goes anyway.

And the real kicker is our trip this year was even weaker than the others before because our trip was to the L.A. Zoo. In the early nineties the senior classes went to Magic Mountain, but the teachers eventually voted on changing locations because too many kids were puking on the bus on the way back home. Just as the trip caused kids to forget that they hated school, it also caused them to forget that they shouldn't smoke weed, eat fifty dollars' worth at the snack stand, and then let themselves be flung upside down and spun in circles for five hours straight.

So then the mid-nineties trip became a visit to Knott's Berry Farm, where the roller coasters weren't especially huge yet and the attractions weren't all roller coasters. Last year saw the end of the Knott's excursion when ride operators caught two seniors (Edward Simon and Veronica Naughton) having sex on The Kingdom of the Dinosaurs. As Edward put his smooth moves on Veronica in the second of the animatronic professor's time travel tunnels, the lights came on and the epic soundtrack slowed. A minimum-wage worker came over the loudspeaker and reminded everyone that all passengers should stay separately seated at all times. Security was waiting at the end of the ride, and that's why today I was getting on a bus for a place where ninety-nine percent of the attractions are out in the open. And those that aren't still require walking.

When I got to school, seven large yellow buses were waiting in a long line at the front of the parking lot. The bus drivers were all leaning against the fender of the first bus and taking turns rolling their eyes and yawning. I immediately spotted Ainsley in the middle of the student crowd that was hanging around. But only because she was standing next to her mom, whose hair is actually much brighter in the sun than it is in her house.

When I reached them, Elizabeth (in head-to-toe white linen) was saying, "I'm worried she's not going to get a window seat—she gets so nauseous" while Ainsley stood there, making fierce eye contact with me.

"Hey," I said.

"Oh, hi." Elizabeth nodded at me and an elegant platinum chain sparkled each time her collarbone jerked. "Are you excited for the trip?"

"Sure," I told her, "I like looking at elephants and monkeys as much as the next girl."

"I'm just worried," Elizabeth repeated to no one in particular. "They're starting to load the buses."

Ainsley rested her head on her own shoulder, looking like she was going to tip over. To me she said, "Ashley's across the street getting coffee."

"You know what?" Elizabeth asked. "I'm just going to run over there and let her know they're loading the buses."

"Okay," Ainsley said.

"If they load the buses, save us seats, okay?"

"Okay."

Without waiting, Ainsley and I boarded the seventh bus together and took our places in the last row on the left-hand side. Our bus filled quickly and by 8:15 there weren't any spaces left. Ainsley watched out the window as her mom crossed the parking lot with Ashley, two flames with matching no-spill cups in their hands. As the two of them passed in front of the first bus and out of our view, she slumped down in her seat and asked, "I'm not being cruel, am I?"

When I said, "No, not at all," she rested her head on the window, convinced. And while I knew I had given her the right answer, I wasn't exactly sure how decent I felt about suddenly becoming her source of truth.

Mr. Litwack, a computer teacher known for his habit of pacing through the entirety of class, paced up and down the aisle of the bus as he wrote down the names we yelled out on his roll sheet. Of course when his turn came, Jared Delaney called out "Your Mom." And then when Mr. Litwack sighed and asked for Jared's real full name he came back with "Your Fat Mom."

After we merged from the 405 freeway to the 605 North (the trees lining the sides getting messier and increasingly dry), I realized that the teachers were even going to have to arrange for alternate means of transportation for next year's trip. In the seat across from mine, Brett Rios had his hand down Tasha Meyer's pants.

Ainsley and I rolled our eyes and lowered our voices and pretended we were scripting a romance novel.

"I can't help it, darling," I said, "but the smell of vinyl seating strikes me as very erotic. Perhaps I have a residual memory from my infancy, in which my diaper was changed on a bus seat and I felt the alluring surface for the first time."

Ainsley (whose voice gets even more like microscopic

gravel when she lowers it) picked off a loose piece of vinyl on the back of the seat in front of us and husked, "I don't know what to do, sweet Brett. I've always liked carpet. I find that around you though, I'm doubting myself."

I suggested, "Tasha, have you considered that it might be the incredibly sexy smell of old puke scrubbed into the floor? Or is it truly the vinyl itself, the way so many sweaty thighs have stuck to it on their way to zoos and museums and amusement parks?"

Ainsley laughed a hushed laugh. "It could be the sweaty thighs."

"I'd be willing to bet my personal fleet of school transportation vehicles you never thought you'd meet a man so sensitive to the things around him."

We passed by a sign announcing the Hawaiian Gardens, which is actually a city on the poor side and not an attraction. I used to picture an oasis of hibiscuses and palm trees, but then I found out it's just squat apartment buildings and liquor store signs with letters missing. Ainsley looked out the window. "You really have a fleet? That's so impressive."

I looked out the window, too. "I know it is. You see, anyone can own a château in France. But a fleet of buses? I am obviously special and superior."

Back at a slightly higher volume, Ainsley asked, "What's a château?" and I told her.

Later our bus pulled off the 5 freeway at Los Feliz Boulevard and a homeless man stood on the corner holding a sign. It read "Gulf War veteran. YOU could make my day into a good one." Underneath all the dirt and facial hair I saw a man who couldn't be over forty, and a few rows in front of mine I heard one of my classmates pondering. "If we all just gave that guy a dollar, can you imagine how stoked he would be? Imagine if we just rolled down all the windows right now and handed him just one buck each. He wouldn't know what to do with himself." I said to Ainsley, "Wouldn't that guy just love to hear that." The light turned and our bus made a left and within a few minutes we were inside the sudden, kind of startling, greenness that makes up Griffith Park.

As we were filing out of the bus, Mr. Litwack proudly held his attendance list in the air while enjoying his greater pacing area on the asphalt. He repeated over and over again, "You must get back on the same bus you came in, or this attendance list will not work. Three o'clock on the dot. Back here. Three o'clock. Same buses."

At the zoo's entrance sign we were met by Mrs. Taylor (a Spanish teacher), who was circling her arms toward her chest like she could bring the whole world together if she just continued to beckon us toward her breasts. "Everybody over here! You will not receive your passes to the zoo until all the buses arrive and we can go in together. So there's no point in going anywhere, guys!"

Without saying a word to each other Ainsley and I slipped behind the group and went to the ticket window and put down our $8.25 each. We pushed through the turnstiles, finally free. Proof what the dollar can actually do.

There was really nowhere pressing to go. It's not like there's any sense in sprinting off to go see the red-flanked duikers. They're going to be there all day. But still we headed for the aquatics area because Ainsley spotted the sea lion on the sign post and gave a jump. "I love seals. Let's go there first."

The seals were much happier than they should have been, living on an island made out of concrete and swimming in a glass tank. When they glided by in front of us they actually looked like they were smiling, and I figured they're just born with naturally pleasant dispositions. They always see their glass tank as half full. Ha.

Leaning on the safety bar with her arms folded, Ainsley said again in nearly inaudible voice, "I love seals. I really do." A heavy man with a boy on his shoulders whipped his head in our direction after Ainsley spoke, and I knew he was wondering if he had just heard someone talking or if a bug had flown too close to his ear. Having understood every word of hers I realized that when around other people, being with Ainsley is like walking around wearing a pair of headphones.

One of the seals on the fake rocks rolled over on his back and stuck his fins in the air. Ainsley leaned forward like the seal was solving algebra equations with his eyes shut. The points of her brown hair, all separated, hung below her chin and out in the air. She asked, "You know what my biggest dream is?"

I shook my head while watching the seal. "No, what?" I wanted to hear it badly.

"My dream is to work at SeaWorld and be one of the people that swims with the dolphins and feeds the seals. That's in a perfect world though." I found this dream incredibly worthy. Not because I think swimming with dolphins is objectively the best career a person could have, but because of the way she said it all. I realized that for Ainsley, swimming with the dolphins seemed as impossible as wishing for world peace or curing cancer. Her voice told me that when she dreamed of something, she held that thought stationary—forever a dream. It was like she didn't even comprehend that when the rest of us say we dream of owning a house or being famous or living to a hundred, we actually plan on trying to do it.

"You know," I played along, "you could actually swim with the dolphins for a living."

"No, I thought about it for a while when I was younger. I can't."

"Why not?"

"Well, you have to be good-looking because you do tricks with the animals in front of a lot of people. It's like show business. And plus, I think you have to have a science background."

I told her, "I don't know. I bet you could do it."

"Nah. It's a dream."

I turned toward her. I studied her and wondered if this was the kind of talk experts would classify as a symptom of planning mind, of her brain already being halfway out the door. I wondered if this was the kind of talk I should have been dishing out. But the thing was, she didn't look purposeful. Wistful instead.

I said, "I honestly don't think you even have to go to college to work with the dolphins. You just start working at the park and you do the small jobs, like you could cut up the fish and hose off the auditorium seats. If you had patience you could just stay there and work your way up and learn a lot from the trainers. One day you'd be one."

She looked from me to the seal swimming under the water in the same way I remember looking to my mom when I thought Donald was telling me a lie. "Still not pretty enough though."

"It doesn't matter," I said. "You just have to be good with the animals. You just have to learn how to do the performances correctly and look like you're enjoying it."

She didn't ask me how I knew she'd just have to be good with the animals. Instead she said passionately, "I would always be good to them. People put them in tanks and it makes me sad, but I'd want to make their lives better. I'd want to help them." She was giving the speech I've heard the aspiring doctors in my classes give, but coming from her it sounded much better.

Shaking a finger at me she said, "I would even stay late at night. I would work an eighty-hour week. Not making them practice tricks though. Just spending time with them and making them my life."

I saw how perfect this life would be for her, with doe-eyed animals floating at her feet and listening to her every word. I imagined that they'd hear her voice before they could even see her. I got it, I really did. And so there was a short pang of disappointment in me, and I felt it underneath my bottom ribs like fingers there, poking me. I began to change my mind about her. Her brain was still firing images and hypothetical situations and future dates, and we were not twins. "You should look into it," I told her. "I guess. Screw Irvine Valley College"

She gave me a sort of cryptic smile, higher on one side than the other, and said, "I was planning to anyway." And then instantly I was confused again, thinking that maybe I read her wrong. She was going to do something.

I asked, "What were you going to do instead?" just as Karen Baronsen came up to me and leaned on the rail and asked me if I wanted to get a cab with her and her friends. I looked behind me and Paige Rand and Melissa Gluckman were waiting.

Karen said, "We're going to go to this restaurant we love on Sunset—really good Mexican food. And then we have to stop by Crazy Gideon's because Paige needs a new stereo."

I wasn't incredibly suspicious, but Karen and I have never done anything together outside of class. So I asked, "Why are you inviting me?"

Karen took this question like a soft slap and changed her focus to the hills behind the exhibit. "I don't know. You were just standing here alone, so I thought you might be into it."

I glanced at Ainsley and she was still looking out toward the seals, still wearing that cryptic smile.

"I was hanging out with Ainsley," I said. And I thought, "How funny it is that we look like two people alone." And then I thought that that's sort of nice. It's not a friendship for the outdoors. If there isn't a set of walls around us, it's like our being in the same place appears completely coincidental. And when we talk, our words only go to each other and then it's like they evaporate. You'd probably remember a bird tweeting in the trees more than you'd remember hearing an actual conversation.

Karen considered the two of us for a second, struggling to understand the connection. But then she just said, "Oh. Have fun." And left.

Next we went to go see the sea lions, who were putting on a hell of a show, diving down and doing somersaults and skidding across their concrete slabs on their stomachs. It was like they actually knew they were smaller and friskier than the seals next door, and were completely attempting to make you forget you just wasted time fawning over their fat teenage sisters. The sign explaining their origins and characteristics said that despite their sweet appearance they're big biters, and I didn't doubt it for a second.

We took up our positions on the rail again, and Ainsley said, "I guess that means the rest of our class is here."

"We can always stay a step ahead."

"We should do that."

A minute later I asked, "What were you going to say before? What were you going to do instead of going to college?"

She leaned back and checked all around her, making sure we were still ahead of everyone. There was only an old lady with a sun umbrella and a woman with small, small features holding a baby next to us. The woman was clapping at the somersaults of the sea lions and asking her baby, "Did you see that? Did you see that? Did you see that?" I was sure the baby wouldn't speak a first word, but a first sentiment like "Yes! Jesus Christ, I'm not blind!"

Anyway, I guess Ainsley didn't think the people around us were trustworthy because she began walking up the path and I came with her. We passed under some trees (imported from somewhere because they had placards with paragraphs on them) and I was glad for the shade. When we couldn't see anyone in front of us or anyone behind us, Ainsley said, "I was going to disappear."

And then my heart raced and inside I heard, "That's it. There it is," and I almost opened up my mouth so my plans could rush out, too, so my mouth could maybe say the exact same things at the exact same time. "Disappear to where?" I had to hear it.

"I've been thinking lately," she said.

"Disappear to where? Where?" I wanted to hear it out loud.

"I'm going to disappear from Irvine. I haven't figured out where yet, but I'm going to work on that tonight. After I cleaned out my closet I went and sold my clothes and some of my things to a thrift store on Sunday. I got a lot of money from pawning a whole bunch of jewelry though. I did that in Costa Mesa. I figure I have enough to get going and then I can always take small jobs. And live in people's extra rooms that they don't charge very much for."

"Disappearing to another town," I thought. It was like a rubber band smacked me in the part of the brain where I had decided that disappearing had only one meaning. I reminded myself that I wasn't everything. I massaged the muscles around my bottom ribs by wrapping my arms around myself.

We walked toward the Koala House. I asked, "Why are you going? Where do you want to go?"

We went into the house, and the sign told us that we were entering darkness and to look up into the trees. "I'm only telling you this," she said. "You can't go and tell anyone."

The koalas were behind a huge sheet of glass in a fake night, where everything made shadows on the wall behind them and the track lighting above us strained to be like moonlight. "Who would I possibly have to tell?" I said. I felt like we were Woodward and Bernstein meeting in the bottom level of a parking structure. I looked up into the leaves trying to make out the animals.

"I've been thinking about it, and I think that no one will even care that I gave the speech at graduation. I think that fantasy was all in my head. In reality, they'll probably whisper to their friends over my talking. Don't you think?"

I looked at her, wondering if she actually wanted an answer.

She looked at me. She didn't. "I came up with a better plan though. They'll call me up to give my speech. And I won't be there. I'm going to leave that morning."

I said very seriously, "I wonder how long they'll call your name for. Do you think it'll be a huge pause where everybody's just turning their heads around and the microphone's crackling and Mr. Frankel's tapping it going, "Check one, Check two. Check...check?" I was so serious.

And then we both started laughing and couldn't stop. It hurt so bad that we had to kneel down to the ground while keeping our arms extended up to the rails for support. We tried to make our laughing quiet when the other, more serious, koala watchers turned to us and stared. But then our humor just came out windy and even more painful, like the air was desperately trying to find more routes out of our bodies.

She wheezed, "And there's more?"

"So tell me."

"I'm going to do something noticeable today, so that people start talking about me on the bus. I have to be a topic of conversation. If I do something out of the ordinary today, then when I disappear people will wonder what happened."

A pack of children entered the exhibit and screeched, "What's in here? Where are they?"

"Where will you go tomorrow?" I asked.

"I bought some maps of California from the gas station. I'm leaning toward San Francisco." And then she jumped a little, like she had when we were going to the seals and said, "What are you going to do this summer?"

My organs churned and my stomach started battling something far worse than butterflies. I didn't want to lie. I had made eye contact with a koala up in a tree and she was staring at me, accusing me with ridiculous cuteness. So I told Ainsley, "Nothing." Which, in retrospect, was a really decent response and I'm glad I went with that one.

Ainsley's bushy eyebrows lifted, opening up her face — not attractive at our school, but maybe attractive elsewhere. And she asked, "Would you want to come with me? I know you're going to college in the fall and so you could only stay for a couple months. It could be great, though, right? I thought I was going to have to be alone. I didn't want to be though."

It was like my brain was playing a game of Tetris and suddenly a long piece fell into a gaping hole in my pattern, eliminating four levels at once. My mind raced ahead trying to figure how this move would impact future moves and what would actually happen the day after tomorrow, but I stopped myself and forced myself to recognize that there's only so much a person can do. And essentially, I figured, a person can get the ball rolling, but can't always be responsible for whether or not the ball makes it safely to the other gutter or gets run over by a car.

"Hold on a second," I said. I took off my backpack and

unzipped it and searched. At the bottom I found the piece of paper with the Del Mar address on it. I offered it to Ainsley. "If you're not set on San Francisco, then my friend is renting a house in Del Mar for the summer and we could go there." Could.

She held it and studied it like a fortune from a cookie. I chose to watch the hedgehogs scurrying across the bottom of the exhibit, looking for either insects or a way out. I tried to avoid the eyes of the koala in the tree, who seemed too smart for her own good. She knew it wasn't night.

"The thing is," I said, "that's really close to SeaWorld. You could go and get a summer job there. And then when the summer was over you'd already have roots somewhere."

Ainsley's freckles seemed to spread across her nose and cheeks like the remnants of fireworks. They were left up in the sky after the explosion and they were sparkling, having just seen themselves do something amazing. And I saw it, too. I saw her in a wet suit, her hair sopping and slicked back all the time. I saw her talking to the killer whales before a show and because her voice was such a low rumble, her coworkers would begin to call her the whale whisperer and they'd view her with respectful eyes. I saw her moving, breathing, and doing *things,* but when I tried to do the same for myself, I just saw the shine off the glass in front of me.

"This is crazy though. I thought I'd be painting people's homes," she said.

"You could go and drive out there and my friend will be there by one o'clock for sure, and then just tell him I sent you. You could pretend to leave for graduation and then drive down to San Diego instead."

I knew that would buy her at least a day, even two. And I helplessly hoped (great song) maybe that short period of time would secure her dream so that she couldn't leave it when they finally found out I wasn't coming.

Ainsley said, "Jeez." Five seconds later. "Jeez." She rested her mouth on her upturned fist and her eyes searched the carpet. "This plan turned out better than I ever thought it could."

"I'm happy," I said. It was dark in that koala house, but at this point I knew I couldn't find a place dark enough.

Later in the day we stood at the top of the zoo, looking up into trees that actually grew toward the sun. We were at the red panda exhibit, and the placard told us that she was only visiting the zoo for a month and that she mostly hid all day and night. In an encouraging font the sign said, "Look up into the trees! The red panda likes to hide herself in heavy leaves. Very few people are able to spot her, so if you catch sight of this exotic animal, consider yourself lucky!" This message was punctuated with three paw prints, as if the red panda had personally signed off on it.

Ainsley held her hand up to shade her eyes and grimaced as she studied a bunch of empty branches. "Where is she? Do you see her?"

I took in each bunch of leaves, inch by inch, determined to find this thing systematically. "No, but I've only gotten through three-fourths of the area so far. Give me a few more seconds."

Four guys from our school were coming up with different sounds they thought a red panda might respond to and shouting them at her. Malcolm Castelle went with "Awhoowr, awhoowr, awhoowr, awhoowr" while Omri Fogel preferred,

"Deekha, deekha, deekha, deekha." Jung Allen's and Chad LaBonge's aren't even worth trying to figure out phonetically, since they were basically orgasmic moans. There wasn't an inch of movement in the trees.

Resting her eyes, Ainsley said, "That's kind of funny. Everyone comes out to the zoo to see this animal. She just hides though."

I told her, "You know what? You're like the red panda. Tomorrow everybody will be staring at the crowd and looking for you and you won't even be there."

"That's right," she said. "I won't."

On our way back to the bus at three, Ashley suddenly brushed up against Ainsley and said, "Where were you all day?"

"The zoo," Ainsley replied.

Examining her tips furiously, Ashley told her, "I can see that I've outgrown our friendship. I don't have time for these immature games, and in the future, I know that I'll make friends that can offer me more." She walked off arm in arm with Jeff Mahoney.

Ainsley and I lazily walked along, like friends coming out of a bar at four in the morning. We kicked our feet forward and didn't care how heavy they landed. Our hips swung wide from side to side every time we took a step.

As we ascended back into the bus and Mr. Litwack called, "Same buses! Thank you. Same buses! Please, please, same buses!" I elbowed Ainsley and said, "Don't forget to do something noticeable."

She took a sweeping glance around the interior, looking for inspiration. And then as Darren Pinsky stopped at the fifth row and turned forward to take his seat, Ainsley reached out and grabbed his crotch. Poor Darren Pinsky. He was totally a victim of circumstance. Ainsley shrugged at him. As he sank down, completely confused and maybe a little excited, Ainsley and I continued to the back where we took up our residence in the final row again. In twenty minutes our whole bus would know what had happened. By five o'clock tonight, the other six would know, too.

"I wish I had remembered to think it out. Not what I was planning," she said as she settled into the corner where the seat and window met.

I sighed and said, "At the end of the day, it's getting the job done that matters."

Now that vodka-filled Evian bottles had been finished off hours ago and the exhaustion of a day spent tanning on the zoo lawn had taken its toll, the rest of our class was hushed and still on the way home. When we reached Woodbridge, even the bus seemed to have to put all its effort into making the turn into the parking lot. The metal linings on the wall shook.

Back on the ground again, Ainsley and I stood on the curb. The light made her look bronzed.

"I'm excited," she said.

"Me, too."

As she headed off toward Elizabeth and Ashley, waiting at the car, she yelled, "Bye, I'll see you later," and for a second I envied her dream. Then I headed through the palace facade, passing by the stiff guard, and went to the pay phone to make an appointment with Lenny Ansen for tomorrow morning.

Fourteen

I must have woken Lenny up because he came to the door squinting and in actual flannel pajamas, his chest hair sticking out above the top button. When I stepped into his house I was smacked with a wall of cold. The air conditioner must have been set to keep the house at sixty.

Lenny struggled to string words together before having his morning line. "Ehhhh, uhhhhhh, business?" he asked as he led me to the kitchen.

"What?" I asked.

"Are you, ehhh, going into business? Because we'll have to ehh, talk about that if you are." His voice boomed against the high ceilings of the condo and bounced back to me.

I tucked my skirt under myself and took a seat at his distressed steel kitchen table and folded my hands together.

"No, no. I'm not going into business. I'd be no good at it since I'm not really a people person."

Lenny leaned against his kitchen counter for support and stared out the glass doors behind me, getting lost for a good five seconds. I turned to see what was so entrancing and found the empty lake, without boats and without waves, like a giant sheet of stained glass.

"Lenny."

He looked back to me, wiping the crust out of one of his eyes with his ring finger. He said, "I was thinking of, ehhh, learning how to sail. Maybe I should take lessons."

I told him, "Hmm."

"But back to the issue at hand. I run, ehh, franchises. I'm like the guy at the top of food chain at, say, Burger King. I don't have freelancers."

I repeated, "I'm really not going into business."

He tilted his head and tried to size me up. "So what are you going to do with eight grams of freebase?"

"It's going to be a long summer," I said.

He seemed okay with that and left the room, calling behind him, "Don't steal anything." I didn't so much as move. I just sat in that chair and looked at the paintings of the empty Spanish towns and kept my hands folded, thinking how thin my fingers feel where they meet with my knuckles.

When Lenny returned, he was holding a lunch bag and wearing terry-cloth slippers. He sat down at the opposite end of the table from me and stretched his arm out across it like I've seen jail prisoners do in TV movies when they're reaching for the hand of their pissed-off wives. "So," he said, "You've got my, ehh, money?"

I did. I'd been to World Savings that morning, where I cashed some of the U.S. bonds my parents left behind. They used to keep them in an envelope under their bathroom sink. The teller had widened his bloodshot eyes after taking a look at my transaction and had bitten the inside of his bottom lip. "These bonds haven't fully appreciated," he panicked. "They're twelve-years. You're only in the eighth. You'll lose a lot of money."

I told the teller, "Oh well."

At the kitchen table I pushed two thousand dollars toward Lenny. He picked the cash up and counted it slowly, licking the tip of his right thumb before flipping through each bill.

As he finished counting, I said, "I know there's more there than you actually charge. For the extra few hundred, I figured you could do me the courtesy of throwing in a pipe."

Lenny raised his hands (the money still in his left fist) above his head and stretched happily, saying, "That sounds fair."

And now I'm back in the sedan, getting ready to leave Lenny's condo. I have the car because Shana and Simon are both riding in his to graduation. I'm supposed to be at the field twenty minutes early to line up for the grand march in.

When I walked into the family room to get the keys earlier, Shana was washing peaches in the sink and Simon was sitting in the blue armchair. The doctors recommended that he stay off his feet as much as possible for the next week or so.

"I came to get the keys," I said. "It's time to go."

Simon flatly remarked, "They're on the counter" as Shana turned off the faucet and looked over her shoulder.

"Do you have your cap and gown with you?" she asked.

I twisted my body so she could see them tucked in their plastic package underneath my left arm. "I've got them here."

"I didn't see them before."

I picked up the keys from on top of the newspaper and took one last glance at the two of them, who resembled nothing so much as Italian children I've seen in pictures taken after the liberation. Shana and Simon looked war-torn and tattered. Like they had been snapped at the exact second they stepped outside of their hiding places and there hadn't been any time to wipe the bewilderment off their faces. I thought, "Have I really done this?"

I'm starting the car.

Now I'm at the light on Main before the 405 North. I know my writing is shaky but it's not because I'm really shaking. I'm actually just leaning this up against the steering wheel so I have a flat surface. The car vibrates and you know, makes my hand bounce up and down. When I get nervous in the room, I will remind myself that this is like when I was younger and ate mounds of peas for the sake of health. I believe in the richness—oh crap, green light.

I just walked into the home, and Lupe just blew me a kiss as I passed. Now I'm sitting on the bed trying to concentrate and Donald is lying across it horizontally (on his back), saying, "Put that down. We need to talk."

I just said, "Hold on." I'm telling him, "I need to describe what you looked like when I came in and told you."

He asks what else I've written in here about him.

I say, "I'll tell you in a minute."

He says, "Now."

I say, "Wait."

When I came in Donald was in the bathroom, washing his face. He dried his face and said, "There you are, Stella." I told him that I was here to help him, and he said, "So you brought me something?" and I said, "Well, I brought both of us something."

"Why both?" he asked slowly as he leaned against the wall, and I asked him, "What if we have the same reasons except we use different examples?"

And he asked back, "Should I be doing something? Should I be convincing you otherwise?"

I said, "Let's just agree that I was never your responsibility."

"And me?" he asked.

"Yes. You're kind of mine."

And tears started down his face. But he wasn't making a crying expression or any sounds at all. And then the tears started down mine, but I was the same. We didn't hiccup and we didn't heave and still we're like that. Right now, since Donald's on his back I can see a tear go out the corner of his left eye and across his temple and down into his ear. One of my own just went off my nose. I think our bodies cry, sad for themselves, but our minds don't, and that's how come we're keeping so quiet.

Donald asks, "Are you finished yet?"

I say, "I think so."

I have Katherine's box on my lap and a bottle of Tylenol in my backpack just in case.

Donald says, "I was saving a quotation should I write my own letter. I believe in closing things properly."

I say, "I appreciate propriety as much as you, but I don't know."

He says, "I'll write in it."

I say, "No, no. Read it to me and I'll write it."

He's getting up and going to the bottom drawer of his dresser, and he's pulling out a book on Roman philosophy. It has statues on the front, and some of their noses are chipped off. He has a piece of yarn marking one of the pages. He's holding the book very close to his eyes, and wiping the tears to see better.

He's saying, " 'The wise man will live as long as he ought, not as long as he can.' Those are the words of Seneca. He was well-respected."

I just told him I think that's very good, and now I'm going to put this down.